Alexander H. Japp

Hours in My Garden, and Other Nature-Sketches

Alexander H. Japp

Hours in My Garden, and Other Nature-Sketches

ISBN/EAN: 9783337013431

Printed in Europe, USA, Canada, Australia, Japan

Cover: Foto ©Andreas Hilbeck / pixelio.de

More available books at **www.hansebooks.com**

HOURS IN MY GARDEN

AND OTHER NATURE-SKETCHES.

BY

ALEXANDER H. JAPP, LL.D., F.R.S.E.

AUTHOR OF "LIFE OF DE QUINCEY," ETC. ETC.

WITH 138 ILLUSTRATIONS BY W. H. J. BOOT,
A. W. COOPER, AND OTHER ARTISTS.

NEW YORK
MACMILLAN AND CO
1893

CONTENTS.

APPENDIX.

PREFACE.

THE following pages aim at presenting some personal impressions and observations, as well as the results of some reading. The author hopes that he has duly signified his indebtedness to others where this was necessary. He trusts that his essays may not be found other than pleasant reading, and that young folks here and there may derive some stimulus to more systematic study of nature than he was fortunate enough to have the chance of making while still young.

ALEXANDER H. JAPP.

HOURS IN MY GARDEN.

ERRATUM.

Page 181, line 13 from bottom, *for* "with its church tower" *read* "with its old church, and peal of bells so strangely placed, and nunnery with its little tower."

by winds, so gentle as to be imperceptible to the senses, or by the movements of the life around me, which never pauses. In this corner I allow no garden flowers proper, but only wildings of field and wood and hedgerow. It is also a kind of asylum and sanctuary for some of the outlaws of the garden, who here, I confess, do their best to atone for the sins of their kindred in forbidden ground.

I have thus around me the delightful record of many pleasant wanderings—a kind of index or memory-map

HOURS IN MY GARDEN.

I.

MY GARDEN SUMMER-SEAT.

HAVE erected in my garden a little summer-seat, in a spot of my own choice—the remotest corner of all. There, in the sunny afternoons, sheltered by the foliage (for it is placed against a thick beech hedge, which just at that point has been allowed to grow high, so as to afford a canopy of greenery overhead), I sit and read or muse and observe by turns as my fancy inclines. Even on the calmest days there is a faint stir and movement, I know not whether caused by winds, so gentle as to be imperceptible to the senses, or by the movements of the life around me, which never pauses. In this corner I allow no garden flowers proper, but only wildings of field and wood and hedgerow. It is also a kind of asylum and sanctuary for some of the outlaws of the garden, who here, I confess, do their best to atone for the sins of their kindred in forbidden ground.

I have thus around me the delightful record of many pleasant wanderings—a kind of index or memory-map

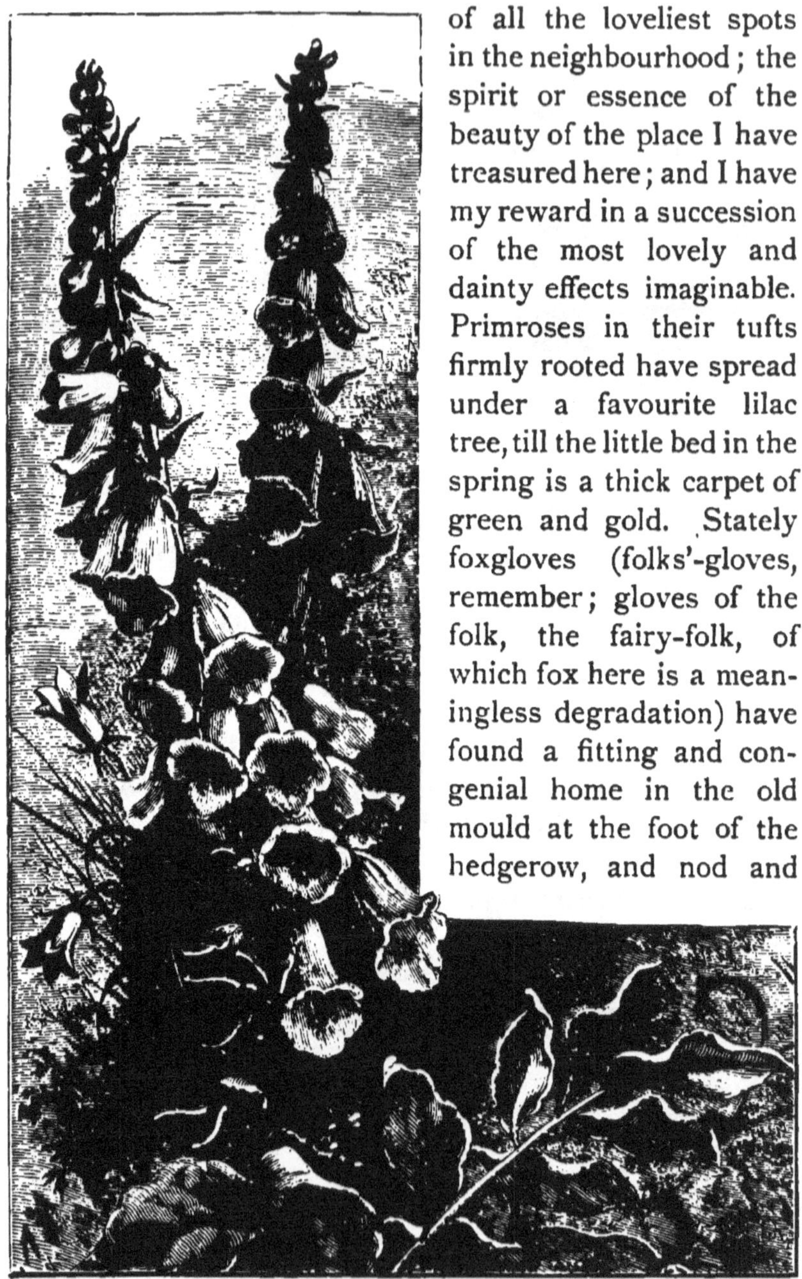

FOXGLOVES.

of all the loveliest spots in the neighbourhood ; the spirit or essence of the beauty of the place I have treasured here ; and I have my reward in a succession of the most lovely and dainty effects imaginable. Primroses in their tufts firmly rooted have spread under a favourite lilac tree, till the little bed in the spring is a thick carpet of green and gold. Stately foxgloves (folks'-gloves, remember ; gloves of the folk, the fairy-folk, of which fox here is a meaningless degradation) have found a fitting and congenial home in the old mould at the foot of the hedgerow, and nod and wave in the later spring and summer—the loveliest colour against the green of the hedge itself. Surely I am lucky in such an omen, and the fairies may visit my garden for their own purposes under the moonlight, for they are not all dead yet. Little common daisies ope their golden eyes, and sometimes, I think, wink and beckon, as if they had some secret to tell. And this I feel the more as the daisy, as an everlasting, knows no seasons and has its secrets accordingly.

> " The rose is but a summer flower,
> The daisy never dies."

Honeysuckle struggles upwards, and the white convolvulus puts forth its fairy trumpets, those flowers of a day, as the French call them, that are born at morn, fall off at eve, but are so soon succeeded by others that we do not notice their loss; and they mix deliciously with the red thorn with which here and there breaks in the hedge have been filled up. Ferns of many kinds wave in a rough rockery built up in the corner, which erstwhile was a rubbish heap; and wild violets peep through with their gentle eyes, and wild hyacinths, blue and even white, and anemones have condescended to blossom, and to impart a touch of lady-like delicacy, grace, and purity, that my corner might not fail of the most exquisite variety. If fortune favours me, I shall try to settle some *droseras* in a shallow wooden box on the rockery slope, and conduct a little jet of water to flow and spread above them, and then my little corner will, to my mind, be finished. But, alas! here as in other things, the final touch is the hardest to succeed in, and there remains the necessity of constant effort. Well, perhaps, that it is so, for else one would fall to drowse in a dull content. A botanist might, perhaps urge that there is an air of irony in my finishing touch, since the droseras would prove the enemies of many minute insects which I profess to have a sneaking regard for; and certainly there is some truth in this, which just shows that in this style of gardening, as in art, too great an aim at completeness may lead to the intrusion of elements that are more or less destructive of the first fresh ideal. But then there is still a good deal of doubt about some points in the manner in which the droseras propagate themselves; and thus scientific curiosity, even in my small way, I must own, comes into conflict with the simple idea of nature and life. Alas, nature *is* like Chronos of old, and apt to eat up her own children by the aid of her other children, and thus the sweet idyllic element will not long remain intact, however much we may strive to maintain it.

SUNDEW (*Drosera rotundifolia*).

To keep order in some degree, and yet not to make my corner too orderly, is the problem. A touch of rustic carelessness is necessary to the effect I desire, but difficult to attain with due regard to the interests of the other parts of the garden; for dandelions will intrude in too strong force, and rag-weed and plantain and groundsel will find a refuge when ruthlessly driven out elsewhere. However, I have an idea that such a corner as this is a fine safety-valve, so to speak—a free lung and breathing space for certain outcasts of gardeners, which yet are very beautiful in their way, and sometimes very useful too.

The dandelion is indeed a very persistent plant, armed as it were by nature with almost magical powers to secure its continuance. With its many edible and medicinal virtues it would seem to contest the common saying that good things either are scarce or are tied up in little bundles. Were its virtues only fully appreciated, it would be much more in use than it is. The rabbits know its virtues, and use it largely, and anybody who keeps tame ones will do wrong not to let them taste it now and then. And man, proud man, drest in a little brief authority, despises the lesson he might learn from the animals; and, instead of enjoying dandelion in coffee or salad, waits till he is compelled to take it in pills and potions. Even as greens the stalks are good : no salad is perfect without them. Were it only scarce it would be eagerly sought after. Dandelion coffee may be bought, but on the word·of a good authority, it is but a poor make-shift for the dandelion coffee that may be grown and made by anybody. Yet few dream of making it, simple as it is. The bitter in it is the valuable element, and the preparation is easy. The roots only require to be carefully dried and ground up, and then infused like coffee, to supply the best medicine for the liver procurable.

Ha! as I sit here musing, dandelion puts itself *en evidence.* There come sailing towards me little soft downy parachutes, dappled or patterned with minute pearly stars, that float and waver, though there is no wind that I can perceive. These are the seeds with their tipped wings ready to take hold of any likely bit of soil that will welcome them. How well they illustrate nature's economy, and even fine art, in ways and means, and in adapting means to ends. But by what secret impulse are they moved in this direction, like little fairy ships or balloons steering through the still air? Of them it cannot surely be said as Coleridge said of his phantom ship in the " Ancient Mariner ":—

> " The air is cut away before
> And closes from behind."

I know not what propels them, only I know that this is a very ancient observation, and that some of the old botanists built a belief or fancy on it—a point of weather lore. They said that if the down of the dandelion or thistle flies away when there is no wind, this is a sure sign of rain. I confess I have not been able satisfactorily to verify this, any more than that other assertion of theirs, that the stalks which support the down of the dandelion huddle together in moist weather under their fluffy umbrella, as if they, too, dreaded the effects of a drenching; and yet I fancy I have seen them shrink together—a mere fancy perhaps.

The plantain—that outlaw of lawn and border—takes root here, and in little open spaces shoots its stalks up to a height of nigh a foot. The persistent efforts of the gardener to exterminate it in the little lawn over there, which had long lain in neglect and got overrun prior to our coming to the place, brought out some evidence that would almost suggest conscious contrivance. As he plied the lawn-mower systematically, the plants more and more shortened the stalks, and grew flatter and flatter under the leaf, contriving in some sort to seed so without showing the flower or seed-pod. There was nothing for it in the third season but to settle matters by taking up each individual root with the daisy-grubber, for it was clear that they would have contrived to live and to spread, though in limited measure, however mowed, if the roots were left, as they also propagate by root as well as by seed. Such is their power of adaptation, which almost makes me believe in some form of conscious adaptation to circumstances. Dr. Taylor's "Sagacity and Morality of Plants" had thus a wonderful experience in its favour in observation of the ways of the plantain on that lawn ; and out of respect for its sheer persistency and its wise adaptiveness, I gladly yield it a little corner in my rustic reserve.

Way-bread, corrupted from waybred, it is called by the people here because of its being bred on the way, and its marvellous tendency to follow in the footsteps of men, as if attached to the white faces, particularly to the British. They say, it has followed our colonists to every part of the world, so that it has been named by the natives of some of our settlements, "The Englishman's foot." Can it be that there are in it hidden elements of healing and purification not yet discovered, which Providence means the white man to recognise and take advantage of ? The balance of nature, indeed, is wonderful, but so are the wise adaptations of nature to men's wants; and mysterious and inscrutable are the potent agents of man's relief still stored up in plant and tree. Bruised plantain leaves, in old days, were esteemed among the rustics an excellent remedy for cuts and bruises, and also for the bites of stinging insects, and in Scotland an ointment is made from them that is sometimes very efficacious. Its mucilaginous properties are remarkable. And what if the uses discovered in it are but prophecies of some still more efficient element in specific disease? Perhaps, then, way-bread is not a corruption after all, and originates in some early conception of edible properties in the plant due to the mucilaginous element in it.

I even allow a nettle or two in my preserve, and have put in a plea for some of the common field nettles to be allowed to struggle through my hedge. This I do, because of my sense of their beauty of leaf and flower, and because certain of the butterflies are fond of hovering over them. But though I have heard much of the excellence of nettles for edible purposes in various forms, I do not affect a utilitarian interest here. In the parish of Dreepdaily, I know they "forced nettles for early springkail." Nettle-tea, I am told, is much liked by some people, and nettles dressed like spinach make tasty greens; but love of these was one of the likings I did not carry away from my native country, and if I have ever enjoyed them they were "disguised." Nevertheless, I believe, they may be of great value in this way, for dried in hay, the cattle are fond of them. One of my countrymen, Campbell by name, complained bitterly of the neglect of these esculents in England, just as the late worthy Dr. Eisdale complained of the neglect of mushrooms in Scotland (to which esculent, I confess, I have however been fully converted in the South), and he said, "In Scotland I have eaten nettles, slept on nettle-sheets, and dined off a nettle table-cloth." The fibre is, however, much more difficult to prepare for weaving than that of the flax, otherwise it might have found much more favour as a fabric. But the more one looks into matters, the more one is convinced that in nature there are no "neer-do-weels," as, alas! there are in the human family.

And I also allow a thistle or two. I have, alas! none of the true Scottish thistle, which, when Burns found

> "Spreading wide, among the bearded bear,
> He turned the weeding clips aside
> And spared the symbol dear,"

but only a few of the milk thistle, which is, however, very beautiful, with its streaks of white on the leaves from which it takes its name. I have also a few poppies, flaunting red in their season, and later displaying their semi-globular seed-head, which gently rattles when shaken, like a toy-drum, the very type and symbol of gay society—the last of a race which it took long to extirpate from the garden, and which are now, like the Iberians of Spain, pushed into the remotest corner, and tolerated

POPPY.

and ruthlessly kept down even there. But he were a very churl of propriety and utilitarianism, who would not allow a representative of the wondrous sleep-inducing papavers in such a plot, to remind him of so much of Homer and the poets, and one secret of mysterious might in the modern pharmacopœia, and also of the wreck of many geniuses in later days—

Coleridge, Hartley Coleridge, Edgar Allan Poe, De Quincey, and probably Byron and Shelley, and how many more? Always comes the question of use and abuse of God's good things.

And among them without any regularity are set some sun-flowers, on which certain bees so love to

SUN-FLOWER.

pasture at certain seasons, that I have found them in the evening quite tipsy, as is the case also with the passion-flower, from some element in the nectar, and unable to take care of themselves and go home like respectable hive citizens. This proves that there is virtue in the sun-flower, which is said to be good as an eatable in many ways. "The fresh flowers, just before full bloom," says Mr. James Long, a good practical authority, "furnish a dish scarcely inferior to the artichoke. The seeds ground into flour make very good cakes, and, if roasted, furnish a drink not much inferior to cocoa. The leaf is often used as tobacco, the seed pods are made into blotting-paper, and the plants, if grown in damp places, for they will grow anywhere, are a protection against intermittent fever."

But I am afraid I only thus provide a preserve for certain birds who find tid-bits among my wildings, and am, in fact, only placing temptation in their way. I can see them eye me sideways, with that remarkable air of rightful superiority which birds, even small birds, can sometimes show, commingled with an indescribable element of disappointment and chagrin, when they are making for my corner of the garden, and catch sight of me there before them.

As I sit here and read and muse, or give myself up to no end of pleasant fancies, I see at the outskirts lime trees in their delicate, semi-transparent green, outlined against the blue sky—the lower leaves, however, taking a darker tinge, while the loftier preserve something of earlier green—and among their leaves sparrows, wrens, robins, tomtits, linnets, and other finches delight to flutter and sport and preen and hide themselves. Between are fruit trees of many kinds, laden with their various fruits, still green and shiny. And, higher than all the rest, and close to the lime trees, is a copper-beech—dark, rich, and effective, drooping in the lower branches almost like a weeping-willow.

I noted a peculiar circumstance about this tree in the spring of 1889. The buds came out soft and green, and—the weather having been unusually favourable—it burst into leaf and became copper-dark almost in one night.

Over a screen of ivy I command a view of a high chimney of the house, in which, during the past season, a couple of pairs of house-martins have had their nests. Often have I sat and watched their steady coming and going with the favourite food for their young ones, admiring their wonderful adaptation to their life and environment. And now my attention is particularly attracted to them by a peculiar circumstance. A number of sparrows have clustered on a branch of a high sycamore tree almost overhanging the chimney, and there they flutter and twitter in a most busybody style, as though they had some very important business on their minds. They have evidently something extraordinary on hand. Now I notice that whenever the swallows wish to enter into their nests the sparrows try to bar the way. I watch, interested and curious. Yes, there is no doubt about it, the sparrows wish to possess themselves of the swallows' nests, and to drive them away. Most pugnacious and interfering of birds are the sparrows,

with no notion of losing any chance, however small, of furthering their own interests; and, if I am not mistaken, they know the secret of union, if they have never read Æsop's fable of the Bundle of Sticks. At last, after some time, and many ineffectual and scattered forays, there is a concerted attack, and a great noise and fluttering. So interested am I, as several of the swallows have disappeared, that I rise to go into the house. I find two of the martins have been thrown down the chimney, and, on my appearance, dash themselves against the windows in what has been for some time a disused kitchen to which the chimney belongs in which the nests are. I catch first one and then the other, and let them free, when they dash right away from the house to the westward. Pretty little things : more than ever, as I handled them, did I realise the perfection of their form for their purpose. In the best sense they are clipper-built, and their wings are wonderful at once for strength and lightness —nerve and muscle are there in their finest quality. When I touched them they gave out a peculiar hissing sound, probably involuntarily.

On going back to my point of observation the sparrows are in possession, and every now and then one or another comes out and sits on the ledge, like a kind of sentinel, to give quick hint, I suppose, if the erewhile possessors, now the intruders, make any show of returning. What a little parable of wars and sieges I have witnessed there this morning. Now, I can believe almost anything of the sparrows. It is the middle of August. I have paid some attention to their proceedings during the spring and summer. They built under the eaves of stables, outhouses, and elsewhere, in covered situations, in February and March, and reared broods there. Then, in May and June, they betook themselves to the trees, more particularly the lime trees in front of the house, being high, carrying off from the nests in the eaves straws and other light bits of material, and also, when it served their purpose, making very free with the thatch on some of the outhouses for the same end. A second brood was hatched in the end of June or beginning of July. Now, is it possible that Mr. Sparrow wants a ready-made nest for a third brood, feeling that he does not have time to build one for himself in a situation that would be sufficiently protected in the cold nights and mornings of later August and September, and deems that he may safely make the swallows victim, as all is fair in love and war?——that is the only inference I can draw from what I have seen to-day from my garden-seat. No wonder the sparrows increase in spite of all the efforts to keep them down; no wonder that in the United States of America they have had to declare war against them by special enactment, branding that man as an enemy of his country who will feed or harbour them in any way. They are most pugnacious when anything arises affecting their rights or self-interests on the part of other birds, and understand thoroughly the principle of trades unions, and work it out practically. I have seen two sparrows on my lawn attack a blackbird who had just managed to get out of the hard earth a considerable worm, and so systematically pursue the attack that the blackbird was routed, and had to leave his prize to be carried off and enjoyed by others. They are the " streeties " or *gamins* of the bird world, these sparrows, with little time or care for sentiment or song beyond a few notes of call, sweet in their way, and all bent on the practical demands of life.

I have heard no end of tales of temporarily disused chimneys in country houses having been utilised by the swallows and the sparrows till the aperture for the ascent of the smoke was quite closed up, and then,

"'SMOKED OUT."

when the fire was lit, there was a fine to-do. " Smoked
out " threatened to be the result till some one ventured
upon the roof to clear the chimney ; and the excitement
caused by the affair would set a whole village astir.

" There are birds and birds," says a reliable writer.
" Of rooks and sparrows we have a surplus, and the
latter promise to exterminate the useful, insect-eating
martins by burglariously entering their nests and ap-
propriating them for their own breeding purposes—a
most objectionable proceeding, which I am under the
impression has only taken place within the last twelve
or fifteen years."

I have many neighbours who belong to the robin
and wren families, who, indeed, are so familiar that
they have both, for
some years past,
built in the hedge
here, quite near to
this seat. The wren
is at some trouble
to disguise the nest
with leaves, the same
as those on the
hedge ; and, besides
his artistic power in
making a beautiful,

WREN.

soft, feathery interior, has indeed quite a wonderful
art in varying the outward effect according to circumstances. In an old tree the nest is made to look
exactly like a handful of dry leaves fixed there by the
wind ; in the ivy the nest has an ivy cover ; while
near to thatch it looks exactly like dry grass. The
wren lays seven or eight eggs, and frequently rears a
second brood in the season—a most nimble, hearty,

and sweet-voiced little fellow. His song is at once spontaneous and musical, gushing, tender, hurried in parts, but very clear, penetrating, full of trills and surprises, if you listen well.

The robins are less particular, and do not trouble themselves, beyond, sometimes, a loose screen of leaves ; perhaps they know that they enjoy a grand immunity in the superstitious fear of destroying their nests or eggs, which is so widespread. And they well reward the immunity they enjoy. Just when

ROBIN BUILDING.

most other birds get silent in the twilight, the robin pours forth his finest ditty, rapid here and there, as if he feared he would not have time to sing all he wanted, and finish off properly, then, recovering, he melts into the mellowest tones, and again becomes bright, clear, and piercing.

But most attractive of all to me for appearance is the beautiful blue-tit, which has established a family here, and often passes me like a winged bit of sky.

He is a most innocent and careful bird, doing not a little service in picking the minute insects off the buds and leaves of certain fruit trees.   And if he has a wonderful tongue for something else than singing, what an eye he must have, also, to be sure ?

The blue-tit is very fond of fat; and if a lump of suet or tallow, or a greasy bone, is hung from the branch of a tree not far off, you will be surprised at the quickness with which the blue-tits will find it out; and you will be forced to admire the nimbleness with which these birds will fix upon it, swing round with it, and speedily eat off the bulk of what is in their view tasty viands, all the time performing the most graceful evolutions for your delight.   Any one who has not witnessed this sight cannot be said to have seen the blue-tit in his glory.   Another peculiar habit of the blue-tit is, that, like the woodpeckers, it either finds, or by great industry, excavates a hole in a tree, and is most methodic and careful in carrying away any chips that may have been produced and dropped to the ground, so that this hint, at any rate, to the position of the nest might not be given to any ill-disposed bird or person.   Cunning little tomtit !

Now and then a bullfinch pays me a visit.   See, there he goes—I must be careful not to startle him— with his fair fawn breast and his dark velvety back, and his occasional sweet note, which he is somewhat careful not to indulge just now, whether from fear of attracting notice or for other reasons.   He is so much hunted as an eater of fruit-buds in the spring that every man's hand is against him here, and he is very seldom to be seen.   He is specially fond of the plum and cherry, and when these are in bud, Mr. Bullfinch won't taste the buds of their wild congeners in the hedgerow. And yet he is so fond of insects, of which he is in search at present in that apple tree, that I am not sure if he does not present an illustration of a degenerate taste. Primarily, no doubt, he took only those buds which were already doomed by the presence of a minute grub; but gradually, as food in some seasons was scarce, he came to form a liking for the bud itself (are not all artificial tastes, indeed, formed in this very way ?), and so has gone on ever since, and has become the victim of a depraved appetite. He is so pretty, and bright, and sweet in voice, though by no means a rich or connected singer, if with a latent gift for mimicry that may be highly developed (the beauty, *par excellence*, for me among the finches), that I really would not like to believe all I hear of him, any more than of my next-door neighbour.

The shy, retiring, hawthorn-loving hawfinch, too, I sometimes see, and now and then a greenfinch will visit me for some of my wilding seeds, and, occasionally, the now, alas ! too rare and beautiful goldfinch steals in furtively to taste, and flutter afterwards in the thistles.

GREEN LINNET.

With thrushes and blackbirds my garden is literally overrun ; they build in the ivy and in the taller trees, and, as they are not frightened off, come from a distance ; and, bold and destructive though they are, I do not have the heart to destroy them : only they cost me annually nearly the worth of my finer fruit, for netting and wire to keep them off.   But I can buy fruit or beg it from my more practical - minded neighbours; but no money could buy that mellow, mellow song, as if blown through fine golden tubes, which indeed it is, that the blackbird gives me from a branch of that tall tree in the gloaming.

BLACKBIRD.

Starlings, too, of a very bold build, constantly look in on me.   See! there one goes, dodging through between those cabbages; he may find a slug or two, but that was not all that he came here for, I'm pretty certain. The idea that starlings do not eat fruit is disproved by my cherry trees. How smooth and shiny his coat is,

STARLING.

and how beautifully marked with gayest colours, and with what a quick eye he detects the presence of anything that is to his taste.

Over yonder is a pyramid Mayduke cherry tree, rising, as you can see, above the graceful feathery plumes of the asparagus, on which *already* the delicate scarlet berries begin to appear, to make a brave show in later September and October; and to that is linked an anecdote, which makes the fruit ravages of the starlings more present to me than would otherwise be the case, and which at the same time throws some light at once on the stolidity and the lazy observant curiosity of a certain class of youthful rustic. At that time I employed a youth of thirteen or fourteen to do odd jobs in the garden, &c., and one day, on coming out and going up to him, as he stood gazing and gaping at something or other across the lawn, and asking the reason of his expression and attitude, I got this very characteristic reply:—" Well, maister, I was just a-lookin' at the starlin' on that ere cherry tree, he do be a picken' off they cherries somethin' wonderful "—the wonderfulness of the starling's. power to pick off the cherries having so impressed the lout that he was disinclined to take the trouble to drive it off. I at once went and did this myself, and had the tree netted, as it was small, though a splendid fruiter. But this did not prevent the starlings returning and making many efforts to pick the fruit through the netting, and one of the birds was caught by the feet in the net and suffered the penalties of his audacity. I have not since shortly after that event had any boys in my garden, believing, with one of my old, shrewd, experienced, observant, farmer friends, that " one boy is a third a man, two boys a sixth a man, and three boys no man at all."

But, notwithstanding all this, the starling is one of the most delightful of birds. It is animated, clever, full of resource, and is capable of being domesticated and taught no end of things. Some of the class have been found able to say certain words more or less distinctly; and on this fact Dr. Norman Macleod founded his tale of " The Starling." The bird of that tale was able to say, " I'm Charlie's bairn ;" and as he would do so on the *Sawbath* day, and thus attract the attention of the youngsters on their way to church, Mr. Porteous, the minister, severe with all the severity of the Scotch Calvinism of half a century ago, insisted on the poor sergeant putting away the bird. This the sergeant would not do, because the starling was associated in his memory with a dead child, and the manner in which Mr. Porteous was brought round and even reconciled both to the starling and to the sergeant is very touching, and well shows the strength of Dr. Macleod as a story-teller of the simple, mixed humorous, and pathetic kind. Mr. Robert Buchanan, too, has used the starling in a very effective poem, in which a little drunken, swearing tailor has a chorus in his only friend, a starling. Sterne's starling everyone remembers.

The cleverness of the starling, together with a touch of *diablerie* in some of its looks and expressions, make it very susceptible of treatment in this way. It is a most striking bird in appearance, too, when you see it in freedom. You would fancy it is black, with, at certain seasons, a touch of buff on the wings, and other markings here and there ; but it really is predominantly a mixture of very dark green and purple and steel-blue, as you would realise if you had ever seen a starling go smartly over a hedge to escape from you in the sunlight. There then is a flash of indescribable dark colour, like the hidden hues of a black opal, which the strong light only reveals. It is best seen on the bird when flying between you and the light.

It has been well said that, in the fields at a distance, the starling looks as if he dressed in the blackbird's old clothes ; but the writer goes on to add that this is a false impression, "for not distance but nearness lends enchantment to a view of the starling. Even as he stands for a moment in the sunshine on the chimney, you can mark much of the brilliancy of his dress as the beautiful metallic green of his dark plumage gleams in the sun and flashes purple every now and then as it catches the light from a different angle. He is too far off for us to notice the harmony of his spot-markings; they cannot be seen to any effect at a distance, but nearer they greatly enhance his beauty. Add to his other points the brown wing feathers with shiny black margins, and his bill, at this season (the breeding season) a bright lemon yellow, like that of a cock blackbird, and you have altogether a singularly handsome bird."

It has often been said that the more virtuous the birds the less beautiful they are. Those that mate year by year, and are, under some rule of "natural selection," led to assume bright colours to attract the females, thus gain their gay appearance as a lady-killer affects fine dress; but the starling mates for life, and yet he is beautiful and most beautiful during the breeding season, as though, so far as he could, he would form an exception to the rule, and prove that nature sometimes gives a touch of loveliness to the well-behaved and true and faithful.

The author of the article on the starling in the " Encyclopædia Britannica" says, " The worst that can be said of it (the starling) is, that *it occasionally pilfers fruit*, and as it flocks to roost in autumn and winter among reed-beds, does considerable damage by breaking down the stems." Yarrell, in his " British Birds," speaks precisely to the same effect.

The truth is, with a very large number of birds, one

can see how they have been corrupted from insect-feeders or seed-eaters to fruit-eaters. This process proceeds along one or other of two lines, (1.) Either they have been led to taste fruit from finding the insects in it or upon it, and having once tasted it, they become fond of it, form, in fact, an artificial taste, as we have found in the case of the bullfinch. (2.) As eaters of the seeds of natural plants, say, the wild strawberry, which has practically no pulp, birds performed in earlier days, before extended cultivation, a great service in the dissemination of the seeds they had eaten and passed through them, carrying them away and re-sowing them in places very distant. But when man's skill develops the pulp—which, in the wild state, is merely enough to protect the seeds—to such an extent that the fruit is practically all pulp and no seeds, then the birds follow his lead, and form a love for the pulp, which nature by itself never would, and never could, have provided for them. Thus it may be said that the process of fruit development is the corruption of the birds from insect-feeders, or mere seed-eaters, to devourers of soft pulp; and the transformation proceeds in such a way that you are hardly ever safe to say that a bird has not in some degree formed this depraved artificial taste by which he at once, as far as he can, apes man and robs him. Human conduct, enterprise, and example are thus responsible for effects far beyond the merely human circle—beyond even the circle which he influences by domestication and direct·application. Analogous cases of artificial tastes formed by changes of habit on animals under man's influence are hundredfold. Here is one: "The baboons at the Cape of Good Hope have always devoured scorpions, but they have lately taken to killing and eating young lambs; in the commencement they killed the lambs for the sake of the milk in their stomachs, but they appear now to have acquired a taste for meat, and devour the flesh of their victims." *

A more extraordinary case still is that of the New Zealand lory or kea, which from a strict vegetarian has become a voracious flesh-eater, and this entirely since the colonists appeared in New Zealand. Prior to this the kea, like the cuckatoos and macaws, was a mild-mannered, fruit-eating, or honey-sucking bird. But "as soon as sheep-stations were established in the island, these degenerate parrots began to acquire a distinct taste for raw mutton. At first, to be sure, they ate only the sheeps' heads and offal that were thrown out from the slaughter-houses, picking the bones as clean of meat as a dog or a jackal. But in process of time, as the taste for blood grew upon them, a still viler idea entered into their wicked heads. The first step on the downward path suggested the second. If dead sheep are good to eat, why not also living ones? The kea, pondering deeply on this abstruse problem, solved it at once with an emphatic affirmative. And he straightway proceeded to act upon his convictions, and invent a really hideous mode of procedure. Perching on the backs of the living sheep, he has now learnt the exact spot where the kidneys are to be found; and he tears open the flesh to get at these dainty morsels, which he pulls out and devours, leaving the unhappy animal to die in miserable agony. As many as two hundred ewes have thus been killed in a night at a single station. I need hardly add that the sheep-farmer naturally resents this irregular proceeding, so opposed to all ideals of good grazing, and that the days

* A. W. Buckland's "Anthropology," p. 42.

of the kea are now numbered in New Zealand.   But
from the purely psychological point of view the case is
an interesting one, as being the best recorded instance
of the growth of a new and complex instinct actually
under the eyes of human observers."

So fruit-eating, in the sense I mean here, is entirely
an acquired taste, and more and more the birds learn
it.   The sparrow and the bullfinch, no doubt at first
cleared the gooseberry bushes from small grubs or
insects in the spring, but they could not help now and
then getting a taste of the eye-buds as they picked the
insects out, and came to form a taste for the buds
themselves, which now they so ravenously devour, that
in some parts covering the bushes with black threads,
crossed from point to point, is the only protection.
The birds do not see these till they dash against them
and are frightened.   So I believe that the starlings
have become corrupted, or are in gradual process of
being so.

In a later page we shall see how the rook bears the
blame of grain-eating when he only picks out, at a
certain stage, the grains which have become the dwell-
ing-places of the intrusive wire-worm; but it is possible
enough that if insect-food became very scarce through
one reason or another, the rook might resort to grain-
eating alone.

And this suggests a word or two about the eyes of
birds, which are indeed wonderful in their adaptation
to be used alternately as a telescope and a microscope.
We speak of a birds-eye view, and that is expressive
enough, but it hints only at one-half the wonder.   The
birds can see far, but they can also see near.   In some
cases the focal distance is remarkably short, being no
more than the length of the bird's bill, whereas in the

normal human eye it is about seven or eight inches. To
the birds in some cases objects are magnified in comparison to the human eye as much as 2000 times.
The tits are in this respect the most noticeable of our
birds, and the beautiful
artistic   nest - building
long-tailed or bottle tit the
most remarkable of all.
To realise his microscopic
power of eye, we must
regard every object that
comes fully within his
field of vision as appearing to him about 2000
times the size that it is
to the normal human
eye. The blue tits and
cole-tits come next, and
then the wrens and wry-
necks, and then, at a considerable interval, the woodpeckers. In consequence of this wonderful magnifying
power, an insect a quarter of an inch long will appear
as large to the eye of the longtailed tit as the common
mouse does to the eye of man, when held as near as it
can be seen.

LONGTAILED TIT.

We need not therefore wonder at the ability of the
little birds to clear off almost microscopic insect larvæ,
and to peck up crumbs that are to our vision scarcely
more than dust. What a peculiar subject it would be
to represent the various objects as they appear to a
long-tailed tit's eye! Think of man how, when close
to the bird, he must stride a colossus in very truth ;
and how ominous an aspect a dog or cat must bear—
the latter a seeming tiger to the little bird. And the

facility with which birds can change the eye from microscopic to telescopic is proved by the fact that, while the tit is feeding on the eggs of flies on this tree (which eggs must appear as large to him as musket bullets do to us), he feels no difficulty in seeing that whinbush at the distance of more than two hundred yards.

A few wood-pigeons will sometimes pay me a visit in the early morning, tempted by some choice strawberries, of which, like other congeners of theirs, they are very fond. There, they are off, with a whirr upwards high, and glance of light from their rapid wings, a slight movement of mine having scared them. They are far more timid than blackbirds, and thrushes or starlings, whose boldness and impudence are equal to their cleverness and ingenuity. The wood-pigeon depends more on his shyness, and swiftness, and caution, than on his boldness, or impudence, or ingenuity. He is a beautiful bird, and his shyness is seen in the fact that he chooses the darkest corner of the wood he can find for his nest, and then is so impatient, or so incapable a nest-builder, that in the gloom his white eggs, exposed through twigs carelessly criss-crossed, will betray him. I have sometimes seen as many as five here shortly after daylight in search of gooseberries (for which, too, they have a passionate liking), cherries, peas, or lettuce, of which they will take an occasional refresher. But they may take a taste of some of my weedy wildings too, for they are very fond of wild mustard and ragweed, and often do good service to the farmer in clearing them from his fields, when he believes that they are only eating his corn, or wheat, or turnips. But they prefer the weeds to them any day, else from their wonderful voracity they would rank as most dangerous enemies of the agriculturist. They are keen, however, at certain seasons for some kinds of turnip-tops and also of turnips, which, if holes have already been made through the rough outside skin by rabbit or hare, they will almost entirely scoop out. The thought of this rouses the farmer's ire, which is not easily allayed.

They are fond of beech-nuts, and will go long

SENTINEL WOODPIGEON.

distances to get them, and some observers say that, like rooks and pheasants, they will gorge themselves with acorns, and that the art they show, soft-billed though they are, in detaching the nut from the cup, and splitting the core, is astonishing. They will set the acorn in position, and strike it with their bills with the utmost precision.

It seems to me that they show traces of a conscience,

whether generated simply by fear and former experience (as the Evolutionists would say) I cannot pretend to know. When feeding in flocks in the fields among the grain or roots, they never forget to post a sentinel or two, and a settled, regulated method of interchange of position, which I had observed in my early morning walks before I had been fortunate enough to alight on this most faithful observation in the fascinating pages of the late Charles St. John.

" It is amusing to watch a large flock of these birds while searching the ground for grain. They walk in a compact body, and in order that all may fare alike, the hindmost rank every now and then fly over the heads of their companions to the front, where they keep the best place for a minute or two, till those now in the rear take their place in the same manner. They keep up this kind of fair-play during the whole time of feeding."

In feeding on acorns in the woods they seem to proceed less regularly, and are to be found more in pairs.

It is very odd, considering the shyness and cunning and caution of birds, the whimsical and exposed places in which sometimes they will build. It would seem as though in some instances they studiously left room in their choice and style of building for after-ingenuity and resource. A wren last year was actually guilty of the innocent enormity of putting her nest in a cabbage plant left for seed right over in that corner. Notwithstanding the presence of this seat, which, as I am often here, one would have fancied would have scared off the birds, there are many nests quite close to it. At my right hand, almost overhead, in the ivy overhanging the old wall, there is a nest of blue tits, and

oh! the whispering and signalling that goes on if I give
any sign of consciously watching their performances.

BLUE TIT.

They are now quite
at their ease, unless
I stand on tiptoe
in the endeavour
to look into their
nest, and then
the whispers and
chatter begin. But
how cunning they
are! Being thus
often observed, and
desirous of hiding
their nest as much as they may, they have constructed
or placed it so that they can enter it both from above
and below; and when I am watching, how they dodge
and dip and enter it either way.

A chaffinch last year built in the corner of a disused
frame, which had become a receptacle for empty flower-

THE CHAFFINCH.

pots, &c., and reared
a brood in spite of
the gardener's con-
stant going about
the frame. The
chaffinch is not al-
ways so easily sat-
isfied. Do you see
that old apple tree
there just beyond
that cherry tree
and next to the
plum? Well, just in the little hole where the branches
part from the bole a chaffinch has had its nest for three

years past. It is so low that by standing on tiptoe you could almost put your hand into it; but they have so wonderfully lichened it over to an exact resemblance with the bark of the tree that it would be a very quick eye indeed that would notice it, unless it followed the bird returning—a beautiful illustration of what is now called the protective instinct which nature has so strongly bestowed on many of her children. The chaffinch is in some ways a very noticeable bird; it is indeed almost the only one of the small birds which pairs for life, and it has been said that it learns its song anew each spring. If this is so, the chaffinch soon regains his mastery. He is in many ways a meister-singer among birds. He is never failing. He begins with a lovely lilt, as it were; a passage of old song, blithe and debonnair, passes into the softest warble, and after some mixed flourishes, with the finest sense of contrast in them, closes with a sudden abrupt kind of clash of notes. Mr. Waterton wrote thus well of the chaffinch, and expresses the thought of many a bird lover :—

"Next to poor cock robin, the chaffinch is my favourite bird. I see him almost at every step. He is in the fruit and forest trees and in the lowly haw-thorn; he is on the house-top and on the ground close to your feet. You may observe him on the stack-bar and on the dunghill, on the king's highway, in the fallow field, in the meadow, in the pasture, and by the margin of the stream. His nest is a paragon of perfection. He attaches lichen to the outside of it by means of the spider's slender web. In the year 1805, when I was on a plantation in Guiana, I saw the humming bird making use of the spider's web in its nidification, and then the thought struck me that our chaffinch might probably make use of it too. On my return to Europe I watched a chaffinch busy at its nest. It left it, and flew to an old wall and took a cobweb from it, then conveyed it to its nest, and interwove it with the lichen on the outside of it."

The little busy goldcrest, very unlike the wren family, to which he is related, in personal appearance,

GOLDCREST.

goes about his business in a careful cheerful manner, and at the hot hours of noon in summer days sends out soft bursts of song, when else silence would almost reign in garden or wood. His tiny nest is hung on the end of the high branch of that cedar tree on the lawn, and so neatly that, looking from below, you could hardly see it, the feathery ends of the needles falling round it.

What a delight the bees have found in these foxgloves, which seem as if nature constructed them to show what she could do in building a perfect floral pyramid, or perhaps more properly, floral obelisk, and to afford a ceaseless series of newly unfolded flowers through a whole season. Unlike the grand builders of the Nile, she does not aim at hard permanence here; but she combines what they did not and could not do, perfection of line and curve, and ceaseless change in sweet gradation. They are now losing the lower flowers that pale off and shrink away, while those at the top are spreading out into a lovely crown of pinky purple. The arrangement is one of the most exquisite in nature, illustrating beauty long drawn out. First, we have a true obelisk, the upper tiers yet immature, and small and darker in colour altogether, without that transparency and luminousness which marked those below, but lending a wonderful grace, poise, and charm to the flower and its movements. Then tier by tier in series, step by step, the colour and charm are taken up from those below, till at last all that remains is a kind of glory-crown, over ranges of seeds : lovely foxgloves

" In whose drooping bells the bee makes her sweet music."

Almost behind me as I sit a mass of firewood has been built stack-shape in view of winter. There a discontented barn-door fowl has wandered from the others and from her proper nest in the hen-house, and has found a hole in this stack into which she has managed to crawl, and has made a nest there, and is now busy in laying her complement of eggs; but with the inconsistency of her kind, in which apparently opposite instincts maintain themselves in full force, she has no sooner laid her egg than she exultantly informs all the world of her feat, which she purposed to keep a great secret. Her cluck, cluck, cluck, iack! is shrill and penetrating, no effort spared. What purpose can that cackling serve, save to betray the hidden nest ? Is the secretive instinct a faint survival even from far-off ancestors, and the cackle a sort of vain, self-conscious something, developed under domestication and intercourse with man—as it is certain now that the bark of the dog is? Wild gallinaceous fowls do not cackle as does the domestic hen. The two instincts seem totally opposed to each other, and are mutually destructive. But then it is very easy to condemn the poor egg-layer. What worse is she than the human weakling who has a great secret and shows that he has it, forgetting that very wise warning Goethe makes Wilhelm Meister give his boy, that to keep a secret you must be careful to hide that you have one.

Bees of all kinds daily visit me. The common humble-bee and sometimes the moss or carder-bee, the "foggy-toddler" of Scottish boys, and a peculiarly long, thin, black bee, with the faintest tip of red on its tail, and at times clouds of my neighbour's hive bees mix with my own—giving evidence that there are some Ligurians imported. Last year they accomplished an odd feat. I had brought some beans of a very fine kind from Belgium. The beans are pure white and in long pods which run up poles as high as hops or even higher; not far off were some scarlet runners, of both of which the bees were very fond. One half of the plants grown from my pure white Belgian seed yielded a cross—not pure white, but speckled as if with the colour of the scarlet-runner bean—and the pods were not nearly so long and flat as in the Belgian bean. It was at all events quite a new variety, never before seen in the district. The wild-flowers near my garden-seat particularly attract them. By what secret magnetism is it that they know when any new species is in bloom, and come simultaneously to it, as it were, from the four winds of heaven? But, in spite of little *contretemps* of this kind, I can heartily say, with that sweet American poetess, Miss Celia Thaxter, whose eye for nature is as keen as her love for it is passionate, when in her beautiful poem titled "Guests," she celebrates, as I do, her—

> " Quaint little wilderness of flowers, straggling hither and
>   thither,
>   Morning glories tangled about the larkspur run to seed ; "

and proceeds to express her welcome thus :

> " Welcome, a thousand times welcome, ye dear and delicate
>   neighbours,
>   Bird and bee and butterfly, and redbreast fairy fine !
>   Proud am I to offer you a field for your graceful labours ;
>   All the honey and all the seeds are yours in this garden of
>   mine !
>   I sit on the doorstep and watch you.   Beyond lies the infinite
>   ocean,
>   Sparkling, shimmering, whispering, rocking itself to rest,
>   And the world is full of perfume and colour and beautiful
>   motion,
>   And each sweet hour of this new day the happiest seems and
>   best."

I spoke of the high branch of the sycamore tree, but
it has points of interest beyond its being beautiful and
affording a good resort for many birds.   If it does not
quite match the chestnut—the " gummy chestnut buds "
of Lord Tennyson *—in the thickness of the gum which

* The verse in " The Miller's Daughter " originally stood thus :—

> " Remember you that pleasant day,
>   When, after roving in the woods
> ('Twas April then), I came and lay
>   Beneath those gummy chestnut-buds ? "

The critic of the *Quarterly Review*, who noticed the whole volume in
a fine strain of mockery and sarcasm, was especially funny and quizzical
over the " gummy chestnut-buds," and so the nice observation had to
give place to more fanciful and amplified and less effective phrases in
the later editions :—

> " But, Alice, what an hour was that,
>   When, after roving in the woods
> ('Twas April then), I came and sat
>   Below the chestnuts, when *their buds*
>   *Were glistening to the breezy blue*,"

which, by the way, any bud with dew or moisture after rain would
do.   Such are the fine ministries of ignorant, cynical, self-conceited
" crickets," as Artemus Ward named them !

it extrudes over the little buds formed in later autumn, in preparation for the next spring, which dries and hardens, and is a most efficient protection for them against the frosts and snows, often glittering like amber between you and the sunset, it has a kind of honey in which it encases them very effectively, through all the cold and frost ; and when the sun once more begins to look forth with a certain heat, this melts away and drops to the ground in the most minute globules like dew when the tree is stirred.   Hence the truth of the line—

"The sycamore drops honey when 'tis stirred."

But the seed of the tree is even more curious and wonderful than the bud. As I have sat here in later September and October, I have seen them part from the tree and come with a peculiar wavering kind of flight on the wind. These seeds are called samaras, because they are really winged, or perhaps because the seed in its envelope has a soft furry, silky lining, either from *simarre*, a woman's dress or scarf, or simarre, a bishop's upper robe. The wings of the samara are beautifully adapted to float a heavy body, which they do, as any one may see, at the right season,

SYCAMORE TREE.

when favourable winds are stirring. They dry into a very light-veined brown skeleton wing, and may be seen in certain spots in thousands in the later autumn and early winter. The late Laureate, in the "In Memoriam," wonders why it is that

> "Often out of fifty seeds
> Great Nature brings but one to bear."

Multitudes of these seeds of sycamore perish; many are eaten by cattle; many are trodden and destroyed. Doubtless, thousands on thousands perish for one that grows in spite of nature's wonderful device to spread them. And yet the sycamore asserts how well nature can cherish her children. Wherever there is a sycamore, sycamore seedlings will spring up in profusion within a wide area, if any spaces whatever are left to nature; it intrudes into all manner of hedges and takes root, particularly liking the gravel. Nature's economy and care of the type is hardly in anything better illustrated than in the sycamore samara.

Do you wonder that I love to sit and read and muse and brood and dream and observe in this sheltered garden-seat, with my wild-flowers close around me, a screen of cultivated garden further off, and all manner of birds and insects continuously sounding soft accompaniment? Yes, even in days when I feel it chilly, I am surprised to see the bees bumming away at their work, and the birds singing! The peculiar manner in which, at certain times, all the various sounds blend into a sort of harmony in the warm summer afternoons has often surprised me, till I doubted whether it was not possible that, after all, the harmony was not an illusion that dwelt in my own sense and soul alone. Any way, the effect is the same; and if the soul is so attuned

that it thus makes harmony for itself, then it is only a
further witness for the harmony of the world, since
through the soul alone can it be apprehended, as through
God the soul, we believe that it was made.   In a green
field philosophy is somewhat out of place; and so it is
in such a corner as this.   I will leave the subject, with
a devout hope that all who desire the kind of sweet
solitude and society I enjoy here at one and the same
moment will soon succeed in realising their wish.   For
this kind of enjoyment is the most remote from selfish,
and feels that to share is doubly to enjoy.   Therefore

> " Blame me not, laborious band,
>   For the common flowers I brought ;
> Every blossom in my hand
>   Comes back laden with a thought."

II

MY POND.

I FIND a world of delight and sweet companionship at all seasons here by the borders of this pond. Its position is just what that of a pond should be to take most advantage of the sunlight and the sunset, of moonlight and stars. It lies open along almost the whole breadth of its eastern end, with a soft level grassy platform there, as if nature had intended, and art—pleasant helpmate—had done its best to reinforce the intention, that you should advantageously and easily see how she can distribute her tree-forms and varied tints to the best advantage, as well as cast in a hook with comfort, if you are inclined to try for roach or golden tench, which abound in it, and which at certain hours find a favourite resort and feeding-place in the freshet; for it is, in truth, a miniature lake, with true inlet and outlet, the banks rising at both sides, and showing that the pond is natural—the enlargement of a very old watercourse. As you stand there, rod in hand, the falling water behind you, that had passed through a grating and bricked channel under your feet for a space of six yards or more, falls into a miniature

basin, self-formed, with a lulling slumbrous sound;
and then, after short pause and eddy, works its way,
glittering in the sunshine, through grass and rushes
and waving watercresses of giant size, over the
centre of what was once the bottom of a second and
lower pond, now dried up and reclaimed for pasturage.
Very fond the cows are, if they can find the chance, of
sheltering here, knee-deep in water, in the hot days of

MY POND.

summer under the shade of the old elder tree, which
had once looked on its image in the sheet of glassy
water below it.

Round both sides of my pond run trees and shrubs
of many kinds, most of them old, and probably self-
sown: grey-green willows, spreading branches over
the water and lightly dipping in, hollies, blackthorns,
beeches, ashes, and alders, more retiring, and one or

two black bullace trees, which are more forward to keep in line with the willows, and which occasionally bear fruit in their season, and attract many birds; while on the upper or western end it is almost closed in by three giant forms of oaks, and one magnificent blackthorn, in later spring hoary and heavy with blossoms. A picnic might be held in the branches of that lordly old oak in the middle of the greeny crescent, and indeed has been ; for if you walk round there you may see still the remnants of the circle of seats placed just above where the branches spring from the bole, and would accommodate a tolerable tea-party were they restored and a tea-table set in the centre, as it well might be.

The effect at sunset is sometimes very fine. Often have I stood, rod in hand, in dreamy admiration of the wondrous mixture of gold and green that inevitably suggested thoughts—not all irreverent—of a burning bush, and, momentarily oblivious of the bobbings of my float, have had to mourn the loss of what seemed finer and heavier fish than I ever landed there, and to reproach or congratulate myself accordingly. But it is a weakness of fishermen thus unconsciously to moralise life by a parable of the contrast between wishes and realities. The fish that were lost ever excelled the fish that were caught. But the glory of the sight scarce admitted such reflections then. In quivering bars the foliage seemed turned to gold, and burned as it danced in the brilliance, if a faint wind were stirring ; while beneath the trees lay soft fair shadows of themselves, yet clear and bold in outline, with all the glory of eve about them, and suggesting a wondrous depth ; and in the middle space, nearer to me, the golden rays that stole through the higher leaves flickered and fell, and dappled the water, as it were, with golden rain that seemed to flit and waver and return in wondrous rhythmic regularity, like breathing, or the notes of a musical scale heard at a distance. As the sun sinks, the brilliant colours die away into a kind of salmon colour on the sky in long soft bars, tremulous if not palpitating, growing fainter and fainter at the extremes ; the shadows deepen ; but the twilight is pleasant, and I often linger till the darkness falls, and I can listen to the owl's cry heard not far off. Indeed, on one or two occasions, these wonderful winged cats, so intent in search of their prey, have flown so close past my ear as to give me a surprise and shock, till I assured

BARN OWL.

myself, as the eye caught a glimpse of the soft white figure gliding on, that it was only an owl. The farmers now like to encourage these settlers, knowing their value as mousers and destroyers of other vermin, and the army has been reinforced quite recently. The barn-owl, when she has young, is said to bring to her nest a mouse every twelve minutes, and as both male and female hunt, the lowest computation is forty mice a day. That is something surely !

The intrusion of the owl intimates to me that I must not farther dilate on nature's inanimate shows at morn or eventide (for that would occupy many pages); I must speak of the living creatures that morning, noon, and night bring to my pond an attraction of their own. A small community of water-hens have found homes here, one couple in the black bullace tree yonder, which spreads its branches over the water, forming a tent-like screen; and as sometimes I sit, half hidden in foliage, on the north side of the pond (for the fish, at certain times and seasons, will quit the freshet and seek coolness and rest in the shadows there), they will lead their broods along the margin with their peculiar, measured, careful tread, and with their peculiar cry—a kind of quickened and sharpened *cluck*, *cluck* of the ordinary farm-yard fowl, suggesting vaguely possibilities of domestication and tameness, which, however, are some-

WATER-HEN.

what rudely dispelled when any cause of fear or alarm arises. The warning or call-note then given is of a very wild, harsh, and grating half-saw-like character— a call which cannot, however, be called a very cunning one, for it would inevitably draw even a tyro's attention to the exact whereabouts of the bird. On the slightest hint of strange intrusion into their domain, they utter this harsh and grating cry, and speedily retreat, marching their youngsters home again to their greeny shelters, under the sweeping branches of bullace, blackthorn, or willow.

The young are very pretty—little balls of soft black down, with a wedge of greeny yellow for a beak. If you look closely at them as they move along the margin, their feet go twinkle, twinkle as they run, with a kind of darting movement, extremely pretty and interesting. They are active from the moment they leave the egg, and if frightened when the parents are absent, will take to the water and swim even on the second day, should the nest be near to the surface; but the moor-hen sometimes builds high, or, as we shall see, occasionally raises her nest higher after she has built it, and then the mother carries the little things down to the water to give them their first outing, and will carefully carry them back again to the nest.

Those who have witnessed it declare it to be one

COOT.

of the prettiest sights to see the young ones lifted by the parents from the nest to the water.   The coots practise the same art, though the young of the coots can hardly be said to be so pretty and original looking as these little balls of black fluffy down.

They are good and careful parents, if sometimes they seem to be rather domineering in manner. But this may be, in some degree, due to the fact that they have so many enemies that not a few of the young never reach maturity. Herons (which occasionally pay the pond a visit), owls, weasels, rats, and even large eels are only a few of those ever ready to prey upon them; so that perhaps the eager surveillance and domineering drill-sergeant air of the water-hen towards its young is not to be wondered at, more especially when we consider the open places it often homes in. Certainly there is no lack of fertility on the part of the water-hen; she lays seven or eight eggs, and has two or three broods a year. Dr. Stanley, Bishop of Norwich (venerated father of the late Dean Stanley, and a minute and careful observer), says that they produce several broods a year, and that when all the broods survive, a second nest is built. This was last year the case with a pair on this very pond, which added much to the parental care and responsibility; and the business of giving warning-calls to the elder brood without leaving the second nest was sometimes so earnest and urgent as to be quite touching. They are decidedly clever birds in their own way, though, as often happens with nature's nurslings, they are unaccountably stupid in other and apparently simpler matters, as some of their calls is enough to show. Dr. Stanley observed that when a water-hen had noticed a pheasant leap on the board of the feeding-boxes the keepers place for them, and they by its weight opened the lid, she at once tried the same thing; but finding she was not heavy enough, she went for a friend, and the combined weight of the two sufficed to secure them a good feed, as reward for their astuteness. In favourable circumstances, too, the water-hens show some eye for beauty, and, like the bower birds, will decorate their nests. If near gardens, they will sometimes pilfer flowers of bright colours—particularly scarlet, for which they have a great fancy—wreaths of scarlet anemones having been carried off by them for this purpose. A friend of mine is certain that in the early spring mornings they have even made efforts at carrying off japonica blossoms from a wall in his garden, which lies not far from their quarters. They always cover the eggs before leaving the nest, either for concealment or for warmth.

And what is perhaps more extraordinary still, as we have said, is that these water-hens will, in the event of flooding or the rise of the water, raise up the nest—which is formed of the leaves of flags deftly interwoven —to a considerable extent, probably by supporting it on their backs and fixing it *pro tem.* to the most available branch or spray, till they have reached a perfectly safe elevation. Most frequently the nest is supported on a branch or branches just a little above the water, so that it is secure from certain egg-eating neighbours, like rats or hedgehogs, who pursue their callings, in most cases not far distant from the water-hen's nest.

There can be no doubt about the water-hen's power in raising the nest in floods. Here is a passage from the description of a reliable observer :—

"The nest was placed a few inches above the water, and about seven feet from the river-bank. When we first observed it, it contained eggs. These were soon hatched, and great was the delight of the children to watch the old birds scuffle away from the nest and then to peep in and mark the progress of the brood. One sad day heavy rain fell, a high flood followed, and great was the children's grief over the little birds, which they thought must be drowned and their nest swept away. Our first excursion on the subsiding of the flood was to the river-side nursery. What were the delight and astonishment of the young folks at beholding the nest firmly fixed to some of the reeds and waving in the air fully five feet above the surface of the water! As we watched, we saw the mother-bird travel down an inclined plane made of bent rushes, which led direct from the nest to the river-bank. Her brood followed her, and soon all dropped into the water and were hidden among the reeds. Within an hour we saw them all return to the nest up the inclined plane, and so things went on for several days till they forsook their home. On examination it was clear to us that as the water rose the old birds must have placed themselves under the nest and gradually lifted it on their backs some five feet. But it was not in their power to make it descend, so they fastened it securely to the reeds, and constructed the roadway to the shore for the egress and ingress of their brood—a beautiful instance of parental care and of the instinct God bestows upon His creatures for their preservation and that of their brood."

Here the water-hens have laid their eggs and reared their broods for many seasons—for seven now to my own knowledge and observation—not much frightened, apparently, by the horses that come down here to drink, and sometimes in the hot days will indulge themselves in a good bath and swim, much to the chagrin of the men, who loudly cry and scream and whistle at them, not liking the extra work of rubbing dry thereby entailed on them, or the dogs that come there from the farm-house to swim and enjoy themselves every day.

And not far from the moor-hens is a settlement of water-voles, who very quietly and unobtrusively carry on their daily life and work. Beautiful little creatures, with that gentle look and soft retiring shyness in their every action which so appeals to the lover of animals

and awakens his curiosity and affection.   Many a time
have I had my train of meditation suddenly interrupted
by the *plop* of one of them from the bank—a sound
they invariably made when descending into the water
thus, and almost the only sound they do make—though
in swimming they will come towards you till they are
within a few yards, and then their brown-grey heads
will softly, suddenly disappear, leaving you doubtful

THE WATER-VOLE.

if you have not been dreaming, till, if you are watchful,
the fact is attested by just one little silvery bubble that
will rise at their point of disappearance.   Long have I
sometimes watched for their reappearance at distant
points of the pond to be disappointed, till I learned
that it is the habit of the creature in these circumstances to enter its nest from under the water, having
at least two openings to it, which leads the family,

when it increases, to do a good deal of harm to the banks by burrowing, though generally they choose an old tree stump, and by preference burrow round about it. Their powers in this way are very remarkable. Man, when he makes a tunnel, needs no end of levels and instruments and calculations, the vole, in the dark, like the mole, can strike his line and burrow along it, and come out at the precise point he wanted. We call this instinct, but when you think of it, it is a wonderful thing. The vole, from his teeth and structure of head is more a beaver than anything else, and indeed he was once so classed scientifically with the beavers, but now forms a leading item in another class of rodents. Unlike the rat he has very short rounded ears, and a short tail by comparison, and his teeth differ in certain important respects. His teeth are yellow teeth like the beaver, owing to the enamel facing they have, and they are precisely of the chisel character. Were it not so they would not be efficient for the work it has to do.

There has been a good deal of discussion about the habits of these pretty little animals as regards food, some saying that they are purely vegetable feeders, and others that they are occasionally carnivorous or fish-eating, and that they will eat the young of the water-hens, &c. &c. We have good reason to believe that they are strict vegetarians, having frequently set morsels of meat of various kinds in their way, which never tempted them that we could see, and were often passed by them with indifference; but these same morsels were sometimes carried off by brown rats that had their holes in the dry ditches near by, an animal for whose depredations our water-vole is doubtless often blamed.

As for the water-hens, they live, so far as I can see, in the most perfect amity with the voles, leading out their young broods fearlessly while the rodents are swimming about, which could hardly be the case, did the voles intrude into the water-hens' nests in search of eggs, or really have serious designs upon their young ones.   This, at least, is no matter of doubt, for at certain seasons of the year we have witnessed it almost daily.   The voles rejoice to browse on the flags, irises, rushes, and green herbage that surround the pond, and are particularly fond of the leaves of the iris, and will sit on their hind legs like a squirrel and nibble contentedly at one spot for a long time.   Their mode of eating is similar to that of the squirrel.   They sit on their haunches and hold the food in their front paws, and nibble, nibble at it in the prettiest way. They do not properly hybernate, but are partially dormant during winter, and lay up a store of food in a shelf or corner, specially prepared.   Mr. Groom Napier found in one of these, when he had dug out a water-vole's tunnelled abode, a large quantity of fragments of carrots and potatoes, sufficient to fill a peck measure.

I have certainly never seen them seeking for worms or insects, or eating them.   As for their eating fish-spawn, they cannot do much depredation in that way, for this pool, which has been always well-fished, increases to such an extent in tench and in roach, that in the evening, when the gnats come out, and disport themselves in their thousands on the surface of the water, you can see the roach in shoals when the sunshine falls at certain favourite spots near the surface, towards the inlet, really making, when you look low along the water, a kind of faint dark-blue or purple patches, from the midst of which every few seconds

one will leap, showing head and shoulders, and sometimes the whole body, and sending a circle of dancing
ripples over the place, with an indescribably lustrous
and beautiful effect. For these reasons I do not believe that the water-voles are, in any respect, carnivorous.* Four years ago, indeed, the moor-hens—in
spite of all their enemies—had increased to such an
extent that my friend, the resident in the place, tells me
he had most unwillingly to shoot a number of them.
They made a favourite feeding-ground in a field at the
side of the pond, and did much damage there—one
corner of it being eaten bare.

Occasionally as I have stood fishing there in July or
August, a pair, or perhaps three of what are called
locally "summer snipe," not the common sandpiper,
however, would suddenly dash over the pond, and, if
I could only keep still enough, or creep silently under
cover of near foliage, would settle on the margin, and
make sundry observations, no doubt in search of some
particular tid-bit, which they do not just then find so
easily elsewhere. Very beautiful are they with their
whitish throats and breasts, and dark velvety back, and
red or chestnut-tipped wings—a somewhat swallow-
like appearance at first glance, though they are much
bigger and long-billed. Their flight is very quick,
and their cry is a sharp short whistle. The last
memorable occasion on which I saw them, and when,
unfortunately in one respect I was not alone, was on
Saturday, August 27, 1887, when my good friend, the
resident on the place, was at my side. He regretted

* Since this was written, a friend has pointed out to me an article in
Science Gossip (1886, pp. 155-158), in which Mr. G. T. Rope says that
even the common bank-vole is a purely vegetable feeder. He has
kept these creatures in confinement for long periods.

(which I confess I did not, though his wish was prompted by the most generous feelings towards me) that he had not his gun that he might have got a brace. But they were scared by our presence, and winged their flight to other scenes—" fresh woods and pastures new "—doubtless disappointed in securing the object of their visit. Speaking of their occasional appearance, my friend said that their visits there were invariably preliminary to heavy rains (it was clear and bright when they came that day), a matter which he had often verified, and which I had not previously done. But, certainly, on this occasion he was right. Rain fell heavily there on the Saturday night, and on the Sunday morning so heavily as to cause very thin church attendances, and again fell heavily on the Monday morning; and the weather the whole week following was broken and wet. It would be interesting to know if the same facts, as bearing on meteorological lore, have been observed in other localities. No doubt the minute observations of the movements of birds, if carried on systematically over the whole country, would be of great use as regards weather forecasting; and, at one time, when Dr. Smiles' hero, Thomas Edwards, the Scottish naturalist, was still alive, there was a proposal to institute such a system by securing the regular aid of such local observers as he to report to headquarters—a kind of wing (or wings) to the Meteorological Survey. But I am not aware that it has ever been carried out.

While I stand fishing on the stump of an old elder which had been cut down some years ago, and is now again burgeoning into beauty, framed like a portrait with greenery round me, a furze-chat pursues its business of attending to its young quite close to me.

I can hear it flying out and in to its nest; and on the slightest noise or movement on the part of the dog I have sometimes with me, it will utter its short hoarse cry of warning or alarm. This I seldom hear from it when the dog is not with me, which proves, I think, that the little bird has some idea that I am too pre-occupied with my own task to interfere with it; though it does not quite trust the dog in the same way, as, indeed, it is quite right in not doing: they are so cunning.

In the summer of 1889 a thrush built a nest in the fork of a small tree right behind where I stand, and sat on her eggs and nursed her brood within a few yards of me. When I withdrew a little to re-bait, I was within a yard and a half of her nest. Yet still she sat; and by raising my head a little as I stood I could see her and she could see me—the dark, honest, bead-like eye with not a touch of fear in it met mine with a kind of confidence which was not unrewarded; for I carefully kept the secret, in response to her trust, till she herself revealed her whereabouts to my friend the proprietor, when he had come round to talk to me, by flying off her young—little yellow-mouthed, broad-beaked things, with wide throats—and I could not save them, for he at once condemned them as prospective eaters of his fruit. And I was sorry, though I could not fully say so.

The perseverance of birds, too, is really wonderful, and on this spot I have seen many remarkable instances of it. In the spring, when nest-building is going on, the devices adopted to transport certain materials to a high branch on a neighbouring tree are hardly credible, any more than is the manner in which the birds are inclined at a stretch to help each other. A couple of wrens who built last year in the hedge just behind where I now stand, afforded me no little amusement and interest, they were so assiduous, and so fond of stealing a moment to pour forth a few notes of song. Some feathers they had no end of trouble in transporting to their nest from right opposite the pond, which they did not try to cross, but flew round. The wind was against them, and was very apt, if the feather was left for an instant for rest or relief, to blow it back again. Finally, they doubtless sought and procured the help of another pair, and the four managed by their combined efforts to get it into the hedge properly. I looked at that nest afterwards, and was surprised to see how neatly the wren had covered it with leaves of the beech hedge in which it was built, so that one would have fancied it was a mere tuft of leaves gathered there—a specimen of the protective instinct in nest-building, which is most noticeable in those birds whose eggs are of a colour which would be most easily noticed.

From this point of vantage, too, I have seen the little robin redbreast on the walk that skirts the pond perform wonders in carrying off to its young brood big worms, which it took care to beat well with its beak—devoting to this end some five or six minutes, and then boldly carrying off the long heavy prize on its bill.

In the dozing heat of the summer afternoons a small variety of the green dragon-fly will sometimes be found in considerable numbers about the pond. Often they fix themselves on the top of the float, and will stick there until the float is moved with some decision. I have often wondered what of attraction there could be for those insects in the float, and would be glad if any one would tell me. Of course, every one knows that they find their food in the small microscopical creatures which infest ponds, that they lay their eggs in the water, and in it their nymphs emerge from the pupa and develop their wings, and that, unlike most creatures, they breathe through their tail, which, though long and large, is not therefore a useless appendage. But all this throws no light on their love of a float, which cannot be appetising; and, as the *libellula* are all so greedy, it is the more to be wondered at that they can choose to spend their time in this apparently profitless way. How apt and clear and exact is Lord Tennyson's picture in "The Two Voices" :—

> "To-day I saw the dragon-fly
> Come from the wells where he did lie.
>
> An inner impulse rent the veil
> Of his old husk ; from head to tail
> Came out clear plates of shining mail.
> He dried his wings ; like gauze they grew,
> Through croft and pasture, wet with dew :
> A living flash of light he flew."

The lesser denizens of the pond are equally active. You may see the water boatman swimming on his back —pleasant pastime mixed with business in his case, for this is the law of nature; if they do not take their pleasures sadly, business is never quite neglected. There he goes swimming on his back, making faint triangular ripples behind him, as he propels himself swiftly by the long cilia or hairs on each side of him —natural oarlets, which far surpass the finest featherings yet made by man. And that little blue-black bloodthirsty "whirligig" is here too, who, but half the size of the boatman, will descend upon and capture him, spinning round and round in circles like a tiny dervish of the waters; only there is no sacredness in his devices, but only a disguise that he may dart the better, and the more surely secure his prey. Crowds of water-bugs are also at times to be seen, and water-measurers with their most dainty aquatic appurtenances. With what delicacy nature has furnished and armed some apparently unworthy creatures! Of course, my pond has its due share of the more common visitors, such as water-wagtails and swallows—the latter sometimes dipping into the water and causing a sudden bright flash in the sunshine. Water-beetles, large and small, reveal themselves at as many points as you look.

Angling in such positions may well be called the "contemplative man's recreation." It is, at all events, a good introduction to nature in some of her phases, for it would seem as though to take a rod in hand and to appear completely absorbed in your pursuit was a magical way to put all the denizens of the place quite at their ease. They are indeed either very penetrating or very cunning. It has been well said that—

"In some instinctive way these wild creatures learn to distinguish when one is or is not intent upon them in a spirit of enmity; and if very near it is always the eye they watch. So long as you observe them, as it were, from the corner of the eyeball, sideways, or look over their heads at something beyond, it is well. Turn your glance full upon them to get a better view, and they are gone."

To sit perfectly still, as Thoreau said, is a good means to get all the wild things of wood and field to come and show themselves to you in turn; but I believe fishing, which does not demand such unchanging cramping positions, is a yet better one. A very good essay

might well be written, and I am not aware that it has
yet been exhaustively written, though Izaak Walton
and many of his disciples have glanced at it, on angling
as an aid to the study of nature and natural history in
certain of their aspects. It ensures that you shall not
defeat your own object, even by too actively and hotly
pursuing it, as too often happens, at all events to the
tyro or amateur. Nothing, indeed, is more difficult to
acquire than that patience and willingness to reserve
action for the sake of observing new traits of character
and unexpected actions. This is the test of real culture in the sportsman, this capability to forego sport,
when any exceptional trait will reward observation;
and nothing in the Badminton book on "shooting,"
has so much delighted me as the many evidences of
this quality, which has made the work a happy treasury
of natural history, and wise incitement to scientific
observation, as well as a most excellent and practical
guide to sportsmen, and especially young sportsmen.
This it was which gave colour and character to all the
writings of the late Mr. Charles St. John. Without
this, indeed, they would have had but half their value.
Charles Waterton's instinct in this regard rose to
genius. This, too, it is which gives charm to Charles
Kingsley's open air chapters, his "chalk-stream studies,"
and so on, and often communicates a delicate freshness and gracious felicity to the pages of the Rev. G. M.
Watkins. Without its presence, indeed, to a greater
or lesser degree, all writings on sport are simply so
many incitements to cold-blooded butchery, in which
jealousy, vanity, and greed of personal success and
superiority are the chief constituents.

Sir Edward Hamley, in his little essay on "Our
Poor Relations," notes this quaintly, and with sly

serio-comic touch sketches the sportsman of the contrary type, in his education and his tendencies.

"We will now, after the manner of great moralists, such as he who depicted the careers of the Industrious and Idle Apprentices, give the reverse of the picture, in the horrible imp of empty head and stony heart, who has been trained to regard the creatures around him as the mere ministers of his pleasure and his pride, and who, in fact, represents in its worst form the indifferent or cruel state of feeling towards animals. Provided almost in his cradle by his unnatural parents with puppies and kittens whereon to wreak his evil propensities, he treats them, to the best of his ability, as the infant Hercules treated the serpents, and when provoked to retaliate with tooth and claw, they are ordered, with his full concurrence, to immediate execution. A little later he hails the periodical pregnancies of the ill-used family as so many opportunities in store for drowning the progeny. All defenceless animals falling into his power are subject to martyrdom by lapidation. Show him a shy bird of rare beauty on moor or heath, in wood or valley, and the soulless goblin immediately shies a stone at it. Stray tabbies are the certain victims of his bull-terrier, and the terrier itself, when it refuses to sit up and smoke a pipe, or to go into the river after a water-rat, is beaten and kicked without mercy. He goes with a relish to see the keeper shoot old Ponto, who was whelped ten years ago in the kennel, and comes in to give his sisters (who don't care) appreciative details of the execution. As a sportsman, he is a tyrant to his dogs, a butcher to his horse; and sitting on that blown and drooping steed, he looks with a disgusting satisfaction when the fox is broken up. Throughout life he regards all his animated possessions (including his unhappy wife) simply as matters of a certain money value, to be made to pay or to be got rid of. Not to pursue his revolting career through all its stages, we will merely hint that he probably ends by committing a double parricide, and being righteously condemned to the gallows, and is reprieved only by the appropriate tenderness of the Home Secretary."

There is more meaning and practical suggestion under this light, half-bantering vein, than in many a severe treatise on humanity.

Mr. St. John, in closing the fourteenth chapter of his "Wild Sports and Natural History of the Highlands," has this confession: "Though naturally all men are carnivorous, and therefore animals of prey, and inclined by nature to hunt and destroy other creatures, and although I share in this natural instinct to a great extent, I have far more pleasure in seeing these different animals enjoying themselves about me, and in observing their different habits, than I have in hunting down and destroying them," which is the very spirit of the true naturalist and sportsman.

I have spoken of the surprise of the barn owl as I stood by the pond musing in the moonlight, but there are other nightly visitors and passers-by. The truth is, nature has no sleeping time; when one set of busy workers leaves off, another comes on, and she knows well how to provide for them all. If there are abundant supplies of flowers, bright-coloured, and even garish, to front the sun and close their eyes with the falling shadows of eventide, she has also some favourites which open their sweets to the night and deny them to the day, and show their charms only in the darkness, that the night-fliers may also have their work and pleasure. When the butterflies disappear, forth come the moths; when the day-beetles retire, they have successors in as brilliant a company, the glow-worm among them; when the lark and linnet, the thrush and the blackbird, the robin and the wren, retire to rest, and are silent, then come forth the night-jar, that queer compound of swallow and hawk, and the owls and the bats are busy. When the squirrels and the voles have curled themselves up to sleep—the one in his airy swinging cradle at the top of the tree, the other in his nest among its kindly protecting rootage down below—the hedgehog comes warily forth; and often have I seen him, with his quick, scuttling, old womanish walk, making his way about the hedges and the dry ditches round the pond, intently seeking for his food. An assiduous slug, snail, and insect hunter, he has a great deal to bear from the country folks, who blame him for sucking the cows' teats, and for taking the eggs of the partridges and pheasants, and even capturing and devouring chickens now and then. An unrelenting war is waged against him by those who should be his best friends—the farmers. I do not believe that he is guilty of some of the crimes of which he is accused; though, of course, in domestication, he is very fond of milk. He may take an egg now and then, but then he renders good service for it. There is such a meek, self-depreciating look about him —such a reluctant sort of assent to yielding, even to his own necessities, that were I inclined to believe in transmigration of souls, I would say that the hedge-hogs are tenanted by those who regard every act as an atonement for injuries done to others.

All nature's workers are thus, in a sense, only half-timers after all. How often in the moonlight have I stood on this bank and watched and listened, rapt with the magic beauty of the scene, the moonlight silvering the tips of the trees, and the pond reflecting a softer and more poetic image of all the leafy world around it. Ah! the moonlight is a wonderful painter! and with some effects outrivals the sun, as Rembrandt, with his deep shadows, got more powerful expression very often than Rubens with all his high lights.

And the varying tints and tones on the water by day, so ceaselessly changing, are like images of changeful human life. Not the slightest cloud passes but, in the sunshine, mirrors itself here, sometimes soft, fleecy, smitten with golden fire, or gray and quiet and one-coloured, gliding slowly on; then, again, on a dark day, the water is dull, sombre, greenish, and obscure; and when again a breeze ripples it, all seems to move in secret rhythmic harmony, water, foliage, and wind making a music so subtle that it is impossible to discriminate and to attribute to each element the effects due properly to it.

We have some pretty visitors in the shape of butterflies, who find dainty bits on the growths round the pond, the red admiral, the swallow--tail, sometimes a peacock or clouded

BUTTERFLY.

yellow, and the giant cabbage butterfly among the rest.

One or two moths sometimes come this way, and will frequently bump against your head in the evenings if you are quiet enough, and then suddenly recover themselves and go off with wonderful speed—a sort of lightning flash in the dark. I have not seen any of the stately and beautiful *Sphingidæ*, humming-birds of our islands, but there is a small red underwing, and a lovely little eggar. Why is it that nature has endowed a whole race of creatures with such wondrous beauty, such elfin lightness of flight, such silence and velocity, like shooting stars, and practically hidden it all from the eyes of men? How few know the night-moths (only some species fly by day, and they are not the most brilliant). They far outshine even the butterflies in their lovely colouring, the harmony and grace of their hues, and they surpass them in the delicate fairy-like prettiness of their forms. And then that silken silence of flight—their wings how exquisitely perfect in balance, how delicate their movement. No invention of man's can compare with it. The common idea of moths has adhering to it some unlucky association of the hated and destructive clothes-moth—something that suggests dust and musty offensive odours, or only a degree better, the irritating persistence of some smaller species round the candle or lamp in the evening. The moths are, indeed, the jewels of the night—more brilliant than the butterflies, who are, in fact, the moths of day, as the moths are the butterflies of night. The French, indeed, call them the *papillons-de-nuit*, which is truly a poem in a name. Practically there is no difference in the development of the two creatures, either as caterpillar, chrysalis, or perfect insect. The moth is, in fact, a butterfly which has developed too beautiful and harmonious an aspect to escape in the daylight the attacks of men and larger animals; and prudent nature has bred in them the protective instinct, so that only under the shadow of twilight or night do they come out to look for their favourite food. And the protective instinct is further seen in the fact that the upper wings are usually a dull colour, that of the tree on which they rest by day. Over in one of the cottage gardens not far off, there are gay clusters of evening primroses, that nod and waver in the wind as I pass. It may be that our beautiful red underwings and eggars are making their way there to give and take after nature's higher law of exchange. The moths retire at dawn, when nature is just preparing to bring on her army of day-workers, and, like too many invalids, they fall into a profound slumber by three o'clock in the middle of summer, and remain through all the hours of sunlight as completely invisible as though they were not. Lovely moths!

Thus my fishing for roach and tench has led me to love this pond, where I am often to be found; and my love for the pond has gotten me many delightful friends and acquaintances (who are not, like too many worldly ones, prone to leave one just when they are most needed), and these delightful friends and acquaintances have done not a little to widen my sympathies, if they have not helped to quicken my observation, so that you are not surprised—as I, at least, hope you are not—that I have even deemed it worthy of record alike from pen and pencil.

III.

MY WOOD.

Y wood is at no great distance from my favourite pond, which I have just described. A walk of five minutes or so by a meadow, and then down a lane, with high untrimmed hedges on either side, the banks at proper season bright with primroses and violets and dog-roses, and later in the year clusters of the wild hop hanging out luxuriously above, the large convolvulus blowing its trumpets sweetly to the wind; and again through a meadow, by the side of the stream which flows from the pond, brings you to the entrance, where you cross a rustic bridge; for just here the little stream flows into a larger one, which skirts the one side of the wood throughout its entire length. This larger stream flows on with a babbling murmur, as though it were ever singing to itself a quiet tune, as Coleridge has it in "The Ancient Mariner," whether it is the leafy month of June or not. There you see, as you look down, it turns and twists and glimmers, as though it returned your smile, making all look greener, and, where it is not almost overspanned by the overhanging branches, mirroring and mocking sky and cloud in the most unexpected and fantastic fashion.

As you walk into the wood it seems as though the

music of the brook went with you to inform the silence. Silent indeed it is at the present mid-day hour, with only the suggestion of an underhum, whether of newly awakened insects or some faint wind stirring in the tops of the beeches, birches, pines and elms and oaks, it would be hard to say. But you do not go far till you are assured of signs of life. There a tiny rabbit, with that significant white tuft of a tail,* scurries into

THE RUSTIC BRIDGE.

its hole; anon a wood-pigeon, disturbed by unwonted footsteps, flies high up overhead with a whirr, and startles the pheasants not far off. Your entrance,

* The reason why the point of the rabbit's tail always remains white is the same as the reason why the point of the tail in some other animals, such as the ermine (which changes its coat) always remains black. It is to enable the young one to see its parents on a surface the same colour as their fur, though no doubt other eyes than those of the young ones sometimes see it too, and make profit by it.

indeed, much to your chagrin, if you are a true lover of nature's quiet and shy recesses, is a signal of danger, your footsteps are awakeners of fear, your advances heralds of alarm, telegraphed, as it would seem, from point to point before you.   Nowhere hardly could one feel more oppressed, as it were, in realising the truth of Robert Burns's sympathetic words :—

> " I'm truly sorry man's dominion
>   Has broken Nature's social union,
>   And justifies that ill opinion
>   That makes them startle
>   At me, their poor earth-born companion
>   And fellow mortal."

The wood lies along a kind of slope, broken up here and there in its lower sweeps (probably by mould or turf having been dug out in old days) into rough irregular terraces, or crescents more correctly, and in the protecting shelter of the higher ridges so formed there are to be found colonies of the delicate white hyacinth, clustering together, like a group of shy girls, as if they eschewed more common haunts or coarser

neighbours, and preferred their own society ; virginal, pure, the most ideal of wild flowers. Truly, the white hyacinth is the lady of the woods, if there ever was one, with all the airy purity and soft shy graceful retiring mien of maidenhood.   One could almost imagine, as one muses over their chaste and inexpressible beauty, their pure and ideal outlines, that nature had made them to show how plastic and sculpturesque she could be; and how, if she were so minded, she could make simple purity and transparency do the work of colour. A faint light, as of sunshine left there, as if caught by some affinity with itself, like some pleasing memory on a maiden's face, shines through them; the white is, after all, only a medium; and when you look carefully you find suggestions of some faint indescribable colour, just as traces of veins will be found under the fairest skin, and the bluer under the fairer skin, as we all know from the phrase "blue blood." Look closely into the purest, whitest-seeming, and ethereal of snowdrops, and you will perceive the most delicate tint of pink along the tips of the leaves of the flower, as though some subtler kind of blood were coursing there, and came the nearer to an indescribably faint blush as you looked into it. Nature does not do much in positive tones, but mingles and combines them with the most artistic perception, if one may say so, and delights in unexpected half-tones and middle tints.

In this lower part of my wood, intruding into the middle distance, are thickly dotted clumps of wild hazels, their tassels and buds shining greenly where they are caught by the rays of the sun that steal through the higher branches; and in the opener spaces wild anemones are thick as a carpet, with their soft starlike flowers nodding over the green of their leaves; they are in reality of a pinkish shade, but look white at a distance. Higher still, upon the smoother slope, the blue hyacinths, as being abler to fight their own battle, have possession, and are so thick that as you look upon them from the lower ground, it might seem as though a bit of sky had fallen on the earth and remained there, the more that a kind of indescribable thin mist seems to hover over the belt. To what this is due is a problem. The day is clear, the sun shining, and the dew of the morning is mostly gone; though here, truth to tell, from the overspreading branches of the loftier trees which let in the sun's rays only in breaks and glimpses, there is always a sense as of something dewy, moist, and sweet, to which the sense of misty atmosphere above this carpet of blue may be owing. But I cannot be quite certain of anything but the effect.

I am quite aware, of course, of the fact that this effect is attributed to shadows cast by certain leaves; but this leaves the problem exactly where it was, since it is hard to see why certain shades of green in leaves should cast blue shadows. The most exhaustive statement of the law would not in any way lessen the surprise and mystery of the effect when seen again after a lapse of years.

Scarce anything could be at once more fascinating and pleasing to the eye. The fancy reinforces the sentiment that sky and earth are married here under some indescribable and mysterious ritual. But as we approach and examine more closely, we find that something of the effect is due to subtle variations of shade, which are, however, much more marked than might be believed. The general effect, looking from a distance, is that of sky; but, as in all nature's finer efforts, this is due to the presence of mingling shades, graduating through the finest chords, and all in perfect harmony. The bells, at their first unfolding, are like purple spikes, that seem to delight in shade (and give to or borrow from it—one can scarce say which—an indefinite kind of atmosphere), up to the palest blue in the more perfect flowers; and the lush green of the grass, like the finest of backgrounds, may only emphasise the effect of unity and harmony. We all know what effects are secured by painters through laying their semi-transparent colours over darker and more opaque ones. Nature clearly has forestalled the artist here, and does the same in many of her finest arrangements and harmonies.

In plots in the more shaded parts, and often nestling close to the roots of certain trees, grow primroses in thick tufts and clusters; for it is, above all, a gregarious flower, and the wild violets seem everywhere to sidle up to the primroses; and just, as sometimes it appears, as though beauties in society pair so as to set off each other's charms to the best advantage, so one might fancy that some such idea determines the association of primroses and wild violets. And even among the primroses—though to not a few even of those who live in the country, Wordsworth's lines on Peter Bell would apply—

> "A primrose by the river's brim
> A yellow primrose was to him,
> And it was nothing more;"—

Even among the primroses, we say, if you look well, you will find a gentle variation of depth of tint such as will perhaps surprise you. They vary from the palest yellow or straw colour up almost to the yellow of sulphur, and the sense of unity and satisfaction to the eye in the mass may, to some extent, be due to this.

Blue and gold! The colours of the stars and the sky! Well might the poet sing of the flowers as the stars of earth—if he had only more emphatically celebrated the sky of earth, which the violets and the hyacinths are!

In the middle of my wood is a piece of water, fed by numerous tiny rillets, with willows, wild bullaces, and an ash or two, surrounding and hemming it in so closely that, save in the very centre, and when the sun is high, the water is dark and cold looking. But the smaller water-lily grows in it, and irises—lovely in their season—shoot up and supply provision for the water-voles which have their homes here. The frog-bit and the water-crowfoot in season gather and spread there in drifts of snow, and the yellow ranunculus contests with them the place of honour, looking forth with its golden eye set as if in its very heart. The spot is utterly lonely, seldom does a footstep pass that way; so lonely is it, indeed, that one might fancy it was just such another spot as that in which Thurtell and Weare threw their victim.

A broken, ragged bit of hedge runs along the higher side of this lonely pond, and the speedwell spreads along it, and the white starwort looks forth pure, but as if with inquiry, and the forget-me-not follows, and white marguerites, and corn-flowers and poppies bloom in their season with the richest effect, for it lies on the side nearest to the corn-fields beyond, and draws something from them.

If you ascend to the top of the slope here you catch a glimpse of the distant church tower of Frating, rising so nicely amidst its trees on the height—very picturesque and beautiful.

The tiny water-shrews, which you have to wait and lie very silently even to see, are always active hereabout, whether you see them or not. Though gay and playful, they are so cautious and shy, that, unless you are very watchful indeed, you may never notice them, even though looking on the banks or in the water where they are. Yet their mode of propulsion in the water is peculiar, depending mostly on the hind legs, the feet of which, unlike those of the voles, have the nicest arrangement in the way of a fringe of strong hairs to help them, and a similar fringe is found on the lower surface of the tail. But they go with a kind of irregular swaying motion, as they use the hind feet alternately in pushing themselves along, and, when closely seen, have a somewhat peculiar shape in the

WATER-SHREW.

water, owing to the skin of the flanks widening and flattening out. The water-shrew's fur is sleek and soft, of a warm brownish colour, with occasional silver hairs and a silvery belly, which give it a very bright glistening appearance when it comes fresh from the water. They are easily recognised by their long snout and a peculiarly musty odour.

Unlike the voles, again, they are carnivorous, and eat almost anything, but are very partial to small water insects, and are apt at turning over little stones, &c., to find the tiny crustaceans underneath. Some say they do this nimbly under the water at the bottom, and assert that they have seen them do so, a privilege, I must confess, that I have not enjoyed, though I quite believe it to be accurate. Very possibly the water-voles are often blamed for their depredations on the eggs of fish. The superstitions about the shrews, both land and water-shrews, are very numerous: one of them was that if a cow had been touched or run over by a shrew it was sure to die, and the only means to prevent this was to bury a living shrew in a hole in the ash-tree, and then a twig from that tree, or even a few leaves from it, was held to work a cure.

The water-shrews are perhaps the most playful of all our small animals. Old and young in the warm afternoons turn out, and describe the funniest circles, chasing each other, turning over each other, and indulging in half-a-hundred of the maddest pranks. The young ones are not by any means the foremost in these romps. They seem thoroughly to believe in the maxim that "all work and no play makes Jack a dull boy." They are certainly not dull. They even carry their gambols into the water, and will sometimes have the nicest races, or it may be games of "touch," when the young ones will suddenly duck and disappear, only to be followed by the pursuers, and when they come to the surface again the game is renewed—only those who had been pursued in the former bout are now the pursuers. But if ever you are privileged to witness this unique and pretty sight, be sure you do not stir, or even raise a hand, or in an instant all will have disappeared in the twinkling of an eye, as though the earth had literally swallowed them up; for, as has been said already, the water-shrews are perhaps the shyest and most easily frightened of all our small fauna, and they have the greatest dislike to any unusual sound, and are a long time before they recover from any fright.

And if you will only muster up courage and come back here at the twilight hour, you will see life indeed, and know that nature pauses not, but has her constant relays of workers, and that her machinery neither rests nor rusts, nor knows any Sabbath day. The hedgehogs are numberless, notwithstanding the war waged against them—the wary, silent, secretive ways of the creature, as well as its natural armour, protecting it from many of its enemies. Oft have I, when walking here or near by, with the proprietor or gamekeeper in the evening, seen them ruthlessly slaughtered, when scented by the dogs and surprised, as they ventured out on their evening quest along hedgerow, or down their walks in the wood. Having coiled themselves up, poor things, the dogs were generally at a disadvantage, and would bark and whine in a way that told only too well what excited them; and it was a point with my friend to proceed to the place, and despatch the creatures by forcibly treading on them with his heavy foot, producing in me, I confess, a squeamishness I could hardly venture to acknowledge; as, by doing so, I would probably have risked losing any little character for manliness and sportsmanlike instinct that I had, for the poor hedgehogs are credited with no end of sins and crimes—whether with truth or not, I cannot say—amongst others, with destroying eggs of pheasants and partridges, which is, of course, an unpardonable offence, and also with stealing into hen coops and eating chickens, and sometimes even biting and injuring hens.

A few late lingering daffodils may still be seen near this bit of water, and waver and gleam in the light of the sun, bending and beckoning, though no wind seems to touch them. Do they really move, or is it an illusion of the eye or of the mind? Anyway, that discovery of Darwin, that every part of every plant is constantly making little circles in the air, moving many times in every minute, comes to the mind, and seems to find evidence here. Here and there, a tree that has been cut down burgeons afresh, and the green twigs that spring round it in beautiful circle shine as if with some reflected light, which you cannot rightly trace to its source; for it would seem as though they were completely overshaded. The hazels that have been coppiced put on their airy green, and whenever you come to the border of a moister spot (for water trickles down the wood in wet weather in many indefinite courses), there are a few oziers, which, as you attempt to pass through them and push them apart, by their swinging afterwards to and fro for a short while, recall Mrs. Barrett Browning's fine image in "Lady Geraldine's Courtship":—

> "The book lay open, and my thought flew from it, taking from it
> A vibration and impulsion to an end beyond its own,
> As the branch of a green osier, when a child would overcome it,
> Springs up freely from its claspings, and goes swinging in the
> sun."

Along these watercourses always, except in long periods of dry weather, more or less moist, are alders, sallows, and here and there a willow. It is almost incredible the rapid growth of some of these. The hazel-stubs, dotted in here and there, have their own story to tell of progress, marked to the eye by the difference of bark in the yearling shoots—some of them six feet or so in length, straight and beautifully regular, tapering, like a fine fishing-rod top, with a grey greenish dusty lustre upon them, which they lose when they develop branches in their second year. It is these yearling hazel twigs, taken just where they fork with each other, which are used for divining purposes; and my friend to whom this wood belongs, though a very practical man, is inclined to believe there is something in it. Held in a horizontal position by the skilled operator, they tremble and vibrate, and dip downward when right over springs, however deep.* The hazel stems or twigs lose their sensitiveness and power in indicating the presence of springs when they have grown older, but are profitable for thatching and other purposes. There are many groups of stubs of ash and alder much in request in the making of hurdles and such purposes. My friend tells me that in well-arranged and well-kept woods, with partially open spaces, free or comparatively free from larger trees, where these can be grown successfully, the yield is more profitable than that of arable land, amounting to something like £7 or even £8 an acre, so that woods are not only ornamental but profitable; here, as in so many other things, beauty and use going hand-in-hand together. Here and there we see,

---

* This, too, it may be remarked, is one of the few points on which De Quincey was not quite accurate. In his note on "Rhabdomaney," to "Opium Confessions," p. 291 (Masson's edition), he writes: "The remedy is to call in a set of local rhabdomantists [to divine for water]. These men traverse the adjacent ground, holding the willow rod horizontally. Wherever that dips or inclines itself spontaneously to the ground, *there* will be found water;" and the same thing is repeated in "Modern Superstition." The willow may be used, but the hazel is the usual, and is accepted as the more powerful medium. De Quincey, like my friend, though on definite Baconian principles, was inclined to believe there "was something in it."

through the network of branches, the bole of an oak which looks white and hoary, as though it had been dusted with whitish powder. This is the sign of age, and a suggestion to the woodman to operate; for oaks, like men, do turn grey with age.

There is a birch, queen of the woods in very truth, beginning to put forth the first tender tresses, to grow luxuriantly in the summer; and the bark seems to brighten and shine responsive, with a flicker in a wavering silvery lustre, lightly dappled with gold, as the rays of the sun steal in and fall, now and then, in patches full upon it. The proprietor has shown his taste and skill in dotting in here and there these lovely trees; but like a delicate family, they arc apt to succumb to rough treatment, and here and there you see that they have been blown down. Sometimes, even in the prone condition, the tree will continue to draw from the portion of the root still in earth sustenance sufficient to sustain its leaves, a parable of life in some of its most touching aspects, of the disappointed, the fallen, the degraded, who still draw as much of strength from their native soil as to put forth green leaves of hope and cheer, though so sadly down in the world and deserted.

The ashes are often spoken of as though they were slow to display their charms, and we cannot help recalling Lord Tennyson's beautiful sentiment in that, perhaps, loveliest of his songs in " The Princess ":—

> " Why lingereth she to clothe her heart with love,
>   Delaying as the tender ash delays,
>   To clothe herself when all the woods are green."

But the ash has been declared in mild seasons here to be in full flower early in April; and it is certainly not always tender in popular legend and folk-lore. The irregularity of its blossoming has found record in popular rhyme, which bases on it a weather forecast.

> " If the oak's before the ash
>   Then we're sure to have a splash ;
> If the ash comes 'fore the oak,
>   Then we're sure to have a soak."

It is pre-eminently the tree of weird fear and charm. It is a lightning-tree very often to be avoided. It is to be conciliated only by certain dues.

> " Beware the ash,
>   It counts the flash,"

is an ancient saw, in which the old idea of the lightning tree survives. Then it surrenders its charm. Amid the tree-myths, we find that some of the early men traced descent from it, and used it as their totem ; so it is a tree to be reverenced as well as feared. Dr. George MacDonald, in that fine romance " Phantastes," where, without learned pretension, he plays fancifully with a great many such ideas, has this, among many other things, about the ash, put into the mouth of the fairy mother :—
" Trust the Oak," said she, " trust the Oak and the Elm and the great Beech. Take care of the Birch, for though she is honest, she is too young not to be changeable. But shun the Ash and the Alder; for the Ash is an ogre. You will know him by his thick fingers; and the Alder will smother you with her web of hair, if you let her near you at night."
The whole romance is in this spirit, and the fairy needs to give the hero a charm against the ash :—
" But now I must tie some of my hair about you, and then the Ash will not touch you."

This charm compelled the ash to be not only friendly, but to surrender its charm for protection and aid.

The fateful powers of trees, too, more particularly the ashes, are fabled to be more active by night than by day; and in a wood at night, when not only the "trancèd senators of mighty woods," but the smallest plant and bush, seem to whisper mysteriously, there is no room to wonder at this, though, perhaps, it was only an old-world way of signifying that nature in none of her phases of activity ever sleeps.

And nature truly knows no death. See how the ivy has made a pillar of the stump of that old pollarded willow, that shows something of grace even in its lopped and desolate condition, with something like a ring of rubies round the outer edge of the stump—the first signs of the new shoots that by-and-by will adorn it. Nature's secret is to transform all decay and dislocation into new beauty; and, as she runs through the cycle of the year, to cover up, soften, smooth down, and to weave a glory round all disorder and dismemberment and death. At the foot of certain of the trees later on will grow the loveliest of fungi, that sometimes contest their right with ground ivy and wood sorrel—fungi of the most beautiful colours: pearl-coloured, fawn, purply-pink, and flesh-coloured. Not edible; ah! no: they are rankly poisonous mostly, these agaric children of the woods, and their radiant colours are only put on to warn.

Often as I have moved along here at different seasons I have noticed on a branch a little patch of glimmering pearl-like lustre, just as though some one had set a jewel there, which had been made by a very skilful artist, some fourteen or fifteen spiral rows running from the centre outwards. You go and touch them, and find that they feel like a part of the tree. Is it some wonderful exudation, then, as resin from the fir? No; these are the eggs of the lackey moth, which shows its skill in arrangement, and its wonderful farsightedness. It attaches these pseudo-pearls one by one to the twig, as it produces them by means of a powerful gum it secretes; and when it has finished its work it runs this same gum in between the rows, so that they are at once safe against the frosts of winter and the efforts of enemies. You try to pull them off. Well, no; you cannot do it. The name often given to them by country folk is "bracelets." Wonderful little artist the lackey moth! And the vapourer moth does the same, though not so artistically.

And yet this is no more wonderful than the craft of some other moths in covering their eggs with down or hair stripped from their own bodies. Some, before they lay their eggs, make thus a fine felting of hair on which to lay them, and then they construct the neatest little thatch roof of hairs to cover them. And notice this, that in laying the felt which is to be under the eggs, they turn about the hairs anyhow, but for the roof the hairs are arranged exactly like straw in a thatch, so that all water may run off. And all this we slump under the name of instinct!

Squirrels work their way across my wood, and dodge and show their acuteness in finding the trees where the bark is most of a colour with their fur. If you follow them too persistently for their liking, they will at last look down and squeak defiance at you in the shrillest key, like that of a magnified mouse-squeak. Moles are active at parts too, and amid the tufted grass in the opener spaces, one sometimes almost stumbles over their heaps. How is it that the mole, whatever the soil he works in, always manages to turn up such deliciously soft powdery earth?

My wood is not always so silent as it has been to-day. Alas, no! It is a great harbour for rabbits, which find the rich undergrowth a protection. Periodi-

SQUIRRELS.

cally there are rabbitings here, which usually yield a good result. Then all the normal life of the wood seems to be disturbed, paralysed. Not only the hunted rabbits, but the birds are scared, and go flying wildly in all directions; and the squirrels go bounding off from tree to tree to the furthest corner; the jays scream, and the crows left at home to guard the nests and the young go off caw-cawing and protesting, as I take it. The wood is properly marked off, and each party takes its own portion. Ferrets are put into the holes, and the dogs are active, and packs of boys gather from the district round, and shout and halloo and add to the uproar. In some places where paraffine or kerosine has been run into the rabbit-holes—a famous device for making short work in some places now-a-days—there is great slaughter. Occasionally a ferret will "lay-up," as they say down here, and have to be dug out, and spades and forks are called into requisition. One can only turn away, lamenting the necessity that forces men periodically to spoil the idyllic repose of such a lovely spot, and to leave the most impressive tokens of their presence in holes, long runs, and heaps of earth, which, in such a place—so seldom trodden of human foot—it takes a long time to get worn down and effaced. About equally exciting are the forays against the poor wood-pigeons in the early spring and autumn.

And, as if permanently to emphasise the fact of man's superiority, and also his, perhaps, pardonable rapacity (for nature sometimes needs help in adjusting her balance so to keep down destructive predominancy, all too corroborative of the survival of the least worthy, if not of the fittest, as respects beauty, whatever may be said of use), here and there one comes on little huts roughly formed of the fallen and lopped branches of trees—not so closely put together as to shut out the light, yet closely enough to afford complete concealment and shelter to gamekeeper and sportsman, either when watching poachers by night or intent on securing some specimens of very shy and retiring creatures. In the

midst of life here, too, we are in death, or, at any
rate, amidst the means of it. Often have I lain in
one of these huts, later in the season, stretched comfortably on a soft carpet of dried moss, and leaves and
grass, and—far from murderous thoughts intent—have
watched, unseen, the ordinary goings-on of life around
me in this sylvan paradise.

One deprivation this kind of pleasant ordeal has
however, it is that no tobacco must be indulged in.

WOODED SCENE WITH HUT.

You light your pipe, and instantly the charm is gone.
These wild creatures are not only quick but suspicious
—the slightest fading curl of smoke, the least strange
scent on the air, and you are left to regret the lack of
good company. Even in a walk through a wood, or
by a hedgerow, the pipe in your mouth is an additional
warning which the wild things not only note, but are
smart to telegraph onwards before you. " No tobacco
smoking allowed" must be the motto.

So cool, so shaded is the hut, with such a sense of

soft retirement and secrecy, that one could not help falling into a Robinson-Crusoe mood—a kind of middle mood between primitive ease and restful indifferency, and the curiosity bred of civilisation and science, which could not be set aside. The wood-doves would sometimes descend and sit· on the hut close above me, and talk to each other in that confiding full-hearted goo-goo-gooing language of theirs, and shed a soft feather or two that would cling to the dry wood for days; the jays would intrude— the mischief-makers

RING DOVE OR WOOD-PIGEON.

that they are—chattering and scolding near by, as if, like interfering gossips and scandal-loving neighbours, they could not let a little love-affair pass without an unseemly interruption and rude comment on it, and many derogatory remarks; the rooks busy in their nests would startle the silence with a caw-caw to a companion, intimating something still to be attended to; and a solitary bee, attracted by one knows not what, would come boldly bumming into the shadowy shelter and settle, apparently seeking for something, one could not guess what, and show no hurry to go away either. Slouching, black, beady-eyed rats have sometimes peered in, but with that quickness of sense characteristic of them, soon smelt the presence of something unusual, and were off; and the weasel, too, with its twining gliding walk (as though it had a snake for a spinal cord, which, perhaps, it has), and with pink eyes, peering, hungry, remorseless, has sometimes entered—perhaps with an eye to Mr. Rat—and startled me; and then with the sharpest thinnest cry on earth —something between a squeak and a hiss—has quietly turned and disappeared, when I stirred to warn it off. The silence and restfulness of my wood is only emphasised by all this gentle language and movement common and normal to it.

Yes; moments of complete silence supervene now and then on these various voices. "Waiting for the next thing" is then the feeling that abides with me. Hush! hark! there comes a something worth waiting for —the sweetest note—soft, rich, mellow; now piercing clear, now falling sweet as the subdued murmur of falling water. Is that the nightingale? one might question, for it is a very common error to suppose that the nightingale does not sing by day. But no, it is not. It is the beautiful, shy, little garden-warbler discoursing his sweet music from the top of the tree he loves. He is a migrant and comes late, with

GARDEN WARBLER.

his wealth of sweet music to add to nature's choir. What is it Tennyson sings? "All precious things discovered late;" for discovered read "arriving," and it applies to the garden-warbler. A shy bird, yet he haunts the abodes of men, and is often driven from them by intrusive companions, and retreats to the deepest recesses of the woods, as he has done now, to enjoy himself in quietude. Perhaps his partner is near by, building a soft little nest in place of the deserted one, where the eggs have been handled—four or five greenish-white eggs, spotted brown or yellow. Though he loves to sit high when singing, he builds low in a little bush, or even amid rank herbage not far from a tree's foot. The nest is rough-made of tough grasses, interwoven with wool, hair, and fine fibres loosely shaken-in forming the lining. The garden-warbler is a fine grub and insect-killer, only when the fruit is ripe indulging himself a little; and, on the whole, deserving entertainment and that little indulgence for the earlier service he does. But he is being hunted off the face of the earth; at all events he is becoming scarcer, save in a very few favoured localities. He deserves this good word for the sweet song he has sung to me, and I must not spoil it now by dwelling on any other. But I must not move, else he will be off, and I may yet have another sweet little shower of song. I will wait quietly and see and hear.

IV

THE DELIGHTS OF HEDGEROWS.

HAT a delight and how rich a sub-ject of investigation is the smallest bit of hedgerow! To my joy, at the bottom of my garden, separat-ing it from the nearest wheat-field, is a beech hedge, instead of any more effective enclosure in the shape of fence or wall. I really would miss much in the interest I have in this corner of mine were there a high wall here in place of this hedge. The hedge, however thick, is still but an airy screen or veil which half hides and half reveals the life without and stimulates curiosity. It is all living, breathing, constantly changing, if you look well, and sounds like a wind-harp to the wind. It refines the view beyond, and does not really inter-rupt or close it; and you can feel the pulse of life, as it were, stirring in it. Birds pass through it almost as free as the wind, weave their nests in it, and near-by sit and discourse the sweetest music, morning, noon, and eve. It does not shut off, but kindly encloses; giving free let to all the sweeter winds, even refining and scenting them, while it tames down and breaks the force of the fiercer and colder winds, and takes the sting from the frosts of winter.

A volume might be written on hedgerows cultivated

and uncultivated; beech, privet, blackthorn, redthorn, ivy, sycamore, holly, laurel, and the rest, for each has not only its own characteristics from a practical or agricultural point of view, but its specific interest from a picturesque or natural history point of view. As for an evergreen hedge, what better symbol of homely protection could you have? As it grows and grows, it weaves, as it were, an outer nest round a dwelling, close, kindly, familiar, and compact as a wall, with a whole world of breathing consciousness about it. What were England without its hedgerows that give an individuality and distinctive countenance to every field, which they at once beautify and shelter from the frosty winds of winter, and from the fierce burning heats of summer? They present to the careful observer in a kind of epitome, the life of the district in which he may be. He cannot be far out for study if he is near a bit of hedgerow. They are natural trellises for wonderful climbers and creepers as beautiful as the vines of Italian climes, and they gather the fairest of our wild flowers to shelter under them. As for the former, think of the convolvulus, white and pink, and of the honeysuckle, and of the sweetbriar or eglantine! How the May in its season spreads its blooming clusters, as has been said, like a bride's train, and how the redthorn blushes! How the bryony creeps and peeps, and, as other beauties fade and pass, still wreathes its festoons and puts out its brilliant berries! How the elder spreads its creamy flowers and shows its dark berries, and the wild hop hangs its clusters to the wind!

Then, for the wild flowers—what an array in constant succession! In the spring, a grand advance wing, come the violet, the primrose, the speedwell, the celandine, herb-robert, and the sweet anemone, drooping bashfully its white head, or nodding to its later-come neighbours, the blue and white hyacinths not far

off; later on, follow the campions and hare-bells, the for-get - me - nots, the stately fox-glove, with its pyramids of purply pink bells; and the succession is quite as full, and their array of flowers is quite as large all through the summer and autumn.

> "By ashen roots the violets blow,"

sings the late Laureate, but the violet loves other than ashen roots; it is very fond also of hazel and birch— a fact which Sir Walter Scott was clear on when he wrote—

> "The violet in her green-wood bower,
> Where birchen boughs and hazels mingle."

Hedgerows have thus managed to assert the characteristic element of English landscape and life, and are rich in associations. Did not Mr. Robert Browning miss the hedgerows of his native land amid the glorious sunshine of Italy; and has he not recorded this feeling as with a lightning-flash of inspiration? And no wonder, when my small morsel is of such importance to me! He sings his song under the title, "Home Thoughts from Abroad"—

I.

" Oh, to be in England
  Now that April's there ;
And whoever wakes in England
  Sees, some morning, unaware,
That the lowest boughs and the brush-wood sheaf
Round the elm-tree bole are in tiny leaf,
  While the chaffinch sings on the orchard bough
    In England—now !

II.

And after April, when May follows,
And the whitethroat builds, and all the swallows :
Hark, where my blossomed pear-tree in the hedge
  Leans to the field, and scatters on the clover
Blossoms and dewdrops—at the bent-spray's edge—
  That's the wise thrush : he sings each song twice over,
  Lest you should think he never could recapture
  The first fine careless rapture.
And though the fields look rough with hoary dew,
All will be gay when noontide wakes anew
  The buttercups, the little children dower,
  Far brighter than this gaudy melon flower !"

What an exquisite sense of English bird-song there is in these lines; not to speak of the " wise thrush " singing his song twice over, " lest you think he never. could recapture the first fine careless rapture," is that reminiscence of the chaffinch not exquisite, " on the orchard bough," and of the whitethroat in May, with his keen varied song—rick, rick, chew, rick, a-rue, rick, rick-chew-chew-ke-rick-a-rew-rew ?

And with what exquisite grace the trees in the hedgerow do sometimes lean from them and dip, and look over into the meadow or field beyond !

Within my vision, too, I can catch a glimpse of something leaning to the field, in the words of Browning, whereby hangs a tale or a curious fact or two. At the extreme corner there of my hedge is a holly tree of some height, which has been for long years left to itself, unclipped, untrimmed, and hangs at one side right over into the field. Even that unwieldy holly seems to stoop down to meet the grass and clover and buttercups beneath; and there is one other still more peculiar circumstance to note. At a certain height it ceases to have spines on the leaves, and preserves them more highly by a foot or two on the side that is towards the field than on the other towards the house. Can the plant really know (from experience of years) the side on which it is most exposed to cattle, and so guards itself most resolutely at the right point? Certainly it is an economist and a soldier in its own way—a combination, after all, not so common. It reserves all its points of defence for the parts where they are really needed, and does not waste its powers. I learn that Southey alone among poets has noticed this fact, and set it in rhyme :—

> " Below a circling fence of leaves is seen,
>   Wrinkled and keen,
>   No grazing cattle through their prickly round
>   Can reach to wound,
>   But as they grow where nothing is to fear
>   Smooth and unarmed the pointless leaves appear."

Hedgerow timber, how much the landscape owes to it! How gracefully the oaks and beeches rise from the deepened ridge where the road dips, their roots sometimes showing bare in gnarled twisted clusters towards the roadway, such as Doré often represents and Millais magnifies! I have in my mind an avenue, where in summer, even in the hottest sun, there is from this cause always coolness and a kind of soothing repose, like that which is found in a southern cathedral in July, when the light, the dim religious light, comes through coloured glass, old and mellow. How often have I, because of my admiration of the place and the effect, lowered myself in the eyes of the peasants, who declaim against those trees as "a-shuttin' in the place so as 'tis never rightly light, and but seldom dry, and allus as 'twere a-droppin' o' suthin' or other—damp leaves, or rain, or dew, or what not—such as is a'most terrifyin' to delicat' females as 'as to be a-passin' of it, partikler in the dark ?"

Notwithstanding all such disadvantages, I would not have my favourite hedgerow trees cut down. In some places with which I am familiar, elms and sycamores assert their own dignity, and occasionally a lime tree glimmers in its lighter green. And in the more enclosed and remote parts you will be sure to find due share of nuts, especially the wild hazels, deliciously sweet, and all the better for the rough cuttings the bushes receive at the hedger's hands. Hollies are, as I have already hinted, beyond praise, not so much the clipped and trimmed specimens in the carefully attended to shrubbery, but the holly of the common hedgerow. How delightful in its permanency, preserving, like the truly heroic nature, its chief charms for the period of trial, when all else is stripped and bare, its red berries shining in the dull light of winter, or throwing a faint rosy tinge on the snow that feathers all the twigs around, the little birds, in finding their dainty but frugal breakfast, having with their sweet breasts cleared the snow from the bunches of fruit, from which they have picked their morning supply.

Then we must not forget the elder, with its creamy flowers in summer, and its bright berries in later autumn; nor the sloe, with its clustering flowers and its fruit, with that unapproachably delicate purply bloom in autumn.

And this suggests another delightful centre of associations—the harvest of the hedgerows. Did you ever, dear reader, go a-blackberrying in the sweet days of autumn, when the clouds are high, and there is a delicious clearness in the air, and a sense as of wider horizons, and soft expansiveness and ripeness and warmth around, as if, to atone for the shortening days and the more abundant joy of summer, nature had resolved to concentrate all mildness and sweetness and variety of tint into one sweet hour or two of light and beauty? Idyllic symplicity, the sense of close communion with nature, is easily realised then; and even into the bucolic mind, little touched by sentimental or æsthetic influences, a sense of poetry will often steal, while, at the same time, a good practical end is served; for nothing could be more wholesome than the blackberry, which is indeed in many forms often recommended to invalids, for which purpose it sells at something like fourpence a quart. It makes delightful puddings, still more delightful jam, and has the true wild flavour eaten fresh from the hedgerow.

Some people are apt to speak of the rustic as utterly without imagination or fancy; but if this is unqualifiedly so, how about the folk-lore and legends which are so common, which touch more or less closely almost everything, and certainly have been as busy with the natives of the hedgerow as with anything else? For example, in some places it is believed that when the blackberries begin to hang limp and shrunken, the devil spit upon them in his Michaelmas travels.

Then there is the barberry, not to be neglected,

though sometimes it is held suspect as a propagator of mildew; and the elderberry, from which good wine is made; and the sloe, from which is drawn more delicious wine still. After a long dusty journey, even those who are in some things fastidious might enjoy a glass of well-kept sloe wine, such as is to be found in many a peasant's cottage. And then we must not forget the wild strawberry nestling among the grass, and peeping forth with its delicious miniature berries. At the proper season old and young turn out in force for the work of picking, and no more pleasant pictures of rustic life are to be seen than then. Even the babies toddle about, and, with lips purple from the juice of stray berries handed to them, laugh and chuckle and dance and are glad, as it befits childhood to be. The farmers are in nothing more liberal than in their willingness to let those who are known to them thus enjoy the harvest of the hedgerow; but, naturally, they have a strong objection to tramps and strangers, who are apt to make such liberty an occasion to pick up unconsidered trifles, and, if not so bad as that, to leave gates open behind them and make inconvenient gaps in fences, which sometimes leads to awkward results in cattle or horses going astray.

And then the nutting; for nutting cannot well be dissociated from the hedgerows, though the nut trees scatter themselves about, like capricious beauties, through strips of plantation and coppice; but they, too, love the hedgerow and flourish there, and you cannot go a-nutting and fail to linger by the hedgerows. Wordsworth knew that too, and has characteristically noted it.

No student of natural history can afford to neglect the hedgerow. He will never become familiar with some of the most attractive and at the same time most beautiful and fascinating aspects of animal life. I do not here refer to the birds, though the hedge-sparrow, and the hedge-warbler, and the yellowhammer, and the larger tits are *habitués*—not to speak of thrushes and blackbirds, and the starlings and jays, who go flashing over and over with a purply gleam wholly indescribable on their black back and wings. But in the hedgerow the hedgehog has his haunt, the delightful little shrews find quarters there, and also the field voles in the bottoms of the dry ditches at their sides. They burrow, and love the proximity of bush roots, though they will also make their nest in the field.

Then the birds' nests, hidden in the most artistic manner sometimes, or so protected by similarity of colour to the surrounding foliage or bark. The wren is one of the most delightful builders. Any one might find in its nest a subject of study and admiration for weeks.

And there is still another harvest of the hedgerows, which we should not forget. What would become of our resident birds—our sweet native songsters—

> " That in the merry months of spring
> Delighted us to hear them sing,"

were it not for the berries of the hedgerow, which too glimmer bright through the frost and snow? And what a pretty sight it is to see, as just said, the blackbird or thrush, or even the little robin, by flutterings and pressures of the breast, clear away the snow from the now dark and trailing branches, and reveal the clusters of red berries to match the breast of the latter. Yes, the hollies and privets and hawthorns, and the brambles, yews, and their brethren then hang out their banners for beauty and their fruits for use! A sad time it often is for the birds in winter, when the snow is deep; but if it is not actually *pelting* snow, you will see our favourites there at work, reaping their harvest of the hedgerow, so wondrously stored up for them ; and when any of these winter food staples fail, through some influence adverse to the insects that fertilise them—as Mr. Darwin once so surprisingly forecasted—how merciful should all bird-lovers be in mindfully scattering to the birds any crumbs or morsels that would else be wasted. If their harvest of the hedgerow to any extent fail, then death by starvation, added to cold, is the fate of our sweet songsters by hundreds and thousands all over the country.

Wild and unkempt as the ordinary hedgerows of road and field may appear, they demand at proper times a good deal of attention from the farmer and the hedger under him. How a farmer keeps his hedges and his ditches is an almost invariable mark of how he keeps the rest. If the hedges are allowed to grow after their own sweet will for years and years, they will certainly at length spread into and close up the ditches, and the farmer's fields and meadows and roads in places will be flooded, to his loss as well as to the landlord's. There is no more frequent subject of quarrel among farmers and country residents than hedges and ditches being left unattended to beyond the proper period; for, of course, in cases of flooding, the surface water is sure to flow on some other one's land than that of the man who is to blame for it. This, however, is not the most idyllic aspect of the subject, and we shall leave it ; but not till we have said a word or two for the hedger, who certainly deserves more credit than he gets. If you fancy there is no skill in his craft, and that only strong muscle and thews and sinews are needed, I would recommend you, the next time you go to the country, to have a try at it and see how you succeed. In hedging, the trained accuracy of eye, which is noticed in the rustic, is especially seen. However careful you might be, you would find that you would leave the hedge in such breaks and notches as would surprise you, and probably make you feel ashamed of your conceit. But the hedger, without any doubt or hesitation, stroke by stroke and without cessation, shaves off as many feet as leaves an exact line along a whole length of field as level as a wall, and without knobs or notches anywhere. If there are a few fancy trees or elevations in the hedge he will, if you give him due encouragement, cut them into the oddest and most *outré* shapes.

Hedges cannot really be thought of without ditches; just as light is invariably accompanied by shadow, so the ditch may be called the shadow of the hedge. In old days, before scientific drainage of land was carried to such an extent as now, naturally more importance was attached to the keeping of them; and so well were they in many cases kept that large reaches were, save in exceptional circumstances, dry; and these dry ditches were very much favoured by tramps and paupers as places of repose before the passing of that most philanthropic, if somewhat repressive, measure (over which the inoffensive Thomas de Quincey mourned), making it an offence to sleep in the open air. "To die in a ditch" may not therefore quite carry all the degrading associations apt to be conjured up by the phrase, however much it may indicate that the person was unfortunate, and fell from the high estate of the respectable citizen and taxpaying householder. In favourable circumstances a dry ditch would not make the worst of beds. Thousands in large cities every night sleep on a far worse and unhealthier one ; the more that for curtain there is the interwoven twigs or lightly rustling greenery of the hedge above, and the sky and the stars to weave a pattern in it.

The boy that has made himself thoroughly familiar with a ditch and hedgerow is on the way to become a fair naturalist ; he has laid the foundations of an education on which, as one may say, it is possible to build almost any superstructure.

As we are about to conclude and look round, pen in hand, our eye lights once again on our own little hedgerow at the bottom of the garden. This suggests a practical paragraph to end with.

Mr. James Long, than whom we have not perhaps a more practical director for any one who possesses a small plot of ground, recommends that all gaps in hedges on a small farm or garden should be mended up with gooseberry bushes, where they will grow admirably. The hint might be made to yield no end of variety to the eye and profit to the pocket. They can be trimmed down into the needful uniformity season by season, and be only improved by it. Then, recently, we saw that some enterprising nursery firm were willing to supply at a cheap rate plants of a very fine kind of blackberry, of American origin if we remember rightly, which might be used in the same way, producing in its season the most luscious fruit. Here, even within the smallest demesne, the occupier may with little outlay, and with very slight labour, intermarry the wild and the cultivated in the .most delightful style, have a tiny but wholly unique garden in his hedgerow, with vari-coloured blossom and flower in their season, and reap the ripe results in the most delicious and refreshing of fruits. Thoreau spoke of the delicate wines stored up in the wild fruits by the wayside, and certainly this plan would have the result at once of giving the trim clipped hedgerow a new beauty, and of bringing a *taste* of the sweet wilderness near to the doors of the house without any, or at any rate many, countervailing disadvantages.

V

UP IN THE MORNING EARLY.

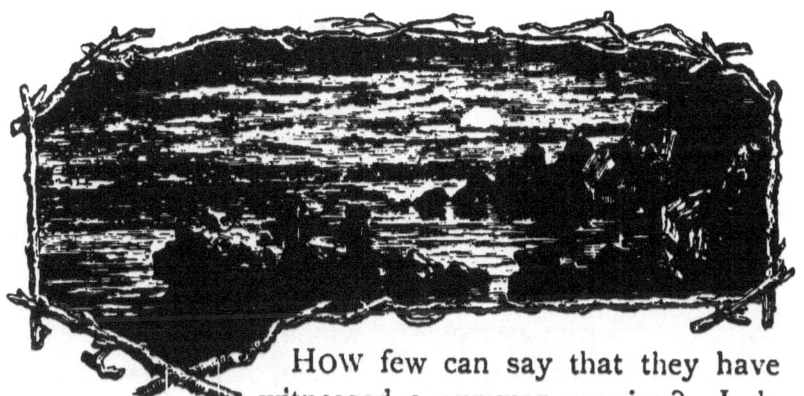

HOW few can say that they have witnessed a summer sunrise? I do not speak only of town-folk, but even of the more leisured country people, who can afford to lie abed, and have no calls of duty or business to attend to. Of course, the toilers in the fields have to be up and about at such an hour as will bring them pretty nearly at certain seasons in spring and autumn face to face with nature, when "o'er the eastern hills the sun's broad eye first peeps." But this class are not observant, at all events of more recondite phenomena, or, if they are, they do not make record. And even they do not see the genuine summer sunrise, when, in the latter end of June and in July, the sun is, as he should be, an example to all the world in early rising. By the invalid, sleepless and weary, the first faint streak of daylight lacing the east is eagerly looked for and anxiously watched as it expands and kindles, and finally transfigures the sky, but, if at last sleep comes not with benignant dawn, the fever, the weakness, or excitement, keeps such an one from true enjoyment of the sights and sounds which really mean, if they are effective, invitations to go forth and join in it. To be really seen, it must be actively seen, in healthy spontaneous outflow of energy, though with that "wise passiveness" which Wordsworth celebrated, and which the gypsy woman, of whom we have heard, must have meant when she said that she did not care for words as she looked on the glorious sights of nature, but rather loved to "let it quietly soak in." To "let it quietly soak in" is the one condition of true enjoyment, and of true insight and observation too; and, unless you observe the old rule "early to bed," you will certainly not gain either the profit or the wisdom promised, however early you may get up, because you will not rise refreshed and vigorous, keenly observant and healthily sensitive to sight and sound and movement, but you will be languid and dull, or morbidly irritable and restless, unable even to sit still—proofs of the effort your early rising has cost you—and the sharp searching air of the morning will penetrate you and trouble you, whether frankly acknowledged or not, because even in summer just before sunrise the air is at the keenest; and to be uncomfortably conscious of this is simply to spoil the finest of the feast. This is a very important point, often—very often—overlooked, especially by city folks when they are spending their holidays in the country.

For the world begins to wake very early on a summer morning. Even by half-past two o'clock, or very shortly after it, you may hear the blackbird calling to his friends from shrub or green, and getting his answer too after a short interval. His matins are early sung, before sunrise even. At certain seasons, that is, from the middle of May to the beginning of June, in some districts at all events, the cuckoo may claim the honour of being the *second* of birds, and some may deem it a reflection on nature altogether that this honour should be held by so arrant a thief and trickster. Perhaps he needs, in pursuit of his own objects, to steal a peep in at some other birds' nests before they have awakened. Certainly, he is like too many human beings —engaged in stealing a march on the more innocent and unsuspecting. But then, bad as he is, he does not victimise his own species—at least, I have never heard that he does; so that, after all, the cuckoos may stand only as a kind of gypsies among birds, constantly taking advantage of other people, if they can, and intruding into other birds' nests; and if not stealing children to disfigure them, stealing service in rearing theirs, to the injury and death of legitimate offspring.

But while we have been reflecting, other birds are becoming active. First the robins, and next the larks, which rise from the dewy grass and mount upwards at the outset with a short undecided flight, as if sorry to leave the nest as yet. Then, as though they had been wakened by the first notes of the lark—buoyant and shrill in spite of indecision—the sweet-voiced thrushes send out hurried notes, in little broken whistles and trills and quavers, soft but irregular, in recurrent but not unpleasing softened discords, like an orchestra tuning up their instruments in preparation for a concert. They are yet but half awakened—Tennyson speaks of "the earliest pipe of half-awakened birds." But this early piping does not occupy Mr. Thrush so closely that, if you watch him well, you will fail to see him suddenly bolt from his place on the tree-branch to the green, and run with sharp darty turns and becks and halts, neatly picking up slugs or worms, as it would seem, at each turn or short stoppage: it looks as though, while trilling his first glad welcome to the day (sweet-throated utilitarian that he is!), he had been carefully observing these slugs or worms, and calculated with the nicest precision how many of them he could thus dismember and gobble up in one run; and having had so good a start for the day's work, he re-perches, and sends forth another stealthy bit of melody more sustained and songlike than the last, but not yet of highest and fullest tone. Perhaps this early morning succulent feed may have something to do with his increasing richness of note. I do not know whether it would be either right or proper to quote the concluding fine lines from Mrs. Barrett Browning's well-known sonnet here; but certainly I must confess they have occurred to me with some quaint questionings, as I have looked on the procedure of Mr. Thrush very early in the summer mornings, whether or not they could in any light be applied to him :—

> " And make the work
> The better for the sweetness of the song ;"

and *vice versâ*.

In this perhaps the blackbird, most greedy and voracious of birds, would not agree. He does not like Mr. Thrush, perhaps—as often happens with human beings—because his faults lie so much in the same direction, and he is a distant relative of the family.

We forgive the blackbird much because of his sweet song; and truly he needs much forgiveness. He is not only greedy and selfish, but more pugnacious and revengeful than might be imagined. I have seen him ruthlessly hunt the poor thrushes if they ventured on what he deemed his feeding-ground, even thus early in the morning, when there seemed plenty of worms and grubs and snails for all of them. When angry or disturbed his note is very sharp and discordant, and far from mellow, as his song is.

Then the tits—particularly the blue tits—begin to flash like light from tree to tree, with their tweenk, tweenk, tweenk; one of the prettiest but most pugnacious of birds; and if you are near water, the wanton wagtails are never long out of it, with their pert and sidelong glance and darty walk;

PIED WAGTAIL.

and they shake and preen and trim themselves, as it were, into harmony with their surroundings, like fashionable ladies at a tea-party. The wrens and robins now turn out in full force in their fine clothing, with a superfine sauciness and audacity, as if they knew that they were still taken for—

> " God Almighty's cock and hen ; "

and on that account no one would dare to injure them.

The sparrows, if you should chance not to be far

from human habitations, will now probably surprise you by the piercing, penetrating, steely vibration of their little voices, as they welcome in the day; and would even seem to have been studying over night how they could be most sharp and resonant in their notes this morning. I have sometimes lain in bed and listened to their chattering, so continuous and intense, till a sort of painful smart shot through the brain, when I would jump up and clothe myself and go outside to escape its keen and unrelieved monotony. A row of lime trees right in front of our house was a favourite resort of theirs; and I confess we were so much of bird lovers and so sentimental as to object to any effort to take down their nests or drive them away, till it became in the way just said, simply unbearable by light sleepers and lovers of open windows like ourselves, when we compromised the matter and had their nests thinned out; but this seemed to make no perceptible difference to the ceaseless shrill of bird-voices close by our windows early in the morning.

Our friendly protection of the birds in our small domain was carried on with open eyes so far as the amiable delusions of the Rev. J. G. Wood are concerned. He really, in some cases, carried his sentiment too far. I should report untruly if I said that thrushes and blackbirds—shameless vagabonds that they are, in spite of their sweet voices — will not delectate themselves on your strawberries early in the summer mornings if you do not have them well netted or protected, or that several other birds won't visit, and speedily thin out, your mayduke and bigarreau and white-heart cherries. The truth is, there are certain things certain birds will have, and these are always the finest, too; and you must protect them if you mean to have any; if you don't protect them, depend upon it you won't have any, because the birds do not understand equity, but only their own tastes and appetites. (If they only took a fair share in exchange for their killing of grubs and insects and worms, I should be the last to grudge it to them; but while your fine fruit lasts they won't touch aught else!) I have sat for hours and watched the efforts of birds to remove nettings, and have seen blackbirds, thrushes, and starlings all labour for half-hours at a time to clear away or scrape off earth tunnel-wise, so that they might enter beneath the net or wire fencing, and, having in some cases succeeded, so exactly have they taken a note of the hole they made, that when you tried to catch them, they flew as direct for it, from the farthest corner of the covered space to which they had enticed you, as a bee-line, and were through as by magic, and off, to your great chagrin. And all this before full sunrise. I cannot, therefore, bird-lover as I am, give quite the same report on this point as Mr. J. G. Wood, because, being often "up in the morning early," I have sat and watched their persevering application and their ingenious devices to outwit you and to eat your choicest fruit; and I have paid dearly for not listening to warnings of gardeners and neighbours of a practical turn of mind who have over and over again looked at my bare beds and my cherry trees with bare stones that rattled on each other gently in the wind, with a sardonic smile, which meant "We told you so."

Goethe has a very fine parable in its way, based on his experiences, when as a youngster he planted a fruit tree, and from day to day watched its progress, to be ever and anon depressed at the inroads of insects, blight, birds, and what not, finally to congratulate

himself that, after all, his tree yielded him as much fruit
as he wanted. But then Goethe did not have some
species of English birds to deal with, else we are
afraid his moral of toleration and contentment would
not have been so comfortable and comforting. And it
is in the early morning that the birds can do most
execution in this line—when they are not watched or
interrupted.

But we rather abruptly left the little sparrows in
their friendly scoldings (or is it their way of saying
"good morning" to each other, and repeating and
repeating it ceaselessly?), though they have certainly
not left off their chattering. It still goes on with an
insistent monotony that would speedily become merely
oppressive were it not that soon it is mixed up with
other sounds.

The blue-tits and the robins are the only birds of
their size who can hold the sparrows at bay; and,
incredible as it may seem, the bold effrontery of the
sparrow will sometimes avail with it against much
larger birds. I have seen a blackbird at early morning
on my lawn, after a spell of dry weather, with much
work and effort secure a small worm or two for her
young brood, and have them daringly carried away by
the sparrows to theirs.

The trees in clumps at some parts seem literally alive
—the leaves stir and flutter as if there was a fitful wind,
which there is not, for it is perfectly calm; with now
and then a sort of subdued susurration, like a dying
sigh, so soft and gentle that you are never perfectly
sure that it does not exist more in your own fancy,
bred of the hush of expectation, than of aught else.
It is not enough, at all events, to stir the leaves in
the trees as we see them stirred. That is due simply

to the ceaseless movements of the birds in the branches, as they flirt and flutter and preen themselves and hop from bough to bough. Very few observers, in the least sensitive, not to say fanciful, would not be inclined at such a moment to admit that there is something in Wordsworth's lines :—

> "The birds around me hopped and played,
>   Their thoughts I cannot measure ;
> But the least motion that they made,
>   It seemed a thrill of pleasure."

Overhead, there is the first flock of wood-pigeons proceeding to my neighbour Farmer Nicholls' fields to look at some very fine early peas he has sown by way of experiment; and an experiment it is also for the pigeons, who know that they are sweeter than usual. And now they are feeding young broods, and make good use of buds and tender pods, and can pack their food for their young ones in some kind of second crop which they have, and in due time they neatly disgorge it, and feed the young ones with pea-pulp admirably suited to their tastes and digestions.

Rooks, cawing in a subdued tone, or it may be that the note seems soft because they are flying rather high, are making their way from yonder elm trees to the distant fields where the soil has just been upturned; and in some cases where feeding grounds are not far off they make a slant downward line for them direct and almost noiselessly, attesting the truth of the old saw about the early bird and the worm.

They are the earliest on wing of our larger insect-eating birds. They have to bear a good deal of the opprobrium due by right to the crow—a distant relation, who has gone on bad lines on two or three points.

The crow is a dirty feeder; the rook is by comparison clean; the crow is solitary—that is, it is seldom seen save alone or in pairs; the rook is social, and loves always to go in bands, to show that it is so, and when high on wing, takes a course always as straight as an arrow. Tennyson is right when he speaks of the old fellow "that leads the clanging rookery home"—he might have spoken of him as leading the clanging rookery out almost at sunrise. An incessant hard-working insect-destroyer, and a true farmer's help, the rook too often comes in for a bad return; for not only is he shot and hunted down, but he is cruelly destroyed, often by poison laid in the fields. A writer in an authoritative paper, and the owner of a rookery, said that one year, to satisfy himself, he now and then shot a rook or two to examine their crops. He got nothing but grubs and wire-worms, and now and then a beetle, up to the 20th of April, when he found some score of particles of oats in the husk; but on carefully examining them, he observed a small whitish streak under the envelope of the husk, and he found imbedded in the kernel a wire-worm. It was extended length-wise, gorged with its milky substance, and in colour exactly the same as the juice it was feeding on. This was the food during the time the grain was in the state of transition; but, after the first week of May, it fed entirely on wire-worms, now of full natural size and colour, and from that date not a particle of grain was found in the stomach of a single rook.*

* It is very surprising to find Mr. John Burroughs ("Fresh Fields," p. 267) writing of "the crows or rooks, as they are usually called," and throughout the whole passage speaking of them alternately as crows and rooks, when it is clear it was the latter he meant. He seemed to fancy that the carrion crow was the only other crow.

As we pass along the edge of a cornfield we hear the harsh *crek, crek* of the corncrake, and from the other side comes, mellowed with the wind, the continuous birring sibilant sound of the yellowhammer. The corncrake has been called the King of the Quails, and one of the most peculiar things about him, as some say, is the ventriloquism of his voice. You might fancy from the cries of one bird that there were a dozen at different parts of the field—a device the bird has to render it difficult to guess from his cry any true hint of his exact whereabouts.* He is pre-eminently the bird of ripening corn, and of the harvest-time— one of the migrants which reach this country after much more slight and tender birds—a fact which has been explained in several ways, but not quite satisfactorily to our idea. Just before us is a clump of high trees, oaks, firs, elms, and beeches, as varied in their green, and as beautifully blended as an artist could desire, and in their foliage the wood-pigeons are cooing in a perfect chorus. In the fields beyond the young lambs are already active, the ewes intent on feeding in the cool of the morning, and the horses in the little paddock to the right, as though they felt themselves superior by their closer contact with man, sniff about, and leisurely whisk and ruminate as though they argued that time was all in their favour, and that good meat would not spoil by waiting.

There already, see, the swallows are on the wing,

* But it should be mentioned that on this point it is said in Yarrell (vol. iii. p. 140), "This bird has been credited with ventriloquial powers, but it may be doubted whether this is not in consequence of the marvellous rapidity with which it sneaks, unperceived, from one spot to another. The Editor has had ocular proof that notes which were supposed to indicate ventriloquism were, in reality, the responsive utterances of two individuals."

attesting that flies are about. As we pass a little bit of road which has been cut through a sandy rise, we see what is very uncommon in our district, a couple of sand-martins—delicate and slender and silvery-dark— who have contrived to find themselves a nest-hole in the bank thus made, and are now busy feeding a young brood. Nature, wise housekeeper, does not long leave

any ugliness due to man's adventuresomeness unim- proved or unrelieved by some form of life.

We are not far enough from the great city not to be aware that the bird-catcher comes this way. We have met him over and over again. He has some of the worst traits of the loafer; but he is very clever in his own way—he can imitate to a nicety the note of the bird he wants—whether it be linnet or robin, chaffinch or goldfinch, bullfinch or yellowhammer; and though he finds his "take" too plenteously for our liking, still the shyer birds abound, while the tamer and more simple or trusting run the risk of being exterminated. Many localities have already been almost cleared of goldfinches and bullfinches, though just here happily the former abound.

By the time the sun shows above the horizon—suffusing the eastern clouds with glory, and running streaks like long fiery fingers across the sky, and repeating in every tree and shrub that lies between him and you the veritable vision of the burning-bush, rose and saffron hues melting softly into one flush all

over the eastern sky up to mid-heaven—the cattle in the meadows begin to move, and emerging from the sheltered corners of the fields, in which, like dark formless heaps, they had lain all night, begin to whisk their tails about in an intermittent leisurely way, which tells that already some not quite so beneficent insects as bees are busy also, and are quite as industrious and methodical, if not so lovable, as bees.

In some of the lower hollows the clouds of mist have hovered close upon the ground; you can almost see them, as it were, fold in and in, and finally disappear like smoke before the full-faced glance of the sun.

There, look you, goes a great green dragon-fly, with his myriad eyes—the first we have seen to-day—his gauzy wings giving a kind of subdued sound, or are our ears deceived between this and something else, say, the first faint stirrings of the field cricket ? We can hardly tell, for the humming in the air increases round us as we sit in this benignant little natural arbour of ours, midway in our morning walk, and we find more and more difficulty in reliably differentiating separate sounds. The distant and the near, too, get more and more mixed up in the sense. Now come soft and faint on the new stirring wind the low lowings of kine from distant fields ; the cockcrows in challenge pass over to and from the neighbouring farms ; and is it possible that that is the distant hooting of an owl even in daylight from some woody recess into which the early sun-rays do not penetrate ? And, listen, can that really be the woodpecker at his work already, tap, tap, tapping the old elm tree ? There goes a little dipper, very rare here, with bright flash on his wing ; he is making his way to the main stream up yonder, the rivulets or branches having waned to mere threads in the recent drought ; and we have now and then the sibilous cry of the willow-wren or chiff-chaff, and the delicious dropping music of the chaffinches from hedge and orchard. Ha ! there goes a bullfinch, as if he had some pressing

BULLFINCH.

business on hand, which indeed he has, and that is to keep himself alive—the only one we have seen on our morning journey—with his exquisitely coloured neck and throat and velvety back. They are not tolerated in our region, having such a bad repute for eating fruit-buds, and in the early spring it moved me to see little strings of them brought in by the young farmers just to show what execution they had done, as I could

not help thinking of the floods of music prematurely silenced—but that was not likely to weigh much with them.

Here we are at a little fence on which I often sit as I pass, just to watch the effect of the first kindling rays of the sun on a bit of water. What a fair world is mirrored there the moment the sun looks in! The little stagnant deep mirrors wondrous heaven with softer sky, clouds already edged with fire, and fleecy bosoms white as wool, and the trees on the banks look down on aërial images of themselves reversed in its borders. And now, listen! there is the croak of the

frogs as they signal to each other, and already the newts are active, and display themselves with their strange eyes; and you may not sit long without hearing the calls

FROG.

of birds who have nests in the trees near by, telling to their mates and their neighbours that you are there, an intruder and a stranger, and to beware of you.

Yonder, see a rabbit scuds home from a too long sustained stay in a neighbouring turnip or wheat field; almost at our feet, a mole puts out his head, and suddenly withdraws it again, though we have remained almost as still as a statue, which proves that Mr. Mole has quick eyes somewhere in his queer, sharp-pointed little head. Yonder goes a weasel wriggling over a turf fence, on the other side of which probably it has its home, gorged, as one can imagine, with the brains of silly rabbits and rabbitlings. He is a symbol of the great blot on creation—the creatures that prey on the weak and innocent, never engage in a fair fight, and are careful to delectate themselves only with the tit-bits. What a peculiar image nature is of human nature in all its phases, lofty and low, pure and selfish!

And now in front, look you, there comes towards us a cat, with a look of intent resolution and business. That cat is a poacher, and has been away at one of its haunts in yonder coppice, and is now making its way home. It is so intent that it is within some thirty yards of us, or it may be even less, before it observes us—sharp as its eyes are; then, with a sudden surprised look that might well bespeak a troubled conscience, it turns and bolts and leaps over a hedge and disappears, making the dew sparkle as it goes. The expression of that cat going homewards in the dawn —tail down, hind quarters low, and shoulders raised —suggests the idea that but for man's constant presence and control, all would at once relapse into wildness.

The late laureate caught this effect, as he had caught so many others in nature, in the first stanza of his song, "The Owl":—

> "When cats run home and light is come,
>   And dew is cold upon the ground,
> And the far-off stream is dumb,
>   And the whirring sail goes round,
>   Alone, and warming his five wits,
>   The white-owl in the belfry sits."

Look, as we walk home through the coppice, we come on tuft after tuft of rabbits' down, and might fancy at first that here was the scene of the weasel's depredations. Not at all. There are burrows in that hedgerow, and here one of the rabbit does has plucked the down from her breast for the lining of the burrow for her young ones; and in the twilight of morning in which she deemed it most safe and advisable to perform this maternal self-denudation, was not so careful as she might have been to remove all traces of her loving labour and near abode. Master Weasel *may* make some use of the information if he has noticed this.

As we pass on we meet a shepherd driving his charges

out thus early to pasture, whistling as he goes, his face shining from hardly yet effaced ablutions; and, turning round, we pass on to a marshy flat, very deserted, the resort of many ducks, the sound of our steps setting the inhabitants to flight, with a peculiar cry and clangour as they dash forth from their favourite resting-places.

As we pass on we skirt the edge of a slope of waste land running down towards the sea; and coming to us across it are the plaintive cries — pees-weet, pees-weet — of lapwings. As we advance, we see them circling round certain

MALLARD IN FLIGHT.

points as they monotonously repeat their rouching cry

—the cry of all nature's voices, to our thinking, of

RESORT OF THE PEE-WIT.

waste and solitary places; so that though mournful, there is no harsh sense of inharmoniousness.* If, indeed, as the poet says, "in nature there is nothing melancholy," it must be because of these nice and often unnoticed adjustments of sound to circumstances, and of circumstances to sound. And there go bands of curlews in their V-like order. We can scarcely imagine lapwing or curlew making home in the leafy coppice or green wood, not to speak of the richly cultivated park or garden.

Nothing will better bring before you than

LAPWING.

CURLEW.

* The French naïvely name them *dix-huit* (dees-weet), from their cry.

a morning walk like this, the fact of *feræ naturæ* in large numbers sustaining themselves in the close vicinity of man, shyly busy at work, but seldom seen. Here, close by a farmhouse, we skirt an unusually large pond with clear inlet and outlet and with high banks around it, particularly on one side. In it are perch, tench, and roach, with a fair store of eels. There runs a moor-hen with her brood along the sedgy edge, undisturbed at our presence, for we often walk that way. She has her home in that little island-looking space over yonder, where the willow spreads a soft screen or shelter for her nest. Wild ducks in colder seasons come this way too, and so do the lapwings in hard weather, and sometimes in summer or autumn a squirrel or two will steal over from yonder wood just to look how the trees are for nuts, and will scream down at you from the higher branches when you stand and closely watch them, as if *you* had no right to be there, and they were privileged. Mr. Squirrel is very nice as a pet, but he is a little exclusive and overbearing in his manners as we find him here. Perhaps, however, something is due to the narrowing of the area of woodland year by year; and he now sees too much of men and their ways for his comfort and peace.

Ha! There goes a brown rat—a very different kind of customer, who, because he can take the water well, and, perhaps, does a bit of fishing on his own account, is often confounded with the vole, who suffers sadly from the ignorant on this account, though really very unlike him in almost every respect. Greed, self-assertion, and low cunning are marked on the water-rat. His quick furtive eyes are as characteristic as the pink eyes of the weasel are of him. He is no vegetarian if he can help it, and after fishing in the afternoon at this very pond side, I have often in the twilight let my fish lie in a kind of dry ditch, to watch as I lay in perfect quiet Mr. Brown Rat steal down to carry off a specimen or two, in which, despite my presence, he more than once succeeded, always, as far as I could see, seizing the fish by one or other extremity—a good precaution, as there was a fair growth of overhanging shrubbery through which he had to make his way with his prize to his hole.

But hark, what piteous sound is that in the coppice we are now skirting—a sharp wail of pain and fear, or rather of terror? We soon discover it—a rabbit in a trap—in torture, palpitating, torn, and bleeding, eyes strained and starting; making a last effort at a bound as we approach, and then dropping helpless, exhausted. It may be there thus for hours, till the trapper's convenience suits. We turn away half sick, our pure pleasure of the morning's sights and sounds somewhat shadowed.

Only a little farther on, in a run we find a snare with a rabbit in it—dead; the poacher is merciful from mere self-interest. He does not like traps, because the animals cry so long and piteously and tell their whereabouts.

Ah! There, as we steal along this hedgeside, goes a hare down the furrow, which attracts us by its peculiar limp. We fix our eyes and see that it has been shot—one of its hind legs shattered, dragging behind, as one sometimes sees a doll's leg which has broken by rough usage, and now only held on by the outside cloth. It is not what sportsmen kill that constitutes the cruelty of sport, it is what they maim and send away to die in holes and corners, torn, tortured, and bleeding. And that is one reason why only *sportsmen* should have sport. But nowadays my yeoman neighbours tell me they are becoming more and more rare; and that lawyers and corndealers, *et hoc genus omne*, who try to hunt and go out shooting, should for most part be prosecuted by the Society for the Prevention of Cruelty to Animals. The former are even cruel to their horses, which they cannot manage; the

latter seldom hit, and when they do, they generally only maim. Very little humanity would suggest a more merciful mode—the cry of a hare in its extremity is exactly like the cry of a child.

The early morning's walk was not to end entirely without incident. Just after I had stepped over a gate going into a field not far from my house, to my surprise I saw a bull with tail in the air making straight towards me. He was a new-comer, and a stranger to me; indeed, I was not aware of ever having before seen a fellow of this sort just hereabout. He made for me with such a wild dash that all I could do was to retreat, and make my way over the gate again. But he was of a mind to pursue the attack, and I was afraid might dash over the very inefficient fence after me. So I clutched at one of the posts, luckily not so firmly fixed in the earth as it might have been, and with it swinging above my head I waited for the attack. On he came, his mouth foaming, his eyes aflame; but before he could make the leap, down came the heavy post on his head, and he turned as though stunned, if not blinded, and I made my way home. One of the few risks of such a walk as this is the presence of such animals in a lone field; but in this case it only imparted the element of adventure and danger, needed to make my early morning walk more and more a true image of human life.

But we must not quit the subject in the sombre strain this incident would suggest. As we regain a view of our house roofs through the screen of encircling lime trees, we see that the pigeons—fantails, pouters, and tumblers, as well as common ones—are already in session on the roofs, waiting for the early advent of those who feed and tend them. In the meantime, they are cooing and doing their devoirs to each other gaily; and, between whiles, doing also a little damage to the roofs by applying their beaks to pick out morsels of lime from between the slates. As Lord Tennyson says of them in the afternoon sun, they are even now, early in the morning, " bowing at their own deserts " — self-pleased, self-admiring, proud, pretty little things : perhaps, indeed, the most self-conscious and sympathetic of all birds, outside certain very sensitive chamber birds. As we enter our little gate, we hear the hum of innumerable bees in the immemorial limes, in the honeysuckle, in the hedges, and in the wild roses and clematis. Butterflies soon follow, some of them of the most lovely colours, giving full assurance of the summer. And so we close our morning ramble of fully two hours—not having met or seen a human being.

The sun is now advancing up his skyey path, and we are concerned only with sunrise. We have seen what delights both ear and eye, but also something to give pain, and pause, and to promote reflection— the tragedy of nature, and the manner in which man so often selfishly or thoughtlessly adds to it.

But before we end our account of our ramble we should like to add a few lines about one point respecting Mr. Cuckoo and his family which is wrapped in doubt. Do the young birds, when they are fledged, learn the call-note of the foster-parents or of their real parents, deserting absolutely the former at this stage, after having

CUCKOO.

got their earlier upbringing out of them ? This query is suggested by the fact that, on this early morning walk of mine, I heard no fewer than four distinctly different cuckoo calls. (1) The ordinary cuckoo call;

(2) this call, in a hurried, startled, sharpened tone, as if of fear or warning; (3) a distinct and prolonged second *koo—cuck-koo-koo-oo*; and (4) a low, tentative *cuck-a-cuck-koo*, the *koo* being faint and indefinite, and more of the broader *a* sound. In addition to the calls being different, the notes sounded varied. I had never personally observed this before, and speaking to a yeoman friend, who has spent all his life in the country, and has been out at all hours, and as a sportsman has observed a good deal, he did not receive these statements of mine with surprise or as suggesting anything novel, but gave it as his theory that the young early broods of the cuckoo in June are fledged, and join older cuckoos, whether their true parents or not he would not say; that the low hesitating *cucka-cuck-koo*, with the *koo* very indistinct, is the note of the young birds, and that the prolonged second *koo* is the note of the old birds, as trainers, now emphasising that note to develop it fully in the young. This is, at all events, ingenious: it could only be verified by evidence as to whether this prolonged second *koo* is definitely heard at periods so early as to make it impossible that it could be due to the circumstances to which he attributes it. He quoted an old saw which lingers in some parts of the country, and is common in our district :—

> " April cuckoo come,
> May he sounds his drum,
> *June he changes tune;*
> July he may fly,
> August he must."

My friend averred that, so far as his broad observation went, these old saws generally had a basis in fact.

Whatever may be doubtful about the cuckoo, there is

no doubt of this, that the young of the cuckoo are armed, as if by special provision of nature in their structure, to throw out the young of their foster-parents from the nest. Their wings at the upper edges are strong and high, and there is a hollow in the back such as is found in the young of no other birds. Their wings and back form, as it were, a shovel by which they may lift and throw out everything else beside them. From the very minute description which Mrs. Blackburn has given of facts observed by her and many of her friends, the young cuckoo works and works till he gets under whatever is in the nest, then he straddles up with his feet fixed in the sides of the nest till high enough, and throws one of his shoulders above the other, and so pitches his fellow-nestling out, and this while he is still almost featherless and totally blind! This only adds to the mystery and the horror which cannot but be felt in studying many of the ways of this bird.

VI

WITH THE NIGHTINGALES AT THE VICARAGE.

THE parish in which I reside is not one that presents much striking variety of scenery, though it is rich here and there in by-ways, in umbrageous greeny nooks, and its hedge-rows are delightful. Not a right-of-way through the smallest farm but you come on "nestling places green, for poets made," as Leigh Hunt has it, in little strips of coppice or woodland, that run like a rich trimming round a plain solid dress of fairest colours.

One little dell I have in my eye, where all is so nicely bright, yet shaded, that you might fancy naiads or sylphs at play among the lush leafage; where, while the ear is charmed with the soft ripple of water, hardly distinguishable from the whispering of the leaves, you can look through the sheltering screen at the distant water-mill, and beyond it the little church-tower— the only things that suggest human activity within eye-range, and by contrast seems to add to the sense of repose, serenity and retirement.

On the boundaries of our parish, to the east and to the west, there are low swelling hills, crested with trees nicely dotted in ; and along the slopes of one of these lies a wood in which it is my delight to stroll, or to lie and realise at mid-day the sense of that Pan-like silence which the ancients fabled to haunt the noon-day woods when Pan was abroad.

In the centre of our district the ground is flat, but fertile ; and the meadows are lush, and, in the season, bright with buttercups and cowslips.

So far as respects tree-planting, the Vicarage is, as perhaps it ought to be, the bright spot of the parish. Art and nature have combined to beautify it.   In former days some of the incumbents were great arbori-culturists—one of them, indeed, went to the East with the idea, solely or mainly, of adding to the store of choice exotics, and in one or two cases he succeeded. The present vicar rejoices in their labours, and has added worthily his own quota to theirs.   You might wander a good way before you came on grounds where, in the words of good old George Herbert, you would find more riches in little room.

The house, somewhat low and angular, lies as it were in the corner of a miniature park; trellised creepers, climbing roses, japonicas, with their faint-red flowers in early spring, and, most notable of all, a lovely magnolia-tree, and a greeny double pomegranate, with scarlet blossom in its season, cover the walls and relieve the harshness of outline seen from whatever point of view; and it gathers its little lawns and rosaries and flower-beds close about it, half-way round it, with shrubberies skirting the outline of these, bright with soft, pink, feathery sumachs, ornamental pines of many kinds—the Glaucus pine among them, with its greeny-frosty fringes, peculiarly beautiful—the Judas tree, the Glastonbury thorn, so rich and rare, or something very closely allied to it, with spikes on the branches an inch and a quarter long, and hedges of varicoloured rhododendrons.

This forms a kind of inner enclosure or sylvan sanctum, through which the farther ground opens up to you in delightful vistas as you look or go from point to point; and from this inner sanctum, at any part, you step at once into the little park of which I have spoken.

On the other side of the road, quite separated from this, lies the main vegetable and fruit garden, with lofty hedges and stone walls for wall-fruit all round it, save, indeed, on the far side, where it gives into a paddock more useful and less ornamental than the park, with which we are more particularly concerned, though it too has some fine trees around it, and one or two within it, on the strong branches of which swings can be placed for the children at merry-making or school-treat; and in one corner there is a pond, exquisitely closed in with chestnuts and other trees, in which a duck will be seen now and then delectating itself.

Round the extreme limit of the park are stately trees of many kinds: beeches, smooth and velvety of bole,

running straight up, "like the mast of some great
ammiral;" oaks of great antiquity; chestnuts in the
early summer, with their creamy pyramids of blossom ;
a horn-beam or two—rare in this quarter—common
willows, waving high, cedars of Lebanon sighing towards their East, and some splendid elms, mixed with
lilacs, and "laburnums, dropping wells of fire" in their

season ; hop-elms, a cedar or two, and a few lime-trees,
with no end of lower shrubbery wood—red-thorns,
black-thorns, white-thorns, &c. &c.

At the lower point of the little park, that is, at the
end farthest from the house, the trees in the outside
circle so arrange themselves in relation to several trees
planted in the grass close to the boundary-walk, that
the branches actually interlace and form arches.   This

the good vicar calls his "cathedral," and the beaming delight with which he will take a stranger to the proper point from which to see this truly Gothic aisle-like effect on a moonlit night, speaks fully for his sense of the picturesque, and his love of the poetry of nature. And indeed, so seen, his cathedral is right well worthy of the name he has given it, for the branches when looked at thus, give the idea of groinings in beautiful fret-work, enriched with the sense as of some divine tracery, flowing in delicious lines and losing themselves in a maze of others like a mist, all due to the moonlight stealing through ; so that you really have something suggestive of the effect of light through richly stained glass—"the dim religious light" in very truth. This, however, only if the moonlight be bright enough, and at the season when the trees are in full foliage, and in that richest tint of green which has the indescribable and almost mysterious effect of throwing some faint suggestion of blue into the shadows they cast. And, indeed, from the sweeping of the pendulous branches over the little walk all the way from the lower gate entering to the park from the road, you have nothing short of leafy cloisters ; so that the vicar has throughout the summer and early autumn a truly cloisteral approach from this point to his cathedral.

Dotted into the park itself, with the most artistic regard to points of view, are copper-beeches, pollard oaks, with sweeping branches, tent-like, broad, umbrageous, walnut trees, birches — graceful ladies-of-the-wood, and a few mountain ashes—"Oh, rowan tree ; oh, rowan tree, thou'lt aye be dear to me !" There are the rich-looking medlar, •fully clad, the graceful spruce, and the weeping willow. And from whatever part of this boundary you may look, you cannot but admire the art shown in so disposing the trees that the limits of the little park on the other side seem to be indefinite and distant.

This park abounds with birds, for the vicar is a great bird lover as well as tree lover, and has even been heard to say, when practical-minded persons have told him of the fruit the birds would eat or destroy, that he would rather be without the fruit (as that *can* be bought), than lose the music of the birds, which make him delightful concert the livelong day, and have even relieved and sweetened to him weary hours of night.

It would seem as though the birds knew it, for they build in the most exposed places here, where one can stand and look on the callow young ones in the nest, raising and opening little beaks as you "tweet, tweet" to them and put the finger near, or into the deep, dark, liquid eyes of the mother-bird, as she sits brooding over eggs or young ones.

Indeed, the vicar has heard of the practice pursued in some parts of America, and pursued too by the famous Waterton, and in order to attract into his preserves some of the rarer birds, has erected in secluded corners of his grounds box-nests like that represented in the engraving, and has in this wonderfully succeeded.

On one occasion a boy had intruded, found out, and carried off one of the nests from a tree in the hedge. The vicar's daughter, passing that way, saw the mother-bird sitting disconsolately on the tree from which the nest had gone. The culprit was speedily found (for all things are soon known here, and nothing can long be hid), followed, and compelled to bring back the nest with its little family, and put it exactly where it was before in the branch ; and the disconsolate mother was comforted, and reared that brood there to maturity.

The robins, in the early spring, will sit and sing their sweet snatches of song almost within arm's length of you.

Our vicar's delight in his flowers, trees, and birds, as indicating a freshness of feeling and capability of youthful joyance, in spite of sad turns of ill-health, is beautiful to see. The park is a haunt of nightingales, which discourse the sweetest music all through the summer night ; and this is an additional delight and source of pride to our vicar, who in no way wishes to keep all his good things to himself.

One evening in the end of May, a year or two ago, we went, full of expectation, to listen to the nightingales. A crescent moon hung in the silver-blue sky, and shed a soft silvery lustre around, strong enough to make a pleasant

light, yet not strong enough to cast shadows too deep
to be eerie. In a little arbour we sat waiting, and
what is waited for is invariably long in coming. But
also it is true, and how delightful 'tis that 'tis also true,
in the words of the French proverb, that "all things
come to him who can wait."

We waited, beguiling the time in talk of many things
—literature, art, and music; and at length the music of

ROBIN SINGING.

the nightingale at once crowned and silenced our talk.
The shadows of the trees, like finer ghosts of themselves, lay lengthened on the grass. The leaves of
the lime and the poplar gently fluttered, even when
there seemed no breeze to stir them, and an almost
inaudible murmur appeared to steal across the thick
long grass, here and there cluster-starred with marguerites, that faintly wavered in the moonlight, in the
pauses of that song.

The pauses grew shorter and shorter as we sat and listened. At first, despite the notion of a challenge, there was more of a complaining plaintive air, varied only now and then with trills, gurgles, penetrating rolls,

and half-whistles (we cannot describe that indescrib-able music, though its subtlely pertinacious, penetrat-ing sweetness is found in no whistle). Gradually the tones grew deeper, fuller, richer, as though the mere act of singing had brought its own comfort, nay, its own delight—the triumphant, mellow, full tones predominated; the shower of song fell on our ears like sweet rain on the wastes of the desert.

We at length arose and proceeded down the crescent path that bounds the park, till we stood close to the tree from which the music came, actually touching its leaves. Still, the bird was so rapt in its song that it did not perceive us, or, perceiving us, was so rapt in its delight that human presences were indifferent to it —or, it may be (who knows?) were even stimulating, as the sense of a sympathetic audience to a great *prima donna*.

And doubtless not far off "the music of the moon slept in the plain eggs of the nightingale," as the poet sings; and that was inspiration too; for the song we have is ever but the herald of songs to come, and an aid to the brooding love that is active to make them come. With the nightingale, as with the human heart, it sings when it labours to prepare and to perfect the life which shall enjoy the love that it feels within, throbbing and prophetic.

Still, the music flowed, gathered, swelled; now piercing clear; now lowly plaintive; again, as if calling some loved one who lingered afar; again, as though that loved one were near—were near. Those pipings, trills, and jug-jug-jugs, how impossible it is to reproduce them, however clearly recalled, and it seemed that, instead of satiating, they grew ever more sweet and intense to ear and heart. We stood—none of us knew how long—close to that sweet heart of minstrelsy; fearless, unseen of us, yet doubtless seeing us; and as we were moved more and more, so more and more the music seemed to grow, and swell and quiveringly vibrate, and deepen and flood all the moonlit fields and meadows round about.   How the other birds can sleep soundly in their nests is indeed a wonder!

The thought of this recalls to us that exquisite legend of the great Sultan Solyman—Solyman the Magnificent —of whom it is told (for he was a great bird lover) that all the birds came by deputation to implore Solyman to stop the song of the nightingale, because his piercing notes spoiled their sleep, and by consequence took from the freshness and the fulness of their song

NIGHTINGALE.

by day.   But Sultan Solyman, after hearing all that the birds had to say, and also the defence set forth by the nightingale (which was mainly to the effect that, if he ceased to sing and tell his tale of longing to the rose, that flower itself might cease to grow, or to shed any longer its sweet scents abroad), gave answer that he was deeply sorry he could not interfere to secure what the birds prayed for.   If the nightingale did indeed rob them of their sleep, he could not in the end injure their song—that could be due only to their own fault—nay, he could but improve it; for they would

K

show themselves very stupid indeed if they did not draw something of sweetness and depth from these longing, plaintive, but triumphant notes of the nightingale.   And so the birds had to go away disappointed.

When at last we turned and bade our friends good night, it seemed that the nightingale's music followed us for a mile or more through the scented sweetness of the night; and that, as at last it grew faint, the notes of other nightingales also came faintly on the ear from far, and more distinctly nearer to us, as though nightingales were sheltered in familiar spots close to our own abode, where before we had never guessed them to be. Or is it that the delighted ear is the only truly prepared ear for kindred harmonies ?

VII.

"THROUGH THE WHEAT."

OFTEN sit at a little latticed window at the back of my house in the country, and look over a wide expanse of landscape. Just beyond the hedge, of which I have given a description in a former chapter, there is, as I mentioned there, a wheat field. I say wheat field, because that is the crop that best I like to see upon it; but, of course, it must pass through the regular rotation of crops, to which farmers, by a most antiquated and short-sighted system, are still bound in lease or even agreement; so that all free action that would enable them, by foresight and prudence, to take advantage of a market suddenly opened, or likely to be suddenly opened, is hindered. The present depressed condition of agriculture may be. due to many causes, some of them preventible, some of them not; this is one of the causes that could easily be removed, and ought to be, so that a man might be enabled to make the best use of his acreage that he could.

Beyond this wheat field lie greeny meadows, often with the most delicious effects of light and shade upon them, and, seen from this point, look as though closed in by trees, though here, as in many other cases, distance lends enchantment to the view; and as you advance, you find that the effect is due to mere clusters here and there coming more and more into line with each other as you retire further and gain this fine effect. Beyond these, again, the ground sinks and passes into the valley in which lies the stream I have spoken of as skirting " my wood." It covers the rising slope ; and behind, still higher, is the gentle hill of Frating, with its church tower rising from amid a screen of trees—like a picture—the very scene which from time immemorial painters have delighted to paint, as if in this they found the highest imaginative hint of rustic and village life in England, the spire or church tower pointing the mind to another and higher life, while below all the squalor and the grimy struggle and want is hidden there behind the trees. Art is said to be the revealer, not seldom it is the concealer too, as I have more than once thought, and looked at Frating from my window, where skilful tree-planting round the vicarage and the church has done much to gain picturesque effect by concealing so much lying below and behind them.

As I withdraw my eyes, they rest on the wheat-field more immediately before me, now crowned with its golden glory. What a wealth there is all through the season, and has been here both for ear and eye ! In the spring and early summer the larks made a perpetual concert, the sweet strains growing at once more piercing, keen, and full as the spiral ascent led higher, higher, and the bird, at last lost to the eye in the sunlight, was still clearly heard, recalling Shelley's rapturous lines, so kindled with the music of the bird. And it is very noticeable that this inspiring singer is the bird of solitude; and he is notably unsocial all through the

spring and summer, each one keeping to his own nest and ground, a thing in which the young ones even follow the parental example, giving the old ones much trouble to find and feed the little things in places apart from

SKYLARK.

each other. Yet they do it. In the winter the larks go in coveys, which makes it more easy for the bird-catchers to find them in many cases.

Corncrakes now fill the pauses with their harsh monotonous cry—*crek, crek, crek,* or something like it;

butterflies hover over the blooming wheat, and now and then alight, and the wood-doves range round the field at certain times. The rabbits dart about, and go with their hirpling kind of walk down the intervals between the "stetches," and now

CORNCRAKE.

and then a mole is seen. The rooks come and make observations in the pauses of their work in the green-cropped fields beyond. A most curious and forecasting bird is the rook; little indeed escapes his attention.

Often have I been drawn out to walk down that winding footpath—a right of way through the wheat —when I should have applied myself to other tasks, unable to resist these magical calls. The walk has thus become very familiar to me. I do not believe that human beings ever entirely escape the liking for hidling corners, which are one of the many delights of infancy. It must be something of this that leads me to seek out enclosed corners where one can listen to the sweet sounds utterly secluded from human sound or companionship, and where one may repose unseen. There are many such corners round this field. Even the walk through it affords half a hidling-place. You walk, as it were, with a solid wall of grain on either side of you, high as your shoulder, and look along a kind of level moving tableland. Mrs. Browning, in " Lady Geraldine's Courtship," says that the heroine's way at a particular point in the story lay through such a field :—

"Her path lay through the wheat,"

and a more delicious or more suggestive background you could hardly have. And the concert you now listened to could not be spoiled, like some concerts, even if you indulged a little sympathetic talk with a companion, if you could allow one, for here the singers will not be put out, nor the chorus break down for your impertinence or interruptions, nor will you spoil it for any other listener, however much you may talk. The eye is as much delighted as the ear—soothed, consoled, as it were, by the variety all in such a wondrous unison. An ever-moving billowy sea with rhythmic waves stirs on either hand. No more delightful impression, I believe, could be produced than by the effect sometimes of the billowy movement, as the wind sweeps over the ripening grain, mingling, as it were, sunshine and shadow in the most delicious interchange as they seem to chase each other unceasingly, while the grain gracefully bends and bows before the gale, and recovers itself to be anew swayed and tossed in a sort of cadenced refrain, continually beginning and being arrested, arrested and beginning again. The late laureate no doubt means this effect when in "In Memoriam" he speaks of—

> "The thousand waves of wheat
> That ripple round the lonely grange."

There is truly something of pathetic suggestion in this rhythmic wave and swell, associated as it is with a low surruration, a pensive music, indescribable, and nowhere else to be heard of precisely the same pitch and quality. The waves on the sea-shore kissing the sand, and sighing as they retreat, only to return again, may have something akin, as may also the gurgling lisping wash of waves round the pebbles by the river side, when vessels are passing onwards; but in both cases the agents concerned are felt to be somewhat more tangible—the effect, the music, is more the result of causes realised to be efficient; but the sea of air, with its unseen waves, when they play upon the fine resistant yet yielding harpstrings of the wheat, has an intensity and penetrating charm of its own, felt to be at once mysterious and natural. I have even fancied sometimes, as I stood and looked at the

> "Reapers, reaping early,
> In among the bearded barley,"

that the awns or beards occasionally imparted an additional keen subtle sibilant sweetness; but this may have been a mere fancy of mine. But any way, whether near oats or wheat or barley, lay your ear close to the ground and listen when the wind comes up once more, and it will seem to you as though thousands of soft human sobbings, not all of sorrow, but not all of joy either, had merged, mingled together, and taken sweetness and soul and penetrating individuality from their union. You may hear wondrously weird tones when "wind, the grand old harper, strikes his thunderharp of pines;" but it is generally too high-set, the resistance is too great, the strings are too far apart for the notes or sobbings softly to intermingle; you hear in a greater degree and in a degree too definite for the fullest effect, each individual voice, so to speak ; and the wonder and pathetic effect are lessened, though under special circumstances it may be that fear or horror might be more powerfully awakened. But the blending and harmony in the other case are complete, and this it is which affects, delights, moves, and, it may be, overcomes you. The wheat especially is a harp, but not a thunder-harp: it is the eternal Æolian harp of nature. In all such sounds heard in solitude, and in a mood of responsive sympathy, there is the strangest suggestion of human voices, far, inarticulate, imprisoned, or diffused, as you may choose to have it; and it is because of this that there are such poetry and pathos in these sights and sounds of nature.

Lord Tennyson has applied the word "happy" to the autumn fields in the first verse of that unique song in "The Princess":—

> "Tears, idle tears, I know not what they mean,
>   Tears from the depths of some divine despair
>   Rise in the heart, and gather in the eyes,
>   In looking on the happy autumn fields,
>   And thinking of the days that are no more."

But "happy" in any sense, save in the idea of energetic rustic effort, the profitable results of toil, and the prospects of a hearty harvest-home, we confess we cannot regard the autumn fields. It may be in this sense that the late poet-laureate regarded it, though that is hardly a very imaginative or poetic sense. They suggest no distinct horizon of hope and promise, like the fields of spring and summer. All the purpose of what from one point of view may be picturesque in human effort has vanished, or is on the point of vanishing, and what is suggested for nature is bareness, bleak winds, the earth robbed of one of her sweetest burdens of music and message to man. It is as bread that man now too exclusively looks on the produce of the fields, and true it is, for poetry as for faith, that man lives not by bread alone.

Lord Tennyson himself in " Dora " makes the heroine take this view of it. She fancies that the gladness of the old farmer's heart *in the full harvest* will make him tender towards poor William's child. This hope has a kind of pathos in it; but Dora's idea of associating the possibility of tenderness with the joy of success has also its truth.

> " Then Dora went to Mary. Mary sat
> And looked with tears upon her boy, and thought
> Hard things of Dora. Dora came, and said,
> ' I have obeyed my uncle until now,
> And I have sinned, for it was all through me
> This evil came on William at the first.
> But, Mary, for the sake of him that's gone,
> And for your sake, the woman that he chose,
> And for this orphan, I am come to you ;
> *You know there has not been for these five years*
> *So full a harvest. Let me take the boy :*

And I will set him in my uncle's eye
Among the wheat, that, when his heart is glad
Of the full harvest, he may see the boy,
And bless him for the sake of him that's gone.'"

And as human feelings, at base, remain much unmodified, whatever the effect of outward custom and observance, it may be presumed that the same sentiment inspired Naomi and Ruth as regards the latter going to glean in the fields of Boaz.

And all this suggests a question: Why is infancy in itself more poetic than adolescence, and adolescence than middle age, and middle age than senility? Is there not something indefinably expressive to the imagination, in possibility, in growth, in the promise of indefinite expansion.? It is not only the purity and innocency of childhood that enchant; it is the spring-like promise, with its unconsciousness, and also its

WILD OAT.

pomp of *passing* beauty. That it is passing is one of the elements that appeals to the heart. In the grown man, with every line fixed and settled, with habits formed, and the countenance become the very index of these habits, what room is there for the brooding forecast blended of hope and fear, which in some circumstances makes the commonest heart thrill to poetry? Childhood is the springtime, adolescence is the early summer, middle age the later summer, and age is the autumn and near winter of human life. Only Wordsworth, with his exceeding reserve and keenness to recover interest by a pathetic colouring, has made old age poetical in the ordinary sense; but even he generally effects this by subtle presentations of contrast—the young child by the side of age—his great and unconscious art lies in subtle contrast, and making the one tell by almost insensible touches on the other, and thus interpret and enforce the treatment of both.

Wheat is the greatest favourite with the poets, though why it should be so is not easy to discover, unless, indeed, it may be that wheat is the tallest, most powerful, and uniformly regular in aspect, looked at from the level. But oats and barley, particularly long-awned barley, have their points of superiority too, viewed merely as picturesque and affecting. The

CULTIVATED OAT.

words corn and cornfields, it is true, would perhaps be found to occupy even a greater space in concordances than wheat and wheat-fields, not to speak of barley and barley-fields; but in a great many instances "corn" is used generically for any cereal, and not unfrequently, indeed, for wheat and barley, as for instance in Lord Tennyson's fine line in " Aylmer's Field "—

" Fairer than Ruth among the fields of corn,"

whereas only wheat-harvest and barley-harvest are spoken of in the Book of Ruth. But we must turn from poetry to fact, and try to find in fact a sort of hidden poetry.

Take a single stalk of wheat in your hand, and bring your finger down to feel how shiny and smooth it is, and then try to break it sharp off; you will be surprised at the resistance—it will crack and split and still hold together unless you are very violent indeed. Nature has built it in the most scientific way for strength, and for the resistance that comes from buoyant yielding. It is a hollow tube, built exactly on the plan of the strongest bones in the human body, and of the great hollow piers for wide river bridges, as seen on several in the Thames. It is perfectly round, and so smooth and shining that any force would be likely to slip from the centre to the sides and past them at whatever point directed. Farmers tell me that strong-strawed wheat, such as the " Suffolk Stand-up," will resist almost any force of direct wind; it is only when the wind circles and changes and " beats round," as they say, accompanied generally by rain, that it goes down. Could God have built better a small stem for resistance first, and also for the power of uprising again afterwards ? Beaten down as it may be, the grain continues to grow, so that despite the evil prognostications from *laid* grain general throughout the country in 1890, the farmers were pleasantly disappointed in a crop which, alike for weight and quality, was far above the average, so that more than once I was tempted to say to them: "You must have your grumble, but no amount of wet can do the harm a month's drought will do; so you may be thankful for the rain—'twas a blessing in disguise." Yes, the wheat stalks are built on the very principle that some of the strongest of animal bones are built, and witness to the same principle in constructing for strength and resistance.

Never before did I observe, as I now did, the great varieties of every form of cereal. To most people not farmers, as I confess it had hitherto done to me, every field of wheat, or of oats, or of barley looked exactly alike. But it is far from being so. Some cereals are short strawed, some long, some more slender, some rounder and more robust, and to such an extent as makes a great difference to the feeling of the scythe-man when he comes to cut it. Some produce an ear longer and more tapered, some rounder, fuller, and less refined to the eye; the grain of some is long, some round, and, to the experienced eye, a very little atten-tion will tell of what particular variety of grain the field is. Some wheats have the seeds standing more straight out from the stem; others more slanting up-wards, and very closely packed together; and I am told that these latter are powerful against lodging rain, and are not nearly so likely to sprout. Some are by their very type large, some small; and it does not always follow that the farmer should be guided by what would be expected to produce the heaviest head. He must have regard to many things—the quality of the soil, the amount of average rain-fall, and many other things. What will do well and yield abund-antly in some soils and situations will do but poorly in others.

Several wheats, indeed, are between four and five feet high; and some of these suffer very much in the case of wind and rain coming together, and are more apt to get laid than others, which, though equally tall, are more powerfully built, so to speak, and are capable of recovering themselves though exposed to great force of wind and rain.

Farming by rule of thumb may do under certain circumstances; hardly can it do when the holding is extensive, and where the soil may vary through a considerable range. Then the mere sowing in of seed according to a hard-and-fast rule of rotation need not be expected to pay. The scientific farmer must be continually on the outlook for new and suitable stocks; and I learn that even a change of stock is often advisable on the mere rule that planting over and over again the same corn in the same land has a tendency, clear and unmistakable, to operate disadvantageously. Farmers in different districts thus very often interchange seed stocks, and, within a certain range of suitability, generally to advantage. But high farming, as it is now called, demands not only much knowledge, but great foresight, calculation, power to enter on experiment, and scientific skill enough to read alike what a certain grain takes in greater excess than another from the soil, and the best manure or chemical elements to supply again to the soil that which was in excess taken from it. This is all quite over and above the consideration due to general effects of atmosphere, soil, rain, &c. &c. Thus it will appear that farming is by no means an unintelligent or mechanical calling in these days. A skilled farmer is indeed a man not only of much energy and resource and capital, but in a certain degree at all events a chemist and skilled meteorologist.

I do not know exactly how many varieties of cereals, pure and hybrid, there may be—a very long list certainly, as seedsmen and nurserymen, as well as large farmers, are continually producing new varieties, many of which are only known locally; but I venture to subjoin here some notes from the pen of one of the leading agriculturists of our district (the north-eastern part of Essex lying towards Suffolk), in which he notes the characteristics of the various cereals most in favour throughout our bounds. I give it precisely as he handed it to me:—

WHITE WHEATS.

Roughchaffed. —The real heavy-land wheat; a great favourite with millers; very prolific in fine seasons.

Talavera. —Very early; a fine quality wheat coming from Spain, as its name implies; not so hardy.

Hardcastle and Lemy's white.—Suitable for lighter soils.

In addition to these many new kinds have been raised by our principal seedsmen. At present they are not so general in use, but are for the most part admitted to possess a stiffer straw than the older varieties.

RED WHEATS.

First and foremost comes *golden-drop.*—A great favourite on all soils; very prolific and hardy, and not liable to sprout.

Old Kent Red.—A good wheat on light and mixed soils, and considered by millers to be nearly equal to best white in quality.

Nursery.—The finest quality of all reds; must have rich deep soils.

Square headed, both *redchaff* and *white*, are good wheats on hollow bottomed soils, rarely going down. Of new crossbred wheats Webb's *Hybrid King* takes first place in our opinion.

Rivets or " *Clog*" wheat is getting more into favour, as it does not lodge or deteriorate through wet harvest.

BARLEYS.

Chevallier.—First raised by Dr. Chevallier of Aspal, Suffolk; is considered to grow the finest skin, but almost equally good are *Golden Melon*, Page's *Prolific*, Webb's *Golden Grain*. Messrs. Webb's *Strain of Chevallier* has taken many prizes of late years—an excellent barley for all soils.

Long-Eared Nottingham is a heavy yielding kind, scarcely so good in quality as the other kinds mentioned, but does well on poor soils.

OATS

chiefly consist of three kinds. The earliest are Winters, and generally come to harvest second or third week in July. These are the heaviest and hardiest out suitable for all soils.

SPRING OATS.

Tartary (white and black) are perhaps more grown than any other variety, but many prefer a white oat, such as *Suffolk Triple* or *Potato*, the latter usually coming to more weight than any other spring variety, but wanting rich soil. Tartary oats in the Fens often produce twelve quarters per acre.

VIII

MY FAVOURITE SUMMER-HOUSES.

THIS little picture carries me in memory to days of
boyhood. In the school vacation how sweet it was
to escape from tasks that were sometimes irksome to
all the delights of freedom, when to range through the
long day by the stream side was to catch a vision of
some paradise that always retreated as you advanced,
but rewarded you with new hopes of finding at the next
advance; when to escape into the firwood, with its sweet,
resiny, healthful scents, and that wonderful blue haze, to
gather fir cones, was indeed a second heaven.   There
were the pools with the tadpoles too; and the wonder
that dawned upon us when we found that these nonde-
scripts of nature were only in a transition state, that
they gradually threw out limbs, and developed lungs

instead of gills, and from something like fishes, became veritable frogs! And then the fishing for sticklebacks, when the sport would be arrested by observing the wonderful playfulness or the surprising fighting-powers of these little rascals of the tiny pools—these finny spiny nest-builders of the miniature lakes that are to be found in almost every bit of our British Isles.

It would have added greatly to our interest had we known more of the life-history of these wonderful little fishes, as we know now. We saw them in their nests; we several times saw one of them hunting off and fighting with others, but we had no one to tell us of the reason that lay behind all this in their economy and habit and style of life. We should then have found a veritable fairy-tale. Our readers may perhaps be pleased if we give them the benefit of what we then lacked. The different species of sticklebacks are all grouped scientifically under the strange-sounding name of *Gasterosteus.* This Greek word literally means "bone-bellied," and is thus finely descriptive. The bodies of the sticklebacks are not furnished with scales, but, instead, are defended by little spines or spikes rising here and there (different numbers of them in different species) from bands of bony matter. The male attends very strictly to his domestic duties, as he sees them, though he is certainly not content with one wife, or with two even; and his plurality of wives has much to do with ensuring the stability and increase of the race.

The very important work of building a nest is associated in the male with the assuming of brighter colours, which make him look more and more different from the females as days go on, till finally he is a very gay and smart little fellow indeed. He begins his task by finding any loose fibrous substances he can about the

stream, very often the soft roots of the willow, and he
works these round the stem of a bush or any protuberance he can find handy and firmly fixed enough.
This is the foundation of his house; and in laying it, as
in after-operations, he is greatly helped by some kind

STICKLEBACK'S NEST.

of slime or gummy substance which he exudes from
his body; and hence, at first particularly, his odd
rubbings of his little body against the bits of fibre
which he brings, and against the little tree-stem or
protuberance. So he works till his house rises; but
before it is finished he has to fight for it. There are

other sticklebacks, many who would fain have a house without all the trouble he has taken of laying a foundation from the very start, and are fain to steal his. He has to give them a touch of his quality, which he does, and drives them off, with no doubt some little quiverings of pain from his spines well applied, as he dashes furiously against them at the unprotected parts.

The nest itself, when finished, is somewhat of barrel-shape, open at both ends however, and will hardly do more than half cover the bride for whom it is intended, the head and tail being clearly exposed, and only the middle of the body in the nest. Well, the next thing, of course, is to bring the bride home to her well-prepared chamber. She is found, brought there, and enters in. The male is very attentive to her for a time, and keeps careful watch over her; but he has no notion of supporting her any longer than he needs her. The moment she has done the work of depositing her eggs he turns her out, and goes in search of another mate, and with her repeats the same process, and again the same process with a third, and it may even be with a fourth. He has made up his mind that he must have a certain number of eggs, and this is the way he takes to get them.

He then closes up the ends of the nest, and keeps strict watch over it, never going away from it further than a foot or two. And he has need to be strict and careful, for not only are there stranger enemies ready to undo his work, but the discarded wives, whether moved by envy or jealousy no one knows, would fain tear the nest to pieces, and eat the eggs, or set them free to be destroyed or eaten of other fishes. For about a month Mr. Stickleback is thus on the closest watch till the eggs are hatched. Even then his hard work is by no means over, for he has to fight for his young as before for his eggs. The old belief of our Scandinavian ancestors was that the strength of the vanquished passed into the conqueror. This seems to be the case with Mr. Stickleback: the more he fights, the more brilliantly coloured he becomes, while the beaten lose all their colours, and subside into mere sober browns and greys. No artist could paint the bright tints that glow and shift and gleam on his sides. When at last the young ones—mere specks of jelly with a dark dot for an eye, by which they may be recognised—are able to move about freely, the father stickleback has still a busy time of it. They are always wanting to wander beyond the bounds he has assigned for their exercises—a foot or two round the nest. Woe betide any little item that strays beyond; he is seized by the parent, dragged back, and pitched into the nest in great hurry and wrath, as it would seem, or has dust blown into his eyes. They gain their liberty bit by bit, as is best for other youngsters as well as sticklebacks.   But at last the young ones are able to shift for themselves, and with the close of this duty the glory of the parent stickleback dies out of him—his bright hues fade away, and will not be resumed until another spring comes round.*

Well, we in our young days saw enough in the stickleback to make us wonder at him and to admire

---

* There are three varieties of sticklebacks. The three-spined is *G. aculeatus*, and is either salt or fresh-water ; the fifteen-spined is *G. spinachia vulgaris*, and is common on the northern coasts of Europe, and is entirely marine—it is larger than the others, measuring from five to seven inches, and is sometimes caught in large numbers on account of its oil, which has commercial value ; and finally, the nine or ten spined (*G. pungitius*), which is confined entirely to fresh water, and is the species with which we have been concerned.

him, and our knowledge of him grew gradually, till we have come to feel that there is a good deal in his life that dimly images the life of we human beings. Yes, these things were veritable revelations then—all was wonderful—every day brought its new surprise, its fresh knowledge, its inspiration, its new hopes. Well may the poet say, " Beautiful is youth, for every-thing is allowed to it."

Never shall I forget a long journey we took from this low, thatch-roofed cottage, with its sluggish stream in front of it, over the hills that lay behind. As we went, it seemed as though life stirred up at every footstep. The place was little frequented ; there was no regular footpath. There were long reaches of heathy common, broken up by patches of fir and birch —that lady among trees truly—and here and there clumps of gorse, with flowers golden in the sunlight. The rabbits ran here and there, disturbed in their feeding or in their play; the curlews called, and ran circling round us, and then flew off away from their nests with the most mournful cries and calls; the omnipresent rook seemed to follow us, and the wild pigeons cried to us from the belts of fir that straggled along irregularly.

The humble bees were busy, bumming on their way or settling on the flowers; on the furze bushes the webs of the spider still hung dewy and glistening in the sun rays; linnets and goldfinches were busy on the thistles that grew thickly here and there. Our object was to reach the highest belt where the pines were thick, as we wished to gather cones. How delicious were the scents of this plantation when we reached it, and what gatherings of birds and insects there were. The wood appeared literally to be alive, and our presence seemed to create a panic of disorder and dismay among its denizens. Butterflies and beetles

GOLDFINCH.

vied with each other in brilliancy of colour up in that solitude, and lovely birds were there, and even the water-wagtail by the tiny stream seemed lovely. The wood was literally carpeted with fir-needles, and with cones of former seasons now dry and sapless, and ever at the foot of trees we came on fungi that showed like gems and pearls.

We gathered and gathered fir-cones till the sun fell, and then returned in the soft twilight, when the mantle of grey was falling over all, and the glow-worms were

GLOW-WORM.

hanging out their lamps on the hill-sides. We were healthily tired, but we had our prize of cones wherewith to make our much-wished for ornaments, and we went to bed and dreamed of that wood, with its shy and lovely ever-active denizens—dreamt that we roved by still more unfrequented and erratic ways than we had that day traversed, lost our bearings, and ourselves were lost, and went hopelessly from point to point, leaping over tiny streams flowing through miles of fir and pine in endless avenues and glades, till at last we sank exhausted on a bed of fern and dreamt—a dream within a dream—of a hill-top, with fairies in circles on it, like circles of light, into which we were led, and

in the midst of the crowning brightness, and face to
face with the most lovely forms, awakened to find that
we had a touch of cramp from over-walking ourselves,
and wished and wished we could fall asleep and just
begin that dream within a dream again, exactly where
we had left off. " Beautiful indeed is youth, for everything is allowed to it."

Into what a different region, with what different

associations does this second house take one! Sweetly
embowered in greenery, for elms, limes, pines, birches,
and poplars deliciously intermingle with lilacs, laburnums, and hollies, and even a rowan-tree (mountain
ash) or two, and close it in on all sides, save the front
entrance, which you see. It is delightfully situated on
a little shelf on the side of one of the Surrey hills, and
looks like a nest with the bird sitting on it. Seen
from below as you advance to it, it appears literally to

hang on the face of the hill, and with the sunshine blinking on its whitened side walls seems in a kindly way to
beckon you to advance.   How many and how pleasant
are the excursions we have made from these doors!
How sweet the memories that dwell with us still of
those rambles through wood and moorland, over heath
and holt!   Looking from the gate we could see over
an immense area; in the middle distance right in front
one of the most beautiful villages in England gathered
round its green so neatly, with its drinking fountain in
the centre, the gift of one who long lived and worked
there, and with the big house of the squire on a gentle
wooded height looking down on it graciously.   And
though this village was a mile or two distant, in some
states of the atmosphere it looked quite near, as though
close below, while looking from that village again towards our house it seemed as though a step or two
would bring you to the foot of our hill.   You had to
learn by experience that the idea of distance in these
hilly regions was very deceptive indeed.

Coldharbour—that picturesque little settlement, red-
roofed and warm amidst its greeny shelter, one half of
it clustering by the church, as though half nestling in
a cup's-side—was not very far off, and often we found
our way there by Mosse's wood; and sometimes on
our way back we would stay thereabout till the twilight
fell, and watch and listen to the sound—the *eerie* sound
—made by that strange bird, half hawk, half swallow,
the nightjar, which wheels round the tops of the trees,
more especially the fir trees, after the moths and beetles
and the night flyers, which form its food—thence the
name which it has in some parts of the wheel-bird.
We had often been surprised at the strange and unexpected sound it makes when anything startles or

frightens it: it strikes its wings together over its back somehow, and from this circumstance came to be regarded with superstitious fears by the rustics.

It has a peculiar owl-like aspect seen in certain positions, and hence it has been called the fern owl, which is more justified than another name it sometimes gets—the night hawk. But more appropriate is the

NIGHTJAR OR EVE-CHURR.

eve-churr, from the *chur-r-r* of its note, a little like the *chir* of electric wires. It has a peculiar habit of never perching across, but only along a branch—a habit supposed to be due to the peculiar form of its toes, the middle toe having a long flange or comblike extension, about the use of which naturalists are much divided. It has another great peculiarity: from the upper part of the beak there hang down over the lower part quill-like points—really undeveloped feathers. The purpose of this is more evident. It catches its

prey in flight, with its mouth wide agape, and this remarkable development aids it in retaining them in its mouth as it flies—the more that these quills are said to be touched with a peculiar kind of gum it secretes for this purpose, and to which the insects stick till the bird can swallow them or feed its young with them.

HEAD AND CLAW OF NIGHTJAR.

It builds no nest, but lays its two eggs— invariably two, but no more—in a depression at the foot of a tree, either among sand or stones or decaying fern and leaves ; and the bird as it broods is so like the sand or stones or fern, that naturalists find in this a good instance of what is called protective colouring. Indeed it knows so well what colour of bark best matches its plumage that you can rarely see it unless it moves, which it is not very keen to do, and will keep quite still till you are about to touch it, or even tread upon it ; then it flies off, pretending that you have hurt it, goes tumbling about as though wing or leg were broken, all to tempt you to follow it and divert you from its " nest "—cunning wee thing ! This instinct according to Thoreau and many other observers is developed in the young ones from the moment of their emergence from the egg, and so wily are they

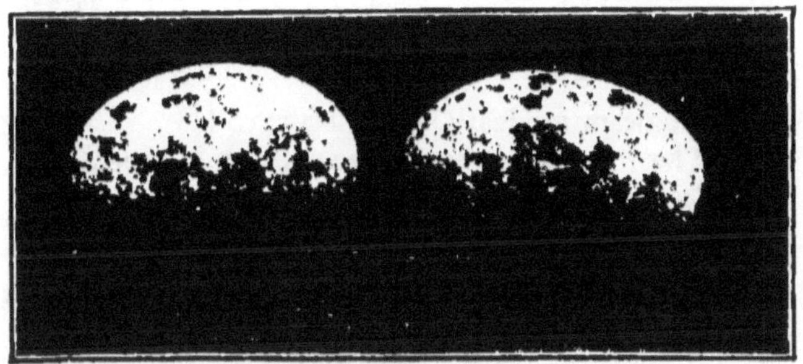

EGGS OF THE NIGHTJAR.

that, as the brightness of the eyes alone would betray them, they close the eyes and look through the very narrowest slit when any strange animal or person comes near.

What a delight it was, too, to turn out into the loftier parts of the hill, over large spaces of which grew the whortleberries, locally called "hurts," and lie and enjoy their delicious tonic flavour, and think of Thoreau's celebrations of the wines that lie stored up in the wild fruits by the wayside! And, after having enjoyed this, to go on again dipping down into the valley by the most delightful footpaths—all round you seas of fern and heath—on to Tillingbourne, to watch the fall, slipping down, white and foaming at foot, or to wander refreshed by the stream-side, or to journey by the almost Swiss-like Friday Street, with its lake lying still below you as you suddenly emerge into view of it from the wood, and so on and on by sweet paths to Abinger, there to range over the wide furzy common —truly a common—and see the pretty quaint old church—restored some years ago—and the picturesque little churchyard, and the old stocks by the main gate as you enter or emerge.

> " Arcadia found at last for our reward !
>   The village lies in swathes of sunshine sweet ;
>   Green grass is soothing for the weary feet,
> Even though it be too luscious burial sward.
>
> To maiden modesty what fit award !
>   The rose-trees year by year the tale repeat
>   Of young life ended pure, without defeat,
> Of hopes long cherished or a heart grown hard.
>
> And there what uncouth forms the glad eyes greet?
>   Are these the stocks that once for penal pains
>   Familiar stood as warning to all swains
> Inclined too lightly other's rights to treat?
>   They moulder now in parody of time
>   When this fair village *had* its petty crime."

Then, if we will, we may pass by the Hammer— sweet hamlet—on to Gomshall and home again. Who can tell how much of the healthful effects of these wanderings is due to the wonderful mixture of aromatic scents—the resinous odour of the pines, the scents of fern and whortleberry, of heath and beech, and oak and elm ?

And then, how often have I taken visitors down past Coldharbour to the Redlands Wood—that delightful pine wood—with its clumps and clusters, its waving ferns and giant firs—one indeed a veritable monster, a mark for miles round, rising high above his fellows—head and shoulders over all—a very Saul among pine trees. Often, often have I, pointing at this great tree from a little distance, asked my companions—new to the place —what their notions of his girth was, and would get the most contradictory replies ; and as we neared and neared the trunk of that tree, it appeared literally to grow as we looked and came closer, till, to the surprise of my friends, it was found that it would take three persons with arms outstretched at full to go round its mighty bole. Many giant oaks and beeches have I seen in the New Forest, at Bushey, down in the rich park lands of Suffolk, and have looked on great firs in Scotland, but I never remember to have seen so great a pine as this—"Fit to be the mast of some great ammiral," to quote Milton. Why, the ship that could take this pine for a mast would make of the *Great Eastern* but a tiny dwarf.

And then there is the middle walk, with the pines so regularly ranged in line on both sides, that the place veritably looks what it has been called, The Cathedral —the mighty branches interlocking overhead, and the light, passing through them, taking that mysterious blue tint and making the looker-on think of the " dim religious light." It is not difficult to be in a certain way poetic in such a place as this, and so I may be excused quoting here what was indeed suggested on this very spot :—

> A sea of fern, far-sweeping, wave on wave,
>   With rhythmic answer to the wind that steals
>   Through pillared stems, and yonder arch reveals
> Blue glory islanded like faëry cave,
> Withdrawn from touch of all rude winds that rave
>   Round men's abodes ; blue-dim the light that seals
>   The sense of worship, making mild appeals,
> Like mellowed sunshine through Cathedral nave,
> When low the organ notes swell out and die,
> ∴ And rise again to flow in fuller strain :
> The spirit of the woods is waiting there
>   To wed the mystery of tears and pain
> In human life with solace soft and fair,
>   Still found in nature's holy constancy.

And then did I not once make a journey down there in mid-winter, after a heavy snowfall, just to see how that pine wood looked in white? Still and calm, like a fairy world of silence and wonder, where no sound may mar the witchery of effect. No, not quite so; listen, what is that? Is it the snow with crispy whispering, or are the sounds ghostly, or are there spirits abroad? Hark! don't you hear something go scratch, scratch, with momentary pauses between? Is it in the tops of the trees, or down on the snow-covered ground? You listen hard and satisfy yourself it is borne to your ear along the surface of the tell-tale snow. It is the rabbits over yonder busy clearing the snow from the mouth of their burrows, and trying to scrape off enough of the mantle of white near bye, to let them get a nibble at the green herbage below.

And as you listen intently, a soft sound of tap-tap-tapping comes to you from the other side, where beyond the firs there is a circle in which there are some beeches, birches, and "immemorial elms." That is the green woodpecker, who, despite the frost and snow, pursues his calling without pause; but just now you might wait long enough to hear his strange laugh, which has led him to get the name of "yaffle" in some parts, for that cry or sound, *pleu, pleu, pleu,* he only emits before rain, which has led him also to get in some places the name of the "rainbird" or "rain-fowl." His green body and red head present a fine contrast to the bark of the trees on which he climbs and taps; but he is a shy and cautious fellow, and has a clever knack of always retreating to the other side of the tree on the slightest hint of his being observed. It is very funny to see him working the trees—a business he does quite systematically. He proceeds up each tree from the foot, taking slant lines across and across it again, till he has reached a considerable height. When he has done with that one, he flies with a peculiarly undulating kind of flight—up and down, up and down—to the foot of another tree, and goes through the very same process with it, rising up and up in slanting lines, ever tap-tapping as he goes. Though he prefers the elm, he carefully works, as well as builds, in other soft-wooded trees also, and may be seen ascending the beech and poplar, even the pine and fir. Some ornithologists have said, indeed, that they prefer the woodpecker in the winter-time to any other season: he is such a sprightly, merry, active fellow, always making the best of it. And I am almost fain to confess that so do I. The nest of the woodpecker is a peculiar specimen. He builds it in a hole in a decayed tree, and is ingenious enough, though seldom seen. The woodpecker is a characteristic presence in the winter woodland, and therefore we have felt justified in referring to it here, and doing it honour for its persistency, cleverness, cheerfulness, and activity. It has sometimes, indeed, to fight for its own, and then it fights bravely—that is, when a thieving starling wishes to oust it from the hole it has made for its nest; and as the woodpecker cares for nothing more for nest-lining than a few chips of wood he has dropped down to the bottom of the hole as he was working, and Master Starling, it would seem, knows this, and as a last resort, drops down sticks, straws, and other nondescript articles—and then, much disliking these, the poor woodpecker abandons the nest to his enemy. It may happen, indeed, if there are many starlings about, that the poor woodpecker is thus " moved on," and " moved on " from nest to nest, pitiable bird in very truth, till he is defeated in rearing even one brood for a whole season. Its favourite trees are the chestnut, sycamore, and silver fir.

The Duke of Argyll in *Nature*, May 29, 1890, gave the following account of observations of the lesser spotted woodpecker :—

"I have had an opportunity lately of observing closely the habits of the lesser spotted woodpecker (*Picus minor*), as regards the very peculiar sound which it makes upon trees by the action of its bill.

"It is quite certain that this habit has nothing whatever to do with the quest for food. The bird selects one particular spot upon the trunk or bough of a tree, which spot is naturally sonorous from the wood being more or less hollowed by decay. The bird returns to this precise spot continually during the day, and produces the sound by striking the wood on the spot with its bill, the stroke being repeated with a rapidity which is really incomprehensible, for it quite eludes the eye. It is effected by a vibratory motion of the head; but the vibrations are so quick that the action looks like a single stroke. After short pauses this stroke is again and again renewed, sometimes for several minutes together. During each interval the woodpecker looks round it and below it with evident delight, and with an apparent challenge of admiration. The beautiful crimson crest is more or less erected.

"The whole performance evidently takes the place of the vernal song in other birds; and so far as I know, it is the only case among the feathered tribes in which vocal is replaced by instrumental music. The nest does not appear to be in the same tree; but similar spots are selected on several trees in the neighbourhood, and as the sound is very loud, and is heard a long way off, the hen bird when sitting is serenaded from different directions. I have not seen or heard any attempt to vary the note produced by variations

either in the strength or in the rapidity of the stroke, or by changing the point of percussion ; but I have
observed that the note varies more or less with the tree on which it is produced. During about six weeks the perform- ance has been fre- quent every day, and early in the morn- ings during part of this time it was al- most constant. Of

SPOTTED WOODPECKER.

late it has been discontinued. In all probability this is parallel to the well-know fact that singing birds cease to sing after the eggs are hatched. This instru- mental substitute for singing among the woodpeckers is extremely curious."

And no sooner have you satisfied yourself about the woodpecker, than your ear is attracted by a smart snapping rasping kind of noise. You try to trace the direction from which it comes, and can scarcely be- lieve your eyes when you see a bird which looks more like a miniature parrot than anything else—for it is brilliantly coloured—a delicious mixture of brown or bronze, red and green, and which seems now to be hanging by the bill from a branch and swinging there, clearly defined against the white background as it moves. You can scarce believe your eyes, for you did not believe that the winter woodland held so beautiful a denizen. You try to approach the tree on which it is, and you find it far less shy than the woodpecker, for it remains in your view till you are within a yard

M

or two of it, and keeps on at its business all the while. It seizes a fir-cone in one claw, while with the other it clings to the branch, and with its bill, which you now notice is very singularly shaped (the mandibles curved and crossing each other), and which seems at first sight so awkward, it dextrously breaks open the fir-cone, extracting the seeds, which form its food. This is the delightful cross-bill, rather rare, and so-called on account of the crossing of its mandibles, which show a remarkable instance of adaptation to mode of life. Now this bird, through being hunted and killed, is seldom seen.   Its note, *jip, jip, jip*, frequently repeated, is very characteristic.

"Tap, tap, tap" once more, but not quick and continuous like that of the woodpecker, and consisting only of two or three taps delivered with far more force.

NUTHATCH.

What is that? you inquire. Well, it is only the nuthatch, which is to be found pretty well wherever the woodpecker is; for the nuthatch likes well to get a home in a deserted woodpecker's nest. But the nuthatch being a much smaller bird than the other, plasters up the hole till it will no more than admit his tinier figure; and he colours the mud, or other material with which he does it, to a fine likeness with the tree-bark where it is, and the nest is usually formed of oak leaves. The clay which the nuthatch uses for this purpose, it glues together with a saliva-like fluid, so that it hardens to withstand rain and sun. When roosting, they sleep, like the tits, with the head and back downwards. The strong tap-tap is the sound of his bill against a nut which he has placed in exact position, wedgelike, in some crevice in the tree. Swinging in a branch, with head downwards, he dashes against it with full force of bill, body, and wing, and soon breaks it to find his well-won prize. And yet he is by comparison a very little fellow, only about six inches in length, white throated, blue on back and head, and bright orange-brown on sides and thighs; pretty, smart, active, always cheerful, and he who does much to make the winter woodland gay wherever there are nut-bearing trees. Hazel and beech-nuts he particularly affects, but he will have recourse to acorns sometimes if there is any scarcity in these.

And what is that which now passes over the white like a cloud, disturbing our reflections? It is the owl that, now the snow no longer falls, is out to see if no little mice, or other small deer, are stirring to get a meal once more, that he may make a meal of them. Soft, soft, and silky-downy is his flight; he consorts well with the great, silence-giving ermine cloak in which everything is wrapped. Mister Owl does sometimes, in these circumstances, take a look out through the day, when the light is not strong, and when his prey is very scarce from such causes as this, though when once the mice and birds begin to stir, he has the advantage of seeing them clear against the white ground. The fir-cones not yet fallen slightly wave, though there is no perceptible wind, and as we walk in the snow, the weight of the foot now and then makes the opened cones, fallen below, crackle as we walk, with much surprise at first. Never did we witness a scene more

beautiful, impressive, and poetical, and fairy-like. Our
presence there seemed like an intrusion that only too

much broke the
spell, and some of
the glimpses from
the borders of the
wood showed the
commonplace trans-
formed to poetry of
landscape.

Do you wonder
at my so cherishing
the memory of these walks? Then, if you do, you
have not roamed in these sweet regions as I have

done, at all seasons and all hours of the day, and some
hours even of the night, with friends, some of whom

are dead now, and some are scattered over the wide earth—and before you blame me you must go there and see!

This picture carries me to a very different kind of scenery, to that prettiest part of Essex in my idea—the region of the Stour — Constable's country — not flat as is the prevailing character of the portion of Essex near to London, of which the region of the Lea is typical, but on both sides rising here and there into rounded hills, prettily wooded. Dedham, indeed, lies at the foot of a considerable hill, driving down which, towards the little town, one of the sweetest views possible bursts suddenly upon you through trees; and when you have put up your horse and trap at the inn, passed through the town, and walked to the river, you get a glimpse of Dedham Mill—immortalised by Constable—with its swirling lade and deep backwater, where big roach lie, fed on the floury morsels from the mill, a scene which Constable has painted too, and made familiar to many who have never seen it. And over yonder on the Suffolk side is East Bergholt, with its church tower on the very top of the hill rising from amid its screen of trees, often painted too and no wonder! It is the very ideal of the scenery of its kind. Along the meadows nearer to the river the full-fed cattle lazily browse and ruminate, and whisk the flies off with their tails, or stand knee-deep in the shallower side pools left here and there. In the picture, the house we see is on the borders of one of the tributaries further down, but while staying there it was our delight to work down the main stream, trolling for pike, or, finding some favourite pool, would sit down and enjoy the quieter more contemplative exercise of ensnaring the more delicate-mouthed roach.

The next picture takes us further afield still—to Suffolk. Oh, the delights of that little farm-house, with its back to the water, in which we fished day by day, and saw the sun set gloriously behind the gentle hills. The water, here drawn off into a lade to work a little mill below, kept up a slumbrous sound like a lullaby as it fell with a fine dreamy effect, and would you believe it, imparted some sense of coolness even in the warmest day, for it always set some wind stirring with refreshing effect?

Falling water ! Minnehaha—laughing water ! is that not what the sound always suggests ? Yes, laughing water ! how it foamed and bubbled as it fell, lingered for a moment, as it were, and then, gathering itself together, went on, composed and steady, singing its undersong, to do its work, to flow on the mill-wheel and grind the corn, throwing off, as it did so, diamonds in millions, forming and flashing as it went, rising, falling, falling, rising, for ever "a thing of beauty and a joy for ever;" the green hues on the old wheel sending a reflected colour through the diamonds sometimes in the sun, more especially evening sun, like a magical circle or world of circles, or rainbows within rainbows, and star-lights intermingling.

That old rambling house, with its dovecote high up in the gabled end, was an unceasing delight to us; and how these pigeons sat in session sunning themselves on the roof, as if to challenge our admiration, pouting and bowing, yet expecting nothing but silent admiration from us strangers—vain things! But they showed a very different temper when their mistress, who fed them, appeared. They looked, indeed, as though to them she was the impersonation of Providence, as truly she was, and would sometimes perch upon her shoulders, head, and even her hands, coo-coo-cooing out her praises.

And then the orchard of which we had the freedom. To sit there in the warm afternoons in the cool shady summer-house, and watch the shadows slowly moving round the dial, every now and then to hear the ripened fruit drop on the grass with a slight thud, and to see the little mice come running out and make the faintest rustling noise among the pea-straw, now stripped from the stacks and laid on the ground.

A very favourite excursion we made then was to an ancient abbey not far off, where in old days the monks lived their life, and no doubt attended well to the wants of the body, while they strove to save the souls of others as well as their own. On almost every field on this farm there were fish-ponds, some of which had been artificially made. These ponds were still rich in tench and roach and other fishes; and one of the ponds was really a moat round an island fed from a small stream some distance off. There were little rustic bridges

across the moat to the island, on which were wealth of
trees, summer-seats, and "nestling places green;" and
often have we sat and dreamed there, always welcome,
or in the golden afternoons have lain down and watched
the sullen pike, pleased and satisfied for once, resting
nigh the surface in the deeper parts when the sun was
warm.   Nay, we have even tried to catch them in the
cunningest way, but with small success, owing to the
peculiar lie of the ground and the narrowness of this
moat, which, however, was very deep at parts compared
with its breadth.   This brought us always too near in
view of the fish.   This circumstance raised the question

how the monks in old days could have got out the fish
as they wanted them.   To this the farmer replied:
"Well, I dunno: if they'd 'ad guns then, I should 'a
said as they shot they pike as I 'a done, times an'
times, just as they laid on top o' the water as they do
now; p'r'aps they were good archers, as I've 'eard say
monks and bishops could do a bit o' fightin' in them
days, and shot the pike so; but sartin sure am I as
they never got 'em out there wi' rod an' line, as the
cleverest chaps wi' the rod ha' cum here just for a try,
an' never a one on um did any better than you 'a done,
so you needn't be werry much ashamed on it."

One of the ponds, the biggest, ran close up to the outhouses, and was a fair sheet of water; there we had better luck with rod and line, and many a pleasant sail have we had in the boat that lay moored in the remote corner among the rushes.

IX

THE VILLAGE WELL.

UR village boasts of two special sources of gossip. The shop—a general shop, where everything is sold, from tin tacks to red herrings, from tapes and ribbons to ham and eggs, and from needles and thread to boots and shoes, which scent all the place, there being truly nothing like leather—is an interesting centre, where you could do a good deal in the study of character. There come tripping in the wives and daughters of the small farmers round to sell their produce—butter, eggs, and so on—or to exchange them for various commodities they cannot themselves produce and yet cannot do without. There, in front of the shop and the inn next door to it in the evenings the young men congregate after work is done, and straggle in irregular little groups over to the village green, a silent witness of the fact that the vicar and the rest have failed to do what they might long ere this have done—institute a reading-room, well warmed and well lighted, and where a cup of tea or coffee might be had. Parish councils may do something to end this, though the lounging habit formed through generations will be hard to root out. The other centre is the village well, which is beautifully situated in a bit of road that dips down at the west end of the village, and is picturesquely overarched with trees, causing a moisture almost always to be over that bit of road. There come the women, as in the days of patriarchs and prophets in the East, to " draw water ; " and if you were a curious visitor, intent on studying the ways of the natives, you would soon discover that if the pulse of the village is beating quick under any love affair, scandal, poaching prosecution, or quarrel, it soon makes itself felt at the village well. No sooner does one woman, probably the leading gossip, in the early forenoon make her appearance, than she is followed by two or three more, who by some secret instinct know that she has gone before them, and there they stand, tongues going, their pails on the ground, and arms akimbo, while she makes a very long business indeed of working that handle to recover her pail, which goes swinging and making a clatter midway as she unsteadily goes winding and winding.

Then the same process is repeated by each in turn, while all the others wait ; and then, each with her pail of water, they come slowly along, holding their heads as close together as they can, so that no sweet morsel may be lost to any ; and there is usually in these cases a pausing at the door of each, before she enters to resume her domestic work. The village well is the housewives' parliament, where, if formal motions are not made or passed, a common policy is often announced and adopted, alike as to how some farmer is to be dealt with who has chastised Tommy Jones for climbing over the walls of his orchard or trespassing in his fields, or the gamekeeper who has pounced on some of the menfolk laying snares in the wood, or the policeman who has been too officious in taking notice of some one's visits to some other one.

In the evening, too, it is funny to notice how the young women home from work will be moved to help mother by bringing water for her. Fanny Wilkins will be seen tripping along with her pail, singing to herself, as her left hand goes over her plenteous fair hair, coiled up in a big cushion at the back of her head, to make sure that it is all trim and tidy, and

looking as though she had no idea anybody else was likely to be about there just then. Before she has reached the well, Johnny Amos steals forth from some hidling corner and joins her with "How be you, Fanny?" at which she pretends great surprise to see him of all possible people; and then they walk on to the well, where Fanny takes long to get her water up somehow, and finds it so hard and is so awkward at it that Johnny has to come and help her, his right arm almost passing round her as he takes her place and gently moves her away. Before they have got their water-pail up and unhooked, another pair are there, and as they move homewards they meet another pair; and each young woman goes home and tells that she saw So-and-so and So-and-so walking out together, and that they will soon have a marriage in the village, and the dance on the green in honour of it. Under all disguise of circumstances isn't human nature much the same all round? The village well is a sort of conservatory for these humble folks, to which they retire to have a chat and quiet fun. Verily, there is much human nature in man, and in woman too.

X.

RUSHES.

HO that has read them can ever forget Mr. Ruskin's wonderful passages on the grasses. This commonest of all plants, trode upon with indifference, made commonplace by its wide distribution and persistency, is shown by him to be little short of a miracle. ·Never was eloquence more convincing, nor rhetoric more effectively directed. He glanced at the more ornamental grasses rising in mimic towers to beautify the most neglected corners, often hanging out their seed-like pearls at the end of silken threads to add a delicacy and grace to what else were wildernesses. But his highest praise was reserved for the common grass of the field, to which we owe, among other things, that satisfaction to the eye in looking on a wide landscape. The more it is crushed down, walked over, rolled, nibbled of cattle and sheep, the more robust it becomes at the root, and the more succulent it grows in the young shoots it is ever sending up— the more the true servant of man, the more it is laid under contribution for the needs of man and beast.

Another series of very common and beautiful objects much overlooked and maligned are the rushes. "Green grow the rushes, O," but nowadays few care to attend to the modest rushes that in marshy places, by the sides of streams, and in ditches and corners of boggy bits of land, rise up, like wardens of the waste, and in their season make a brightness of their own. How straight, and clear, and shining they are, with their fresh glancing green, that answers so nicely to wind and sun, and, when their flowering time is come, they look like soldiers carrying spoils, or better still, banners of victory. In old days the common rush had a use. The pith of it furnished the best wick that could be found for the oil-lamp—in Scotland called a " crusie," diminutive of " cruse." It was a common thing for a whole family to turn out for a day or two at certain seasons to gather rushes by the burn and ditch sides. From these in the evenings the pith would be extracted, cut into lengths, tied up in bundles, and put away for future use, stored in dry places with the greatest care. Over wide districts no other light was known than that derived from this rush-pith saturated with oil.

These were the days when no lucifer matches as yet existed, when the only way to get light was by the slow and clumsy process of striking a spark from a flint with steel upon tinder, and then light-ing at this tinder a sul-phur-tipped " spunk " or match.

In our early days away up in Glenesk, beyond the village of Edzell (to which we learn a railway is now being constructed from Brechin, so as to join this old capital of "the land of the Lindsays" with the big world and full civilization), how often have we wandered by strips of wood in the centre of great sweeps of boulder-dotted heath land to gather the rushes; and how often have we lain in a sheltered corner—sheltered alike from wind and sun by the tall rushes among which we worked—and through the whole afternoon gathered and patiently extracted piths, getting more and more up to it by practice till the soft white rounded substance

would whirl, twisting from the greeny case, like the shavings from a plane or a spokeshave, to return proudly, our prize in our hand, and receive praise and commendation—more esteemed, perhaps, than any praise or commendation we have since received.

The only service played by the pith of the rush nowadays, so far as we know, is in making the wick of certain night-lights.

Most beautiful and imposing of all the rushes is, perhaps, the bulrush, which has come in for a good deal of notice from the poets. Few readers of poetry but will remember Lord Tennyson's fine lines in the "May Queen":—

"When the flowers come again, mother, beneath the waning light,
  You'll never see me more in the long grey fields at night;
  When from the dry dark wold the summer airs blow cool
On the oat-grass, and the sword-grass, and the bulrush in the
      pool."

In "The Dance of the Flowers in Welcome of the Spring" we read :—

"The bulrush, safely guarded about
With full drawn sword, was the sentinel stout
That o'er the gathering kept close ward,
As the flowers danced merry upon the sward :
And the water-soldiers their adjutants were,
Who on their shoulders ball-epaulets wear."

The rushes are close associates of the flags and sedges ; they are, in fact, the democracy of which these are the aristocrats. Not a bit of waste water but the rushes contrive to throw some gleam of colour and relief over it ; nor do they seem wholly

out of place on the marshy borders of lonely mountain tarns and lochs, where no such high-bred plant as the wild iris would or could set its foot, having, despite robustness, a certain delicacy of taste which the rush affects not. The water-birds love the shelter of the rushes, and are often found nestling among or under them. . The wild-ducks, the coots, and the dabchicks are their patrons, and are never felt to be out of place in their vicinity ; and efts and newts and frogs, and all their confréres, are easily kept in soft association with the rushes. Even on streams of some little importance, where trout of a considerable weight may be found by the skilful fly-fisher, there are bights and little bays where the water lingers, spreading out into delightful tiny crescents, and where the rush contests the right of place with some of its higher-born brethren, and seldom fails in holding its own. If it does not, like the daffodils of Wordsworth, flash upon that inward eye which is the bliss of solitude, it is gratefully remembered by many for sake of the useful service it yielded in byegone days.

And the rushes and sedges have, for most part, their unfailing company of flowers: the water plantain, with its broad leaves, the yellow iris, and the common high flag-flower, resting amid its handsome greyish-green leaves, so tender that it hardly bears being touched; and water forget-me-not, and loosestrife, and brooklime, and crowfoot yield their welcome variety. The flowers form a goodly fellowship, and in the most unlikely places they grow and cluster and shed their wealth of light and beauty.

XI

BEES AND BEE-KEEPING.

HERE is in our village one bond of good feeling and amity which was so unexpected to me that I cannot but make special record of it. The same thing may exist in other parochial communities, but it did not come before me in any other place I visited in the same definite and effective way as it has in our parish. This is bee-keeping. The country round, owing to the gradual enclosure of heaths and commons, is certainly not so good for this purpose as it once was; but gardens abound, and so conservative are the people in following the habits of their forefathers, that there are but few houses or cottages that do not have their "skeps" of bees; and the business of looking after swarms, in which neighbour willingly helps neighbour, forms one of the most pleasant elements in the life.

But you might live a long time without hearing much of it, if you did not begin to keep bees yourself as I did. Then you suddenly become the centre of a kind of informal society, in which everything about the bees is discussed—not only the quantities of honey obtained, but also points relative to the habits of the bees, and the best means of "strengthing" them through the winter and guarding them; for it is a fatal mistake on the part of many people in towns to suppose that bees simply hibernate the whole winter and never wake up. On the contrary they are very wakeful, much more so than the bee-master always wants, and in certain kinds of weather will give him a good deal of trouble and concern. In the occasional blinks of warmer sunny weather we sometimes have in winter at mid-day, certain of the bees will be apt to steal out, and to become so intoxicated with the sweets of the ivy flowers, that they will stay too long and get benumbed with frost, and never manage to get back to the hive. I have seen them just struggle to get on to the little platform in front of the hive, and die there from frost.

The bee-master must prevent this by dint of various attentions. A small tube slipped into the hole of the hive with honey and sugar is a good one, and a very peculiar thing may be noted with regard to the intelligence of bees (of some bees, at all events) in this matter. As soon as their tube is empty, instead of flying out in the mid-day "blink," they will employ themselves in hauling this tube right out of the hive to the little platform in front, so that their condition or want cannot be overlooked by the bee-master. At first I fancied this was due to intermeddlers, and made many inquiries of those about the house whether the bee's tubes had been touched, but met with decided "noes" at every point. Mentioning this to the man from whom I had got my "swarms," he said, "'Tis queer, ain't it, but that's what my bees allus do; and, would you believe it o' them mites o' things? I ha' seen 'em with my own eyes a pullin' of the tube out, just like a row of sailors a pullin' of a boat down the beach to the water—so many one side, so many t'other

side—one of the prettiest sights as you could ever
see."

I could not credit this myself, but my friend went
just then and took a look at my tube. "Oh," he said,
"I am summat afeard as 'tis too wide for the bees to
do the work so neatly as I have seen 'em a doin' of it.
You make a tube a little bit smaller, sir, just so much
as will let the bees have room to move at each side,
no more, and then, if I ain't mestaken, you will see
what I war a tellin' you on, if you come to them hives
about mid-day the third day after." I did so, and
'twas just as he had said, and certainly 'twas a very
pretty sight.

Then this same bee-master told me that he had
often observed stray bees that had swarmed from a
hive go back, from some cause, to the parent hive.
They were never tolerated there, but quickly turned
out; and not only so, but for most part killed, and not
only that, but the bees proper to the hive would drag
them over the little platform in front of the hive, and
then fly down, work away till they had made a small
hole, and roll little pellets of sod over the bodies, and
thus bury them. He had seen this done not once but
scores of times, for he was an indefatigable watcher and
a thorough friend of the bees. This does not quite
agree with some observations of Sir John Lubbock,
but that may pass.

Then sometimes a vagrant wasp would intrude into
the hive, and the bees had a very short method with
him. They directed their whole power of attack on
one point—to tearing off one of the wings of the wasp,
which they were not long in effecting ; then Mr. Wasp
was helpless, could only buzz and pitifully gyrate, and,
thus maimed, he was bundled out of the hive and

thrown on the ground, but the bees did not do the wasp the honour of burial.

But the bees have sometimes more gigantic intruders, with whom we should suppose it would be much more difficult for them to deal; yet they surmount the difficulty in the most ingenious and safest manner, as the following passage from a good authority will show :—

"There are some actions of bees which we hesitate, for want of confidence, whether to ascribe to an innate instinct or to a more reasonable faculty of their minds. If, as will often happen, a snail steals into the hive, he is at once attacked and stung to death. But the bees are not sufficiently strong to remove such a leviathan; and yet, if he remains, his putrefying carcase will be enough to breed a pestilence in the city. When the Lilliputians wished to kill Gulliver, they were deterred by the selfsame fear. But the bees contrive to rid themselves of their Gulliver in a very ingenious manner. They cannot remove him, it is true; but they can, and do, embalm him. They cover him all over with that glutinous substance called 'propolis,' and this keeps out the air, and prevents the body from decomposition. If, however, the snail be one that wears a shell on his back, the bees merely cover over the door of the shell, and leave the captive to the fate which is inevitable. These processes, though seeming to go beyond what one conceives to be the beaten track of instinct, are, however, so universally adopted, that one is almost driven to the conclusion that instinct is, after all, the motive force under which they are performed. There is, however, a class of cases which it is evident that the bees are accustomed to encounter, and which would, we may suppose, be differently treated in different hives."

The very able observer, F. Müller, states an observation of his own, which must be considered as alone sufficient to prove that bees are able to communicate information to one another :—

"Once" (he says, "Letter to Mr. Darwin," published in *Nature*, vol. x. p. 102), "I assisted at a curious contest which took place between the queen and the other bees in one of my hives, which throws some light on the intellectual faculties of these animals. A set of forty-seven cells have been filled, eight on a newly completed comb, thirty-five on the following, and four around the first cell of a new comb. When the queen had laid eggs in all the cells of the two older combs, she went several times round their circumference (as she always does, in order to ascertain whether she has not forgotten any cell), and then prepared to retreat into the lower part of the breeding-room. But as she had overlooked the four cells of the new comb, the workers ran impatiently from this part to the queen, pushing her in an odd manner with their heads, as they did also other workers they met with. In consequence, the queen began again to go round on the two older combs, but as she did not find any cell wanting an egg, she tried to descend, but everywhere she was pushed back by the workers. This contest lasted for a rather long while, till the queen escaped without having completed her work. Thus the workers knew how to advise the queen that something was as yet to be done, but they knew not how to show her *where* it had to be done."*

Mr. John Burroughs has some very exquisite observations of bees. Here are two :—

"When a bee brings pollen into the hive, he advances

* Romanes' "Animal Intelligence," p. 157.

to the cell in which it is to be deposited, and kicks it off as one might his overalls or rubber boots, making one foot help the other; then he walks off without ever looking behind him. Another bee, one of the indoor hands, comes along and rams it down with his head and packs it into the cell, as the dairymaid packs butter into a firkin." *

And again:

"I have a theory that when bees leave the hive, unless there is some special attraction in some other direction, they generally go against the wind. They would thus have the wind with them when they returned home heavily laden, and with those little navigators the difference is an important one. With a full cargo, a stiff headwind is a great hindrance. But fresh and empty-handed, they can face it with more ease." †

The acquaintances and friends the bees have been the medium of bringing me are many; and from the many conversations I have had with them—conversations as pleasant and obliging and neighbourly as they were informing—I have been led to form far higher ideas of the English peasant's power of observing and of reasoning than I had done before. They greatly err who fancy the agricultural labourer, in our part of the country at all events, is a mere clod, without power of observation, perception, sensitiveness, or delicacy. In some things, the truth is, he puts his town-brother to shame, only to strangers is he shy, and is little apt at expressing himself in such a style as they could understand. The bees with us, at all events, are a good bond of union, doing not a little to break down some of the prejudices of caste and class, a service for which I am not

* "Locusts and Wild Honey."   † Pepacton, p. 104.

aware that they have hitherto been duly or sufficiently celebrated.

Sir John Lubbock, so far as his experiments have gone, has not found the bees nearly so clever and intelligent as the ants; but I am sure he would hardly subscribe to the statement that the bees are as lazy as loafers, and work at the most only three months out of the twelve, considering the many and the long journeys he has faithfully traced day by day. At the same time, I am certain that he would not pronounce the bees to be free from faults either. There is one vice, as already hinted, to which they are sometimes inclined. Like many other animals (and men too!) who bear a high character for industry and respectability, they are only too apt, many of them, to go on the " spree," or to have a " bouse." It is notorious that they will sometimes get tipsy; and if flowers of certain plants are within reach, will indulge themselves by imbibing intoxicants or narcotics with so great avidity, that stray ones now and then will be unable to fly from the source of their ill, and are to be found hanging there quite stupid after sunset, and no doubt perish from cold. Bumble bees often, and hive bees sometimes, have been found in this tipsy condition on the flowers of certain species of the willow.

In the *Gardener's Chronicle*, so far back as 1841, this extract will be found :—

" We regret extremely to announce that some honest humble bees of our acquaintance have taken to drinking, and to such an extent that they are daily found reeling and tumbling about the doors of their places of call—the blossoms of the passion-flower, which flow over with intoxicating beverage—and there, not content with drinking like decent bees, they plunge their great hairy heads into the beautiful goblet that nature has provided for them, formed in such plants, thrusting each other aside, or climbing over each other's shoulders, till the flowers bend beneath their weight. After a time they become so stupid that it is vain to pull them by the skirts and advise them to go home, instead of wasting their time in tippling. They are, however, so good-natured in their cups, and show no resentment at being disturbed; on the contrary, they cling to their wine goblet, and crawl back to it as fast as they are pulled away, unless, indeed, they fairly lose their legs and tumble down, in which case they lie sprawling on the ground, quite unable to get up again."

This was held to be quite in contrast with the temperate habits of hive bees by Mr. Wailes, who wrote in the *Entomological Magazine* (i. 525) that hive-bees, after their visits to his passion-flowers, hurried back to their hive as soon as they had imbibed their supply of nectar. This is not quite our own experience, either in respect to the passion-flower or to the sunflower, both of which, at certain times, contain in their nectar some element which acts as a narcotic, or, at all events, soporific; for we have found both kinds of bees dull, stupid, and more than half asleep on these flowers after sundown, apparently unable to better themselves and go home, emulating only too faithfully the unfortunate human beings who will lay themselves asleep by a beer-house door till they are trundled off by a policeman. We have lifted them off the flowers of both plants repeatedly, and held them in our hands and put them on the flowers again, the insect having no more energy than just to cling to the bed of the sweet poison, and certainly not likely to go home that night, but rather to stay there till they fell off, chilled and stricken, only too like many other topers who are apt to sing, "We won't go home till morning," and, alas! only too often don't go home even then.

With regard to the laziness of the bee, it has to be said that in certain circumstances it may chance that the bees are in too favourable a position, have too much of what they want quite close at hand, to keep them up to the mark for activity and industry, and, like human beings, get corrupt and lazy. But facts attest that the bee will work very hard. It is on record that a famous bee-master kept a line of hives on the roof of his place in the Strand; that the bees, not content with what they could procure in the Temple gardens and other gardens near at hand, travelled at certain seasons miles daily to get at the heath-bells, for the flavour of heath was found in the honey gathered from the hives on the top of the house in the Strand; and, besides, the bees were watched, and there could be no doubt about it. Were the bees so lazy as has been asserted, it is hardly possible that the keeping of bees would be so profitable as it is.

The old straw or thatch hives, such as we have put for initial, were very picturesque and all that, but now-a-days no bee-master would be content with them. He must have a hive the top of which is removable. It is not necessary that great expense should be gone into to procure this improved form of hive, which enables the bee-master to remove honey from the "skep" at certain times, since Mr. Hunter, the well-known writer on bees, has given directions of such simple character that any one can follow how to frame very cheaply, out of stray boards and odds and ends of wood, a hive of the most improved pattern; and his pamphlet can be had, I think, for a penny.

In America there are at the proper places immense bee-farms, where there are perhaps ten thousand hives, and where everything is reduced to a science, and the whole treatment of bees for profitable honey-making followed as a study, and made the one business of life for scores of men and women.

It will probably surprise many readers to hear it suggested that the main end of the bee's sting is not stinging. This notion, however, has its support in several circumstances; one of them is that the working bees alone have stings—the others are stingless. On this point a well-known naturalist has recently written to the following effect :—

" It will be a surprise to many to learn that, after all, the most important function of the bee's sting is not its stinging. I have long been convinced that the bees put the finishing touches on their artistic cell-work by the dexterous use of their stings ; and during this final finishing stage of the process of honey-making, the bees inject a minute portion of formic acid into the honey. This is in reality the poison of their sting. This formic acid gives to the honey its peculiar flavour, and also imparts to it its keeping qualities. The sting is really an exquisitely contrived little trowel, with which the bee finishes off and caps the cells when they are filled brimful with honey. While doing this the formic acid passes from the poison bag, exudes, drop by drop, from the point of the sting, and the beautiful work is finished."

XII

STILL WATER.

STILL water is a very different thing from stagnant water. We know this by the fact of the very different kind of growths that are encouraged, and the different kinds of life that they favour. After floods there is always a certain amount of water left behind in depressions in the lower parts of valley bottoms, but generally it does not remain long; it is absorbed, and passes away under the action of many agencies. All the devices of scientific draining are averse to the stay of this water. Generally it is still water, and any claim such a sheet may have to picturesqueness is due to the character of the surroundings. If the hills have wealth of vegetation, or are bare and rocky, but with coatings here and there of lichen or moss, how beautifully all this is mirrored in the still sheet below! If you sail over it in a boat, you can see the green grass at the bottom giving a kind of tint to the water; and if there are any structures on it due to the hand of man, were it only a bit of paling or a fence-gate, you see the upper part of it still left unhidden, mirrored in the glassy mass. Such a bit does our first little engraving portray.

In some of our great inland lakes, where the spurs of the hills, set forward like an advancing foot, seem to break the regularity of line, we see the fine effects

of shadow on still water.   And in some cases where
little lines of low reefs of earth or stone rise up to
break the monotony of the expanse, with a fringe of
dark against the light, it only adds to the beauty ; and
though it may not be pleasing in itself, yet commends
itself to the eye from the mere desire and craving for
variety and relief in a level which is inherent in the
mind of man.

What gives the sense of weariness and oppression
in looking on a vast desert, or on expanses of still
water, is due simply to lack of relief.   This is not felt

at sea, for example, nearly so much as it would be on
a still lake.   The ceaseless movement of the ocean
is itself a relief; the endless variety of the swelling
curves in its lazy wavelets and ripples, even on the
calmest day, is a delight alike to eye and brain ; while,
our pleasure on looking on such a sheet of still water
as is presented in our next engraving, is derived from
our sense of its contact with the land, and these spurs
that run into it, break it up, and impart some sense
of variety.

The pleasure which one has in looking at the lovely
wooded Ellen's Island in Loch Katrine, is largely due

to this same principle.   It breaks up the expanse, and relieves the monotony that would be felt in looking on an unrelieved level of still water.   In our third little illustration, the reader will perhaps more fully

feel the force of what has been said when he realises the effect in this little picture of the small hut-like islands, which are dotted over the level expanse of lake, each casting its own shade behind it in the strong sunlight.   Here it is easily seen that anything which

breaks the smooth levelness of the middle distance is a benefit, and helps the picturesque effect.   If we allow ourselves to analyse the impression to its roots, we find that the secret of weariness and monotony in land-scape is invariably the lack of shade.   Perhaps some of

our readers have seen pictures of Lake Coruisk in the
Isle of Skye (a subject which, if we remember aright,
Mr. John MacWhirter painted a good many years ago).
This sheet of water would be very gloomy and un-
picturesque indeed, were it not for the peculiar form and
the deep purple colour (at all events at certain times) of
the flat-faced and almost pyramid-sided hills which
throw deep shadows on the darkish waters beneath
them, and thus by contrast a kind of inexpressible
relief is given to the scene.   We know that in the
East the shadow of a great rock in a weary land is
given as the very ideal of shelter and protection.   It
is as beneficial actually as it is refreshing and welcome
picturesquely.   In the poems of the great German
poet, Heinrich Heine, there is a constantly recurrent
idea (which indeed crops up in his prose as well) of
the fir tree longing for the palm, and the palm tree
longing for the fir, which in a fanciful or imaginative
way admirably expresses this principle—the demand
for shade, for contrast; and as shade is only made
effective by the presence of sun affecting objects standing more or less in the midst of level spaces, the true
medium is the middle medium—not the palm alone
amid excess of sun, and single intense shadow in
centre of a quiveringly hot expanse, nor the fir amid
the frost and snow, where the sun, even when it shines,
is so weak as scarcely to cast a shadow over the snow
or frost-whitened surface.   No; but in the something
between, which the poet indicates in the longing of
each for each, when he sings :—

> " A fir tree stands all lonely
>   In the north, on a cold grey height ;
>   He slumbers, as round him ice and snow
>   Weave a mantle of spotless white.

> He dreams of a palm-tree towering
> Afar in the eastern land,
> Alone, and silently dreaming
> 'Mid rocks and burning sand.*

Thus, while the Hebrew Psalmist in one place promises that the Lord shall lead His chosen "by the still waters," his companion yet more powerfully indicates the shelter, and to them the soft benignance of their God, by likening His tender and solicitous kindness to the shadow of a great rock in a weary land—an idea which is made fine use of in that grandest hymn of Luther, "Ein feste Burg ist unser Gott." Art, in interpreting for us the benignity of nature as it affects our spirits, says almost the same. In its selection—its necessary selection—of elements that present a unity to the mind of the observer, it must carefully balance the shadows and the lights, the blacks and the whites, the sun and the shade; so that, though it may be sweet there also to walk by the "still waters," yet sweeter at once in intenser pains and in intenser pleasures, is it to rest under "the shadow of a great rock in a weary land."

* This is from Heine—a free translation—and here is the original :—

> " Ein Fichtenbaum steht einsam,
> Im Norden auf kahler Höh,
> Ihn schläfert mit weisser Decke
> Umhüllen ihn Eis und Schnee.
>
> Er träumt von einer Palme
> Die fern im Morgenland,
> Einsam und schweigend trauert
> Auf brennender Felsenwand."

XIII

A SCOTTISH TROUT STREAM.

HAT a delightful thing it is to wander, as we have often done, alike in Perthshire and Inverness, on Deeside and Tweedside, and in Rachan Valley, about the hills that line Loch Long, by the borders of Gareloch and Roseneath Hill, and far up in the famed Glenesk, and follow the course of a tiny stream leaping down the hill side, now heady and impetuous, now dropping into little pools or basins, boulder-walled, all the waterside waving with ferns and wild flowers, and bright with mosses, not a nook but has its greenery, spray refreshed, hawthorns, the mossy birches, and firs and mountain ashes and elders, hanging on the sides of the little chasm, nodding to each other, their branches in many places meeting overhead; and everywhere the songs of birds making chord with the sweet tinklings and lullabies of that little thread of water; wild pigeons, mountain-pipits, and water-ousels coming to the pools to drink. This last is truly a pretty

bird, white-breasted, short-tailed, and with a happy
faculty for mingling business and pleasure, or so it
seems to me. He comes here to drink perhaps, but
he does more before he leaves. He will perch on a
stone and sit quite still for a while; then he will dive,
and, speedily coming up again, will return to the stone
and perhaps drop a few notes of very sweet and cheerful music, all his own, and liquid as the streams he
haunts. There is a kind of legend that he can walk
in water at the bottom, seeking his food, but I have not
been fortunate enough to observe it so long under
water as to suggest this, which, however, I can well
believe. The Duke of Argyll has told how the young
dippers will take to the water on being frightened, and
will at once show the same diving power as their elders.

The stream has innumerable lesser tributaries, too—
tiny rain-courses, or little more, some of them, pouring
themselves through rough rocky channels, to join and
to enlarge the streamlet as it goes, and making all the
music they may ere they pass and are lost.

We remember one delightful afternoon spent near to
where a little stream of this kind bickers and sings on
its way to join the Tummel—most delightful and most
varied of streams, sweetest mixture of idyllic and of
cunningly dangerous among all the rivers that we
know. "Tummel Falls indeed are tricksy, Tummel
Falls are rare," but do not attempt, as some have done,
to slide, and glide, and get behind that white curtain,
half of cloudy mist, and half of more prosaic element,
as you may regret it. You may slip, plunge, and
be carried away; or, if not quite that, receive such
a douche that you are not likely to forget it, or ever
after fail to speak with due respect, not to say enthu-
siasm, of bonnie Tummel.

But Scottish streams show a different character in many cases. Here is a bit that might pass for a brawling shallow in the Tweed, or in the North Esk, or in the Spey, or in the Ness, or the Ithen. How sweetly refreshing it is to look on such a bit as this! The brown water sails along with a kind of smooth even demeanour, till it meets with opposition from the big boulders, green and slippery, and then it " puts up its

back,"to use a colloquialism, and, since it cannot overleap the obstacle, it will dash and throw itself in foam against it, so protesting. But very different it is when the river is in spate. Then the water overtops the boulders, and goes dashing along with defiance in its face. No obstacle can resist it then. Majesty crowns the " drumlie flood," and all goes down before it. Siller Tweed, broadbreasted Spey, soft Southesk, and leaping Northesk, with its Kelpie's pools, and lovely Dee, and sweet Tay gleaming, are all alike then, and have no shallows; a dull uniformity of dark umber depths then prevails, and wipes out the more attractive marks; all are robbed of their more distinguishing beauties and characteristic traits.

Nevertheless some of our painters have painted splended pictures of rivers in spate when the greeny ordered beauty of the bank or margin was lost in a roaring brown sea, and when all resources of the pencil had to be applied to render the whirl and wild gurgling dash of brown water, leaping, passing here and there into foam-covered swirling eddies. One picture we remember of Mr. Peter Graham, masterly in the general effect as in details, and another, if we remember rightly, from the easel of Mr. J. R. Macdonald, R.S.A., and still another from that of Mr. W. Mactaggart, R.S.A.

And floods have left their mark in literature too. The great flood on the Spey, which wrecked a valley, and was almost as memorable for wonderful and romantic escapes as for the lives lost, has received worthy commemoration. Few that have read it will ever forget Sir Thomas Dick Lauder's thrilling and faithful pictures, or the yet more wonderful effects which Dr. George Macdonald gains from his highly poetical and dramatic presentation of the phenomena in his novel of "Sir Gibbie," which would have a permanent value were it for this feature alone.

It is this great change, sometimes very sudden, which was in the mind of the writer of that famous song, "The Flowers of the Forest," when this fine verse was penned—

" I've seen the morning with gold the hills adorning,
And the red storm roaring before the parting day ;
I've seen Tweed's siller streams, glistening on the sunny beams,
Grow drumlie and dark as they rolled on their way."

Yes, truly, "drumlie and dark," as we have said; and what more finely expressive or symbolic of the sudden change, sudden as the flash of shining swords in dewy light, under which the flowers o' the forest are a' wede away!

But such a storm, with the results that naturally follow, brings the angler's opportunity. Most frequently it is just after such a spate as this has

somewhat subsided, when the waters lessen, but are not yet wholly clear, that the fisherman finds his harvest. The big fish are all astir then, eager to feed, and the angler not seldom exults in the heavy "take."

Then even small streams are swollen to rivers, and the fall, which after a drought dwindles and dwindles to little more than a white thread, becomes once again a waterfall—voice of hungry, hissing, rushing torrent, which carries down with it no end of driftwood,

HARE CRAIG POOL.

drowned sheep, and hay or corn that may have lain on the flooded lands near to it far, far up above.

The Tweed is undoubtedly the queen of Scottish rivers, not alone because of its length and the variety of the scenery it passes through, and its clearer pebbly strand than any other Scottish river enjoys, or the number and varied character of the tributaries it receives, but because of its associations—the aromas of

SPROUSTON DUB.

song and ballad that linger about it, the histories of hero and of poet that are enlinked with it, the human spell that is upon it adding to it, and seeming to interpret its varied beauty. True it is, as the poet sings—

> " Thy lot it is, fair stream, to flow amid
> A varied vale : not mountain height alone,
> Nor mere outspreading flat is dully thine,

> But wavy lines of hills, high, massive, broad,
> That rise and fall, and flowing softly fine
> In haughs of grassy sward, a deep-hued green." *

And truly what a contrast there is between the brawling foaming torrent below Yair and the sunny repose of such sheets as we give of Hare Craig Pool, below Dryburgh, and the famous Sprouston Dub, beloved of anglers! But it is true also that there is a varied music of human hearts, of dim-hued memories, and high ambitions foiled and overthrown, and passions and disappointed hopes that keep time to its music as it flows for ever, inalienable, beautiful, glad and undying :—

> "Great nature mocks us if the heart can take
>   No tribute of high memory to invest
>   Her beauty with the sense of love and good."

In some respects the tributaries of such a river as the Tweed will be found as interesting, or even more interesting, than the river itself. Some of them have been finely celebrated in Professor Veitch's poem, "The Tweed." Not to speak of the Lyne and the Manor, which flow into it from north and south above Peebles; the latter, with its rushing water, leaping, laughing, and rolling through steep and lofty mountains, and high up in whose solitary valley abode David Ritchie, the original of Scott's "Black Dwarf;" or of the Leithen, lower down, which, after sweeping through a greeny vale, throws its ample stream into the more level region of the river, where the gently rising banks are richly wooded, only in the pass beyond Yair to narrow and rush on, foaming, impetuous, as Sir Walter Scott has painted it :—

---

* "The Tweed and other Poems," by Professor John Veitch, LL.D.

> " From Yair, which hills so closely bind,
>   Scarce can the Tweed his passage find,
>   Though much he fret and chafe and toil,
>   Till all his eddying currents boil."

or of the famous Ettrick, oft-besung, or the romance-shaded dreamy Yarrow; or of long-flowing, legend-laden Teviot ; or of Gala Water—" Braw, braw lads on Gala Water ; " or of the ominously named Whiteadder and Blackadder, yet lower down. After all these there are still three tributaries of the Tweed, which, on their separate and contrasted accounts, may claim from us a little more attention. These are the Eden, and the Till, and the Quair. The former is in places a very narrow stream, gathering into bouldery-spread pools, with steep banks on either side, so steep indeed that not seldom the fisher must wade either up or down ; and it has very considerable falls here and there, the most notable of which is the Newton Don Fall (often called Stitchell Linn), where the water gathers into a comparatively wide basin, for the volume of the stream above, and throws itself foaming, and divided, as it were, into different streams, down a series of stairlike shelves, parted from each other again to form a wide basin below, where the water, after slowly eddying round, seems to pause restfully, recovering from the effects of its turmoil before proceeding on again. This fall is, in every respect, beautiful and striking, being something over sixty feet in height. This is a height far beyond the power of salmon to ascend; and it forms a barrier also to the passing and repassing of some kinds of trout, and hence the character of the trout above differs in several points from those found below.

Though sixty feet is far beyond the power of salmon

to ascend, it is very wonderful the heights that they will leap. I have stood by the side of a northern stream at the right season, close by what are called "the salmon loups," where the falls are certainly more than ten feet in height, and have seen the salmon in crowds leaping up, their bodies seen for several seconds clear out of the water—glancing, silvery purple, luminous, beauti-

STITCHELL LINN.

ful. Most of them, of course, fell back to try again, but every now and then one would succeed and pass upward.

It is near to such spots as this that the otter delights to make his home, to prey on the larger fishes. The general idea is that he is a very particular feeder, eating only the more delicate portions for the most part, and leaving the bulk of the fish on the banks, to lead skilful eyes to know of his whereabouts. The

facility with which otters can be tamed and trained
and domesticated has led to no end of stories of otters
becoming the cunning and helpful mates of poachers;
and it is said that in old days not seldom the residents
near a stream where an otter worked winked at his
depredations, and hid the fact of his existence, because
they knew where they could always find a good meal
by going and taking the portions of the salmon which
he had rejected and left on the banks.

SALMON LOUPS.

Later reports—the result of what claims to be closer
observation—go to give the poor otter a somewhat
better character. A writer in the *Fishing Gazette* in
the beginning of the year (1893) stood up for him,
declaring that he was more the angler's friend than
many would credit. "Whilst we write," he says, "we
have in our mind a little river in our own neighbourhood, than which for its size there is not a better in
the kingdom as a trout stream; and yet this river,
figuratively speaking, actually swarms with otters. . . .

Fish forms only a part of the otter's daily meals. The young of water-hens, coots, and other birds breeding by the water-side, and at times rabbits, and even large worms, are common changes in an otter's diet; while frogs, eels, and the crustaceous crayfish are probably thought as great a dainty as the brightest of silvery salmon. These facts are proved by an examination of the animal's 'foil,' while we have over and over again had demonstration of the avidity with which vegetable food is consumed." And the theory of this writer is that the otter chiefly preys on weak or diseased fish, unable to evade his pursuit, as healthier fish almost invariably do, and that he is thus really a scavenger of the streams. We honestly confess to a sneaking regard for the otter, because he has been so ruthlessly persecuted and destroyed, and has shown so much bravery and persistence; and if the facts are as given above, then the habits and character of the otter should plead for him and prevent the wanton and cruel destruction of this beautiful and clever animal which has so long and ruthlessly been carried on. But certainly the "Son of the Marshes" is not wholly at one with this idea, for he says the otter eats only the belly and shoulders of pike, and leaves good bits of eel on the banks. "Less refined creatures," he adds, "can dine on what he leaves on the banks."

Nowadays, in many streams, the proprietors or conservators of the water, to aid the fish in their struggles to ascend these falls or "loups" to the most favoured spawning grounds, have erected what are called salmon ladders or steps—a kind of artificial aid, which, if we mistake not, the late Frank Buckland did much to improve and to commend. In old days, when the legislature with regard to protection of fish, and a "close time" for them, was not so strict as it now is, and when men were more regardless of law, and salmon poaching was largely practised, it was common for the poachers to do a good stroke at the pools at the foot of these falls. A number of men went out at night with torches in their hands, and others with leisters or three and four pronged fork-like implements, with which on seeing a fish near them, they settled it by driving the leister into it, fixing it to the bottom and then seizing it—a most cruel and wasteful process, with which the law now deals very severely, for the fish thus killed were of course on their way up to spawn, and in course of time the rivers by this system were greatly depopulated.

On this point Sir Thomas Dick Lauder well says— "Like many other things that are very nefarious in practice, there is much in the most destructive of practices that is productive of romantic and picturesque effect—the darkness of the night, the blaze of torches upon the water, the flash of the foam from the bare limbs of the men who are wading through the shallows, with their long poles and many pointed and barbed iron heads, or glancing from the prow of the boat, moving slowly over the deeper water, with its strange unearthly figures in it." *

The Till beats the Eden both for depth and for rapidity. Scott calls it "the sullen Till," but it can rush and sparkle too. It is not safe for the fisherman to wade it. People attempting to cross it even at what seemed the shallower parts have had to retrace their steps.

> "Tweed said to Till,
> 'What gars ye rin sae still?'

---

* "Scottish Rivers," p. 45.

Till said to Tweed,
' Though ye rin wi' speed,
And I rin slaw,
Sae still as ye rin and fast as ye gae,
Yet where ye drown ae man
I drown twae.'"

The vale of the Till, here rocky and wild, there alling into gentler pools and forming little lakes, such as is represented in this cut by Twisel Mill, running

TWISEL MILL.

up into the English Northumberland, has its own share of historical interest as well as its own individual character.   The Bridge of Twisel (not far from Twisel Mill), afforded great aid to the army of Lord Surrey. It was by it that the English were enabled to meet the Scottish army at Flodden—a movement for ever memorable in history, and splendidly celebrated by Sir Walter Scott in verses that breathe and burn :—

"From Flodden ridge
The Scots beheld the English host
Leave Barmore-wood, their evening post,
And heedful watch'd them as they cross'd
The Till by Twisel Bridge.
 High sight it is, and haughty, while
They dive into the deep defile ;·
Beneath the cavern'd cliff they fall,
Beneath the castle's airy wall.
By rock, by oak, by hawthorn-tree,
 Troop after troop are disappearing ;
 Troop after troop their banners rearing,
Upon the eastern bank you see.
Still pouring down the rocky den,
 Where flows the sullen Till,
And rising from the dim-wood glen,
Standards on standards, men on men,
 In slow succession still,
And, sweeping o'er the Gothic arch,
And pressing on, in ceaseless march,
 To gain the opposing hill.
That morn, to many a trumpet clang,
Twisel ! thy rock's deep echo rang ;
And many a chief of birth and rank,
Saint Helen ! at thy fountain drank.
Thy hawthorn glade, which now we see
In spring-tide bloom so lavishly,
Had then from many an axe its doom,
To give the marching columns room."

As to Quair, it is surrounded by associations more gently sad and sweet—touching, pathetic, and yet pleasing. It is the symbol of love and wooing and regretful memories of pure passion defeated or elevated through disappointment and ill. Professor Veitch has well apostrophised it :—

Come, gentle Quair, thou dear loved stream of song !
Long consecrate to passion's bootless prayer ;
By thee Love's hope has dawned and dwined and died,
From 'mid the spring, when tender birken boughs

Are growing green, and all the lover's heart
Throbs with upbraiding full and wild unrest
That nature is so kind, and fate so hard.*

And Principal Shairp in his beautiful ballad of the
"Bush aboon Traquair," more than most, has thrown
a new light across the very spirit of the old Border
ballad :—

" What saw ye there,
    At the Bush aboon Traquair?
And what heard ye there that was worth your heed?
    I heard the cushies croon
    Thro' the gowden afternoon,
And the Quair burn singin' doon to the Vale o' the Tweed.

.   .   .   .

    And birks, saw I three or four,
    Wi' grey moss, bearded ower,
The last that are left o' the birkenshaw,
    Whar mony a simmer e'en,
    Fond lovers did convene
Thae bonny, bonny gloamin's that are far awa'.

.   .   .   .   .

    They were best beyond compare,
    When they held their trystin' there
Amang the greenest hills shone on by the sun ;
    And there they wan a rest,
    The lounest and the best,
I Traquair Kirkyard when a' was dune.

    Now the birks to dust may rot,
    Names o' lovers be forgot,
Nae lads and lasses there ony mair convene ;
    But the blithe lilt o' yon air
    Keeps the Bush aboon Traquair,
And the love that ance was there, aye fresh and green.

* " The Tweed " and other poems.

And then for old keeps and peel towers, and famous ruins, and still more famous houses not ruins, on its borders, what river can equal Tweed? There is Melrose Abbey—the prince of them all; there is Dryburgh Abbey, with its celebrated burial-place,

DRYBURGH ABBEY.

and Norham Castle lower down, on Northumberland side, overhanging the steep, a fortress that figured largely in stories of battles and sieges,* and makes

* In Mr. Hubert E. H. Jerningham's interesting volume, published by Wm. Patterson of Edinburgh, will be found the fullest details

us think of Tweed as the poet thought of it when he
wrote :—

> " The symbol thou, O Tweed, of those two lands,
>   The South and North, that long in conflict strove,
>   And from their striving found a greater life."

NORHAM CASTLE.

about Norham Castle.   He gives as frontispiece a drawing of Norham
as it was in the time of Pudsey (1151), a stately pile with strong encircling wall, running so low on the range of the mound that the whole
structure could be clearly seen from a distance ; also a sketch of the
castle in 1680, when the ruinous process had so far proceeded that all
the small square turrets had disappeared.   All that now remains of the
historical pile is presented in our engraving.

Sir Walter Scott, in the opening of " Marmion," has this fine description of Norham :—

> " Day set on Norham's castled steep,
>   And Tweed's fair river, broad and deep,
>   And Cheviot's mountains lone :
>   The battled towers, the donjon keep,
>   The loophole grates, where captives weep,
>   The flanking walls that round it sweep,
>   In yellow lustre shone.
>   The warriors on the turrets high,
>   Moving athwart the evening sky,
>   Seem'd forms of giant height :
>   Their armour, as it caught the rays,
>   Flash'd back again the western blaze,
>   In lines of dazzling light."

From the ramparts of nodding Neidpath Castle, the dying girl bent down to hail the banished lover, recalled, alas! too late, by a sorrowing father. She met the unrecognising glance raised to her changed face, and stricken by the pang of pain, fell back dead, while the lover was hurrying up the stair to greet her. Elibank Tower, the rude home of Muckle-mou'ed Meg, sung often in ballad, and idealised by Browning, over-looks the Tweed, the Siller Tweed, which Scott pined for by " the yellow Tiber and the green, becastled Rhine."

And then there is Abbotsford, sacred to the memory of the Magician of the North, and Ashestiel, his first love on the classic stream (of which we speak else-where), and Yair, the home of a branch of the power-ful Pringles, and many another classic house and home, each with its own history, its own traditions, its legends and song lore.

A very different aspect does the Scottish river pre-sent, when it glides down into something of a lake-like aspect, as it steals round its banks, fir-fringed, with many a bend and circuit, and staying its waters, as though it were loath to leave behind it such a paradise. It seems like a lover looking back at a loved one, lingering and gazing still and beckoning farewell. The more surely is this the case when the full moon looks down and makes a milder softer daylight, leaving his trace upon the water in many a rippling curving

bend—faint images and prophecies of himself, when he shall become but a crescent in the sky once more. Such a scene as this might indeed tempt one to exclaim—

> " Beautiful moon, so soft, so bright,
>   Walking the pathways by the night.
>
>   Over the clouds like a ship you leap,
>   Leaving a track of pearl to keep

A halo, and tell you have passed that way,
In spite of the clouds that eclipse your ray.

Beautiful moon, so soft, so bright,
Like a shepherd watching his flocks by night,
That wander away and wander far,
For your flock is planet and trembling star.

And they seek to serve you in many a guise,
And dote most fondly in your fair eyes ;
And circle you round in river and lake,
With a meek obeisance no winds can break.

If it blows too roughly, you only smile,
The better your followers to beguile ;
And you lift a look of sublime repose
When the calm of a tempest before it goes.

The Lightning shakes out its locks in vain ;
You walk serenely o'er cloudy plain ;
And you look so fair through the fir trees fine,
We wonder not men held you once divine."

All about these Scottish streams are little bits of wild rocky barriers, as it were, where the water is made to leap and toss and curvet, and then fall over green slippery boulders into tiny pools beyond, where the fish—and bigger fish than you would believe—are often found to lie, waiting for the tit-bits brought down by the stream, or lying half hid watching for their favourite flies which often affect these stiller pools. Here is one of these corners, such as is to be found on many a northern stream.

And often these streams pour themselves into lakes which lie surrounded by their mountains, open ever to sun, moon, and stars. A typical lake in this respect is Loch Hourn, with its rocky piers and buttresses and shelving hills. What soft, tender, dewy lines of light lie along such a sheet in the sunrise as we oft have

seen them, and what golden glories flit across it in
the sunset, while the deepening shadows of the hills,

purple below, their summits touched with fire, reproduce themselves in these still depths. Some of the
most magnificent effects of light and shade we have

ever seen were beheld on some of these Scottish lakes,
when, too, the mists were creeping round the mountains, and the wind began to blow its trumpets, an

LOCH HOURN.

the echoes of further hills to make regular reply, and over the eastern sky hung gloomy, bastion-like fringes of rain, while yet trembling bars of sunset glory lingered in the west, pulsating with a redder, bloodier gleam, suddenly to fade and pale and pass, and leave behind a deeper darkness, lit up only by the lightning-flash, and then round all the peaks and scars "rattled the live thunder." But it would need the pen of a Scott to do anything like justice to such scenes and such sounds.

But one thing may be said, unclouded clearness of sun and still air burdened with dry heat are not the mediums through which to behold at their best the beauties of Scottish, and more particularly of Highland scenery : the mists that creep at earlier morning or in storm, like mighty serpents, round the bases of the mountains, and rise up and up till the peak alone is hidden, mist-capped, and then gradually pass, to leave, as it were, gems twinkling about it ; so that the looker-on will sometimes wonder whether morning stars do not linger still near the glancing summits of some of our rocky bens. It is all very well to complain of cloud and mist, of the dull, low-hanging curtains of rain, and the uncomfortable, penetrating, drizzling falls of wet ; these supply the elements that give colour, life, and grandeur to our Scottish hills and lakes— sunny, tearful, laughing, frowning, clear or misty, sun-lit or darkly shadowed by sudden turns. Without our clouds and mists and rains we should compare but poorly with Southern France, with Italy, or with the Austrian Tyrol.

Has not De Quincey essayed to prove indeed that our literature—our higher imaginative literature—owes much to mist and cloud, to the effects of sun and rain and sullen skies with leaden downlook ? He compares, in this respect, the genius of Milton with that of Dante. The latter he holds is the genius of exact, of powerful description—every object he describes could be measured—you could draw it faithfully to scale if you had but canvas enough ; he magnifies, but with definiteness still; while again Milton suggests to the imagination what cannot be measured, great cloudy shapes, phantoms that move, misty, grand, sublime. He delights in vague and measureless outlines and vast masses, and thus gains grandeur and true sublimity which Dante, after all, seldom or never does. And this De Quincey ingeniously argues is attributable to the fact that Milton had seen mists and fogs and cloud-capped mountains, and had been deeply impressed by them ; while Dante had seen natural objects always in clear light, and had no conception of the misty and vague to heighten, if indeed it is not essential to, the grandeur of the sublime.

Mr. Grant Allen may be inclined to press an idea too far when he wishes to prove the presence of a Celtic strain in all our great artists, whether in painting, music, or poetry ; but there can be no doubt that power is in the hills, and that the power of the hills is more or less on them, with their sense of shadow, depth, and passing yet undying glory, which has done much to give to the Celtic genius, nursed among the hills, its inner sense of beauty, of sadness, and mournful change, of lyric love and grief, regretful pathos, and of tragedy.

In a letter received the other day from an invalid friend at Hyères, this point was very effectively indicated :—

" It is curious that these southern climes, so beautiful in some of their atmospheric effects, have nothing of the deep poetic effects of the lovely hills, glades, dells, and rivers of England or Scotland. You require to see everything in the far distance to get any fine effect at all. The most beautiful bit of landscape turns into a mud-heap of olive groves or a market-garden. If we had but a rather better climate, I think there is no place more purely poetically beautiful than the more picturesque parts of our own country—so soft, so dewy, and so deliciously changeful under changing lights and shades, and yet restful too."

Full justification for the sport of fly-fishing on the streams or on the lakes of our northern regions, were there no other, might be found in this, that in scarce any other manner could those indulging in it be so unconsciously impressed and educated in the sense of the truly imaginative picturesque. If as Izaak Walton declared of angling that it was " the contemplative man's recreation " northern fly-fishing may be regarded as the sport above all others that leads to imaginative reverie and to poetry.

Even the rattling, somewhat too boyish, high-spirited " Christopher North " knew this, and acted on it, as is to be seen not only in such essays as " Streams," but in those delightful pathetic tales, " Lights and Shadows of Scottish Life," which are, in great part no doubt, the outcome of Christopher's wanderings by stream and glen, by wood and mountain, and by moor, into which he was led for most part by his keen love of the angle and the fly and the landing-net.

XIV

AN ENGLISH STREAM.

IT has been much the habit of poets 'and essayists to moralise the stream by finding in it a symbol of human life. Such poems as Miss Ingelow's "Divided" savour of it; and Lord Tennyson's exquisite lyric in "The Brook: an Idyl" brings the parabolic element into fine prominence—a point which the famous "C. L. S.", the late Mr. Calverley, very cleverly took advantage of and fully brought out in his well-known parody of it. For the stream has its quiet secluded infancy up in some remote mountain cradle, where the winds fan it, and the sunshine makes it radiant, as it goes laughing play-ful through its sobbing grasses, waving sedges, or by banks bright with starlike primroses, and ragweed and ranunculus in their season, then on, like flushing youth, as it broadens its breast to sun and moon, to receive yet more fully of the light and shade, and to return more readily its offering to the winds in tiny waves and ripples, and swiftly interchanging sun and shadow, exulting in happy "give and take." Onward and on-ward, till over the gravel it goes dancing towards its fullest, where it falls over a little ledge, bubbling and singing to itself, figuring early manhood, with little backward eddies, gusts of passion and desire, when suddenly again it recovers itself, and sighing now and then restfully as it laps the margins, passes on over a slightly rocky fall into broader reaches, and then, as if to mirror the absorbment of the man in the wider and also the more intense and tender ties of life, it pours itself into a bigger current, to find its way, not lost but transfigured, amid many influences, towards the great ocean.

> " The wonder of the water is the song,
>   It sings for ever moving on its way ;
>   Now charm of dropping notelets in the play
> Of sun and shadow ; now the chorus strong
> As tumbling o'er the rocks it doth prolong
>   Its passion-sobs in eddies circling gay,
>   In fretted glory as the branches' sway,
> And then with dreamy murmur sails along
>   To catch a beauty from an ampler day,
>   Broad-breasted under sun or milder moon."

Let me take you for a walk by the borders of a sweet English stream that I know well, where, often I have roved alike at early morn and dewy eve, in the warm noontides of the sweet summer-time, and in the golden afternoons of autumn, when nature spreads her richest tints around, and the stream is ready to reflect it all, showing here and there the golden radiance finely transfigured in its bosom, like a dream, bringing indeed a sense of dreamlike absorption and half trance, as one stood and looked into the wondrous world reversed and almost more beautiful below. Wordsworth, it is true, speaks of

> " that uncertain heaven received
> Into the bosom of the steady lake."

But here very often there is little of uncertainty—the more you gaze the less you realise that element. My favourite walk from my house to this stream is over a series of gentle swelling hills that rise and dip, and rise again, and all along the course you come on little bits of broken ragged hedgerow, where the furze bushes rise and hang out their flowers like lamps along the pathway, where if there is no legal right-of-way, there is a kind of neighbourly allowance and indulgence that makes the privilege the more appreciated, as the journey is all the more quiet and solitary. And now and then the eye is gladdened with a tuft of broom, and a few thistles will rise beside them, and, oh ! the stir and chatter that you are guilty of interrupting at certain seasons, when the thistles are in seed, and the linnets and the gold-finches are busy fluttering over it, and now and then utter little shrill protests against the presence of so many rivals just there.

> " When three gray linnets wrangle for the seed "

sings the late laureate. Three ! In a little patch no bigger than the top of the table on which I write, I have seen twenty, and now and then their motions making the thistle down fly like a mist, and that flutterings on my approach making the narrow space seem alive, as they uttered their cries of alarm or warning, and simply dropped down and disappeared on the other side of the clump till I had passed, and were back again before I was actually out of view.

What a delightful stillness, freshness, and repose there is about the stream at the point where I join it. When you come to the bank, your eye just catches the twinkle of fins — the dart-away from you of some denizen, much interrupted in his business by your appearance. As you look, you discover that the water is wonderfully clear; you can see the bottom and all

that is in it, as you look through the pale brown water, and on the opposite side, under a tuft of sedge, you can see a stickleback's nest, with the tail of the little fellow's wife just escaping from the opening of it.

I walk on a little way, and soon pass by slightly more varied ground, the borders of the stream more wooded, and the current a shade swifter. This is a very nice bit of water for small trout, which are very fond of lying in the deeper pools at the roots of the

trees, at certain hours of the day, and are very active
in the purling runs at other times.   Here I cross a
little wooden bridge, and proceeding downward on the
other side, I find my good friend, Will Hartley, with
his angle, fishing as is his wont.   I bid him good day,
and ask him how he is getting on.

  " Oh, pretty well, thank 'ee" he cries, turning round ;

" can't expec' much—the water do be too clear 'ere-
abouts to-day, we want some little bit o' rain to darken
it afore we can hope for much o' sport. ᐧ But I allus
say as the fisherman's constitutional is in patient
waitin', and so we mun just wait."   I ask him how his
friend, Joe Timmins, the keeper is.   " Well," he says,
" I hear from his goodwife this mornin', as he do feel a

bit better, easier like, but them troubles," he goes on
with a serious look, "wants a good share o' nursin'."
Poor Joe had fallen from a tree he had ascended after
some young owls—the branch gave way, and he fell
from a considerable height, breaking his arm and hurt-
ing the spine, and owing to cold, erysipelas had set in,
and Joe's friends were very anxious about him.   I
express my sympathy for Joe, and bid Will Hartley
good day and pass on.

Further on, how deliciously it winds, and ripples
and eddies, by little headlands, with their fortifications
in front of them of sedges, rushes, and no end of water-
weeds, and in the stiller little bays and reaches even
bands of water-lilies, spreading out their round, broad,
dark green leaves, with the wonderful white cup,
magically astir in its season, in the centre of them.

The ground rises slightly higher on the margins, and gives the idea that the water has had more work than elsewhere in cutting a course for itself through this part, and now exults in its reward; for, not only is the place most beautiful, but it abounds, more than we have yet seen, in life of various kinds. The wild ducks are fond of paying this part a visit at certain times, and the heron, in the still of the evening, will come and stand like a veritable wisp of foam in the swifter currents, under the shade of fir tree or beech; coots and dab-chicks appear and disappear in the oddest and most arbitrary manner, while we now get tokens in many forms of the presence of voles, water-rats, and water-shrews. Wherever you have sedges, flags, and irises, there is a chance of finding water-voles, for they are very fond of these, as we have said already; and wherever there is such a margin as to afford at places the kind of aquatic insects that lie half concealed under little stones, you are almost sure to see signs of the water-shrew if you look close enough. As for the water-rat, he is everywhere, and cunningly takes advantage of the presence of almost everything else, to make himself fat and comfortable. And he is a rare swimmer too. On this account he is often mistaken for the water vole by those who do not watch long, though he swims differently in various respects.

This character of scenery prevails for a considerable distance—the streamside forming a most delightful walk, so delightful that advantage has been taken to lay out a rough sort of path, not seldom the resort of lovers at the sweet eventide, when everything—earth and air, sky and water—seems to be in harmony with the whispers they use to impart to each other the "open secrets," which poets are never tired of celebrating in song and novelists in novels. We shall not intrude on their province further than to say that wherever they can they should set their lovers a walk by just such a streamside as this, whose very course may, as it were, musically mirror theirs, and their soft sighings and whisperings find symbol in those of the running water.

It is just about such parts of a stream as this, with trees and bushes on the margin, and with little deeper pools here and there, that you may see the kingfisher

still pursuing his work, proving that, despite all the persecution of sportsmen and specimen-seekers, a few still survive to show to the careful observer how lovely the halcyons are. You can scarcely tell of what colour he is, he is so full of bright shades, as though burnished, bronze, chestnut, green and blue, and red and purple, with no end of other colours. Even in the distance you would know him with his long bill, his lengthened wings, and his short, little, stumpy tail, that is better seen as he flies than as he sits when the long wings go to hide it, or make it appear even less prominent than it really is. Do you want a sight of him? Then be wary. Stand here silent, and look through this low-hanging sycamore branch. See! he sits still as a bit of the branch on which he has perched, and which overhangs the water. Look, look! suddenly he descends, as in arc of a circle, dives; he has found his prey—a small fish, and is off with it in his beak to feed his young ones, which are very carefully sheltered in a hole in the bank there—the very

strangest of all our native birds' nests. It is formed merely of the bones of the fishes which he has eaten, and which he disgorges, lays them on a shelf he has formed at the end of his hole, with a depression in it, the larger bones below, the smaller bones, as of minnows, above, and he contrives to glue these little bones slightly together by some of the saliva or natural cement which many birds, swallows and others, secrete and use, and which finds its highest and fullest use, as regards nest-building, at all events, in the case of those Chinese birds that build what are called edible nests.

But the halcyon is not very particular in this respect; so loose and careless is he, indeed, that it is almost impossible to carry off in anything like proper shape a halcyon's nest; and these curiosities have over and over again been advertised for by collectors and for museums, and I have even heard that as much as £100 have been offered for a fairly perfect specimen. But such a run there is on Old Halcyon—fly-fishers will give anything almost for certain feathers of his for their hooks—as well as on his nest, that it is to be feared before very many years have elapsed he will be utterly extinct, unless some more strict laws are laid down for his protection. There is, or used to be, a great prejudice against him among sportsmen and fishermen, because it was believed that he was very fond of, and devoured trout-spawn; but that fine ornithologist and careful observer, the Rev. H. D. Rawnsley, in his " Plea for the Birds," defends poor Halcyon, and says that he seeks as much for slugs and watersnails as he does for trout-spawn and minnows. He has fought well for his existence, but now, when no part of stream or wood is untraversed or unvisited by the ruthless beauty-slayer, what hope is there for him? Poor and lovely halcyon!

> " With his plumage shining fair,
>   On the bough he silent sits,
> Then, with sudden circle low,
>   Downward to the water flits.
>
> He has found his prey, and bears
>   A shining fish to yonder nest,
> Where the callow young ones wait
>   For the shining of his breast.

> Welcome signal ! how they raise
>   Their open beaks for morsels new !
> Then the good repast enjoyed,
>   He returns where late he flew.
>
> Sits upon his perch again,
>   Like a figure in a dream,
> Brilliant hues of sun and rain
>   Make a sunlight on the stream.
>
> King of fishes, truly, thou,
>   Patient as was Izaak old,*
> But have you ever in your heart
>   A tender pity all untold ?

The poetical idea of the kingfisher making "a sun-light" or a rainbow on the water in a leaf-shaded place has not perhaps an entirely poetical origin.   We read in a good authority—

"The kingfisher has frequently been observed hovering on outstretched wings over the water, and some writers believe that this is done with a view of attracting the fish to the surface.   Whether this is the case is not yet ascertained, but it is well known that when a light is thrown at night on the water, the inhabitants of the 'finny deep' flock in numbers to discover the cause of the unwonted brilliancy."

And we have ourselves often sat in a shady spot by the border of a brook thickly overhung with foliage, and noticed that where a small ray of sunlight penetrated and struck the water, there the small fish rose to bask in it.   The kingfisher perhaps makes an artificial sunlight which helps him.

In Wood's "Natural History" it is said that the kingfisher is fond of music.   On playing an organ in a room facing a river, it was found that several of the

---

* Izaak Walton, author of "The Compleat Angler," born in London 1593, and died in 1683.

birds were attracted by the sounds. Slow and solemn airs they enjoyed seemingly, but whenever anything lighter or more lively was played they were off.

In a very little time we come to an old-fashioned stone bridge rising high in the middle—a great resort of anglers—a favourite starting-point indeed when proceeding to fish either up or down the stream. It is, too, on certain afternoons a favourite resort for the boys from a school near by, the younger ones running about the greeny margins and searching for tiny eels,

and this and that, while the elders ply the rod and line and return proud of a few small dace or minnows. In the warm afternoons of summer they will occasionally, in protected leafy corners near by, indulge themselves in a stealthy bathe, which is far more leisurely than might be supposed possible in connection with anything *stolen*, for they run about the banks and play games in the water.

Often have I stood by the side of the water here and wondered at the fair reflection that this old bridge makes in the afternoons when the sun is shining. The water just there is deep, and stiller than elsewhere, with scarcely a perceptible ripple. or murmur, and is a fair mirror for all that is in its borders. As I have stood and looked, more especially in the evening time, suddenly a trout would *rise*—a fellow of a couple of pounds at least—after a midge or May-fly, and go down again with a plump, sending a widening circle of

ripples over the glassy water, attesting that the deep holes round about the old arches of this bridge have their finny denizens—so cunning, I came to learn, that no fisher, however skilled, or with tackle however fine, had the slightest chance of killing these shrewd old fellows.

Passing onward, we emerge by-and-by into a barer

region, where the stream, after recovering itself from a passage over a shallower reach, in which the cattle love to come and stand knee-deep in the summer, and thus escape as best they can from the flies, gets enclosed in a narrower channel, with many deep pools and rather dark-looking, slow-eddying corners. It is here, they tell us, that the big fish love to lie, and here that the skilful angler with the worm, after a fall of rain, will be likely to come and try for them.

A little further down, just before the stream loses itself in the big water, our favourite walk is lost—the current spreads itself over a half marshy expanse, with no end of little pools; and not far off is a row of fisher-men's huts—houses they can hardly be named—and their boats, or "cobbles," as they would call them in Scotland and the North, lie there fastened to old oak piles, unless in the season when they are busy at the fishing. In the off-season you are sure to find them in front of these huts making nets or doing other such work, and they will be very willing to row you about on the river, or take you to the best fishing grounds for a comparatively small fee.

XV

WILD-DUCKS, WATER-BIRDS, AND SEA-FOWL.

IF you chance to know any quiet bit of water, either in the shape of small pond or enlargement of a little stream, pretty well surrounded by rushes, sedges, and foliage, you are certain now and then to find a wild-duck upon it, diving and dabbling about in search of food. Some of them are very pretty in plumage. The mallard is every way a fine bird, with its lovely colours and tufted tail. When in full plumage, his head is velvety green, and his body and wings varied of the finest tints of grey and brown and purple. But during the summer months, as if nature had resorted to a device to save the species, or to ensure the maintenance of numbers, the cock-mallard is stripped of his beauty and reduced to a likeness to his "womenkind." This is owing to a very severe and unusual moult. All the primary wing feathers come off at once, and he thus assumes sober colours till he can fly again. Were it not for this arrangement of subdued colouring, he would be too easily recognised, and too easily hunted and shot. No doubt this is a "protective" arrangement in great measure. The mallard is fond of marshy lands, and in the winter, if the weather is severe, seeks the sea-shore, where it is to be seen foraging industriously for small molluscs, insects, and little fishes. The extension of draining, and the taking in of wet heaths and waste lands, has somewhat curtailed its numbers, but in some favourable districts it is still quite common. It is well worth notice, were it only for the fact that it is the bird from which all our common domesticated ducks are derived; and when we contrast it with them, we see

MALLARD.

once more how man, when he tames and subdues the lower creatures to his own uses, at once improves and injures. The mallard is perhaps the swiftest in flight of all the ducks, making a peculiar whistling sound with its strong wing feathers as it goes, and, if suddenly disturbed, it rises up into the air, recovers itself suddenly, and is off.

The common teal is one of the smallest of the ducks, very nimble and light in

TEAL.

the water, and also very pretty, though hardly so handsome as the pintail, but, unlike it, is very far from shy, and will occasionally allow you to come pretty near to it. The widgeon only stays with us during the winter, and appears in vast flocks. It gives grass and other plants a much greater prominence in its diet than any of the other wild ducks, and delights in salt grasses.

PINTAIL.

Owing to the many enemies with which the young of the wild duck would be surrounded did the parents nest near to the water which they frequent, it is the habit with many of the species to build in the most unexpected parts. Some nests may be found at a considerable distance from the water, amid tussocks of dry grass and furze on the moors, or even in heather and in low fir trees. Not the least among these enemies is the intrusive cruel brown rat, to which the young of other water-birds too often fall a prey. The ducks are excellent parents, and are on the watch constantly against the many enemies of their young.

Beside the ducks there are, on or near any pond or retired piece of water, sure to be representatives of other species—coots as well as moor-hens—with many varieties of snipe. The coot is a most nimble bird, with great powers in swimming and in doing work under water. One peculiarity the coot has: though its feet are shorter than those of the water-hen, this disadvantage is made up to it by a slight fringe of webbing, which is no doubt of the greatest benefit to it in quickness of movement in the water. Dr. Stanley tells how the coot differs from the waterhen in the building of its nest. The coot prefers having it floating on the surface, and not supported on stems of rushes, &c., but that it may rise with the water, and not be moved away from its position by stormy winds; it is, as it were, moored to stems of reeds or rushes, by a kind of loose rings, so that it will rise exactly as the water rises. Both coots and waterhens, as has been already said, cover their eggs in the nests on rising from and leaving them, and this they do, with such an artistic eye to carelessness of effect, that you might look on one of their nests and fancy it was a deserted one. A thick foundation of rush leaves and other matter is formed under the coot's nest proper, to keep it from damp. This bird lays from six to nine eggs, which are like those of the waterhen, but larger. The poor coot has suffered much in late years, owing to a belief, whether well or ill founded, that it eats the spawn of fishes; and when once an idea of this sort gains ground among the sporting community, and is taken up by the rustics, alack for the poor incriminated bird. It matters not what good qualities it may have otherwise, it is doomed, as water voles and owls were for so long doomed by farmers and others.

The mallard and the teal are both largely night feeders. They resort after twilight to favourite spots, where their tit-bits grow and half play themselves on the water, and sleep and rest through the day.

The ducks are broadly divided into surface and diving ducks; the first class mostly confine themselves to fresh water, and the latter are properly sea-fowl. In addition to those which we have already named, there are the shoveller and the sheldrake. The second class includes the tufted duck—a fine bird—the scaup, the smew, the scoter, the surf-scoter, the velvet scoter, the pochard with its red head, and the beautiful golden-eye, and the interesting eider duck is frequently to be seen.

The scaup is but a winter visitor, and has not been known to breed here; and of the pochard almost the same may be said, only that it has been known in rare cases to breed here. Of these, the most beautiful by far is the last named. The golden-eye is remarkable for its habit of nesting in holes in trees, sometimes a good way distant from the water, and for transporting its young from thence to the water, like the coots and water-hens when building high, and it is said that the young golden-eyes are held under the bill of the parent, and supported by the neck.

The family of the mergansers, all divers, may next be noticed here. The sawbill, or jacksaw, derives its name from its bill being serrated on both sides, exactly like two saws meeting. It is a very expert diver, and will remain at the bottom walking along in search of food for a couple of minutes or more. If its nest has been placed at a distance from the river or lake, it conveys the young ones in the bill or on the back to the water. Macgillivray says that once he watched a flock of red mergansers pursuing sand-eels. The birds moved under the water with almost as much velocity as in the air, and often rose to breathe at a distance of 200 yards from the spot where they had dived. One of these birds was caught in a net at a depth of thirty fathoms. The swiftness of the divers in the water, and the distances they traverse, are almost incredible. It has been computed that a red-throated diver swims about four and a half miles on the surface of the water, and between six and seven beneath the surface, per hour.

On the larger sheets of water you are almost sure to see some of the more noted divers—beautiful birds and well worth watching. You are lucky if you see the loon, which is very shy and very expert. John Burroughs, the well-known American naturalist, says—

" Its wings are more than wings in the water. It plunges into the denser air, and flies with incredible speed. Its head and beak form a sharp point to its tapering neck. Its wings are far in front, and its legs equally far in the rear, and its course through the crystal depths is like the speed of an arrow. In the northern lakes it has been taken forty feet under water upon hooks baited for the large lake trout. I had never seen one till last fall, when one appeared on the river in front of my house. I knew instantly it was the loon. Who could not, tell a loon a half-mile or more away, though he had never seen one before? The river was like glass, and every movement of the bird as it sported about broke the surface into ripples, that revealed it far and wide. Presently a boat shot out from shore, and went ripping up the surface toward the loon. The creature at once seemed to divine the intentions of the boatman, and sided off obliquely, keeping a sharp look-out as if to make sure it was pursued. A steamer came down and passed between them ; and when the way was again clear, the loon was still swimming on the surface. Presently it disappeared under the water, and the boatman pulled sharp and hard. In a few moments the bird reappeared some rods further on, as if to make an observation. Seeing it was being pursued, and no mistake, it dived quickly, and when it came up again had gone many times as far as the boat had in the same space of time. Then it dived again, and distanced its pursuer so easily that he gave over the chase and rested upon his oars. But the bird made a final plunge, and when it emerged upon the surface again it was over a mile away. Its course must have been, and doubtless was, an actual flight under water, and half as fast as the crow flies in the air. The loon would have delighted the old poets. Its wild demoniac laughter awakens the echoes on the solitary lakes, and its ferity and hardiness were kindred to those robust spirits."

The loon, or crested grebe, is indeed a most interesting bird. Whoever has seen him, as Mr. Burroughs did, cannot but admire him. He pairs for life, and both sexes are devotedly attached to the young. They haunt the same nesting places year after year. They lead out their young ones, and take them down with them under their wings when they dive. The young swim about quite freely as soon as they are hatched. The nest is by no means artistic—a mere rough mass of flags and rushes and grasses, like that of the coot, partly sunk under the water and partly raised above it, and contains three, four, and sometimes five, white or pale-greenish white eggs.

KITTIWAKE.

And certainly not the least among the amenities of the sea-side are the opportunities it affords for the study of the gulls, terns, sea-pies, the kittiwakes, black-backed gulls, herring-gulls, skuas, and others, very remarkable in their manner of life, their powers of

wing, their powers in the water, and so much else.
Who that has watched the sea-gull as it pauses in its
flight, and hangs suspended as if resting on air, absolutely still, observing what is beneath it, and has not
wondered at the beauty of the bird; or when voyaging
by ship, or rowing about near the shore, has seen
some of those birds sit on the waves as though on
some airy swinging nest, and has not admired their
grace and wonderful adaptation to their mode of life.
With the storm-petrel and its movements, most people
have thus become familiar. The sea-pie or pied oyster-
catcher affects localities where it can find oysters,
mussels, or limpets, and these it detaches and breaks
with its bright red bill, which is admirably adapted
to this work, being literally chisel-shaped. Although
for the greatest experts in the diving way you must
go further afield than the most attractive portions of
our coasts, and find the penguins, the puffins, or the
beautiful black-throated divers, which are fonder of
more northern temperatures, though the last-named
may be seen in some parts of the northern coasts of
Scotland. There is a penguin in the fish-house of the
Zoological Gardens at Regent's Park, whose powers
in diving the keeper exhibits so many times a day by
throwing small fishes for it into water in a glass-fronted
tank—the bird, for the nonce, becomes a fish, and the
small fry are soon snapped up: at the end of every line
of movement a fish is devoured, and all with such
decision and despatch as gives one a wholly new idea
of the powers of the diver birds. A shag also dives.

But with the gulls and the sea-ducks alone you will
find plenty to interest you if you watch them well;
and all round our shores, especially on high rocky
cliffs, where the seabirds delight to build, they fly in

countless flocks.   There is a very fine range of rocks
beyond Hastings which they much affect, and another
near Ramsgate, of which we give here a little drawing.
That lovely bird, the great northern diver, is to be
seen at many places on the coasts of Devon and

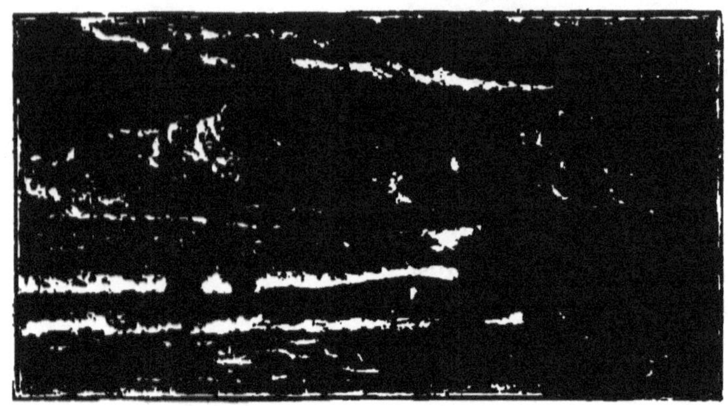

COAST SCENE, WITH SEA BIRDS.

Cornwall, and right well worthy he is of being seen.
Hardly less so the lovely, great, black-backed gull,
which is more common in the south.   Here is an
admirable picture of it from the pen of one of our most
gifted early ornithologists : —

"The contrast between the dark purple tint of his
back and wings, and the snowy white of the rest of
his plumage, with the bright carmine-patched yellow
of his powerful bill, and the delicate pinkish hue of his
feet, render him an object at all times agreeable to the
sight.   No sprinkling of dust, no spot of mud, ever
soils his downy clothing; his bill exhibits no tinge
derived from the subject of his last meal, bloody or
half putrid though it be ; and his feet, laved by the
clear brine, are beautifully pure.   There he stands on
the sandy point, the guardian, as it were, of that flock

of not less cleanly and scarcely less lovely herring-gulls and sea-mews. But, not giving us more credit for our good intentions than we deserve, he spreads out his large wings, stretches forth his long neck, runs a few paces, and, uttering a loud and screaming cry, springs into the air. Some gentle flaps of his vigorous wings carry him to a safe distance, when he alights on the smooth water, and is frequently joined by his clamorous companions. Buoyantly they float, each with his head to the wind, like a fleet of merchantmen at anchor, secured from the attacks of pirates by the presence of their convoy." *

The wild geese, in very severe seasons, are to be found in considerable numbers among the birds at the seashore. They may be known by the V-shaped order in which they invariably fly (for they are social birds), and by the peculiar cry of *hank, hank, hank,* which they now and then utter as they go. There are three main families of wild geese, the lag geese, the grey geese, and the brent geese ; the former are day feeders, and divide their time between the sea or the marshy margins of the lake or the field. The brent geese, on the contrary, are to a large extent night feeders, like the mallard and the teal. They are fond of certain grasses, and will go a considerable distance to feed on the newly sprouting winter wheat ; and when they are feeding in such circumstances, like the crows and the wood-pigeons, they invariably post sentinels, and are very cunning and cautious—difficult to get near to, whether at the seaside, by margin of inland lake, or while feeding in the fields. The man who has stalked and shot a wild goose may consider himself a good shot. The contrast between the wild geese and the

* Macgillivray's " Birds."

domesticated variety is very striking in not a few respects.

Besides those already named, there are gannets or solan geese, with their strange cry, and their fond-

GANNET.

ness for the herrings, so great, indeed, that in the season they live entirely on her-rings, and, it is said, take for their share of the shoals more than does the whole fishing fleet of Scotland. The plan of the gannet in catching its prey is very peculiar. It notes where the fish are, and the depth at which they are swimming, then flies up to what it considers the height needed to give it impetus in diving to the exact point in the water. It has been a subject of dispute whether the bird was named from the Solent or gave the name to the Solent.* The guillemots, too, who are so faith-ful to their young that they will suffer themselves to be seized rather than leave the nest. Cormorants, too, may often be seen, dark and striking figures, among the gulls. The cormorant is to this day, in China and Japan, trained to catch fish. The custom is to pass a leather band round the neck of the bird, so that it

* Though known also as solan geese, the gannets do not scientifically belong to the *anseres* or goose family at all, but are grouped along with the cormorants in a separate class, the *Pelecanidæ*, and the name of the species is *Sula bassana*. It is the more surprising, therefore, that Mr. John Burroughs, in his excellent series of essays, "Fresh Fields," should write of the gannets and solan geese ; for solan here he must mean lag geese, brent geese, or bean geese.

cannot swallow what it catches. A man on a raft has two cormorant assistants—the one is resting while the other is fishing—and the man uses a long pole, which he stretches out to the point where the bird rises, and aids it to come on the raft with its prize. This style of fishing was practised in our own country up, at all events, to the time of Charles the First; for we find from authoritative documents that the fishing birds were procured from Norfolk, and that he had a Master of the Cormorants. Gunpowder made an end of hawking. We are not aware exactly what put an end to cormorant fishing in England: possibly it just passed out of fashion. As in the case of catching fish with tamed otters, where the animal every short time gets a fish to encourage him to go on, so precisely do the cormorants.

As for the petrels, they are everywhere; and the tiny stormy petrel, though the smallest of all, as bold as any, and perhaps most enduring. Petrels have been observed 2000 miles from land. The giant frigate bird, black and bold, has been seen 400 leagues from land, and yet is said to return every night to its solitary roost—which will suffice to give an idea of the power of wing in these sea-birds. But the penguin, which has but undeveloped wings, has transmuted them into the most splendid oars or paddles. It moves through the water at such a rate that few. fishes can surpass it ; and it has been seen quietly paddling at no less a distance than 1000 miles from land.

Certain other birds are very fond of periodically paying the sea-shore a visit to swell the company and give variety. The ring dotterel, that robin redbreast of the sea-shore, which the natives in certain parts will not shoot, is a pretty bird, gentle and trustful, and pipes in a cheerful way as it moves along. The dab-chick, or little grebe, will sometimes pass down from

marshy lands to the sea-shore, and do a little bit of business in the shallower pools left by the tide, moving about them with a quickness and buoyancy all its own. From its smallness and its darting swiftness amid its bigger companions, it has been likened to a torpedo boat among other and heavier craft. The hooded crow with his grey coat loves the sea-shore too, and will sometimes be seen quietly feeding near to wild ducks, black-backed gulls, and herring gulls.

One of the prettiest and most interesting denizens of the sea-shore at certain seasons is the turnstone. It is a very nimble bird, and has good right to the name it bears. Some very interesting points have been noted about the life and habits of the turnstone, which have been very admirably summed up in that carefully edited, well-written and beautifully illustrated work on Shooting (one of the " Badminton Library " Series), edited by Lord Walsingham and Sir Ralph Payne-Gallwey, where we find the following passage :—

" The turnstone is a handsome bird, about as large as a thrush, and having a black, chestnut, and white appearance. It derives its name from its habit of running about on the beach, and turning over stones with its bill in order to obtain the small crustacea that lie underneath. We have often seen one turnstone run up and assist another in doing this, and have even noticed three of them at work raising one stone, like quarrymen with their crowbars. They do not merely lift a stone and reach under it, but gradually hoist it up till it balances upright, then with a great effort the stone is pushed over, and all

TURNSTONE.

is exposed underneath. If a strange turnstone appears on the scene who did not assist in the work, there is a great scrimmage, and the interloper is sent about his business. We once watched two turnstones for a full hour trying to turn over a dead fish, nearly a foot long, without success. We longed to help them in their struggles, but dared not come forward for fear of frightening them away. Finally, with a strong heave and a heave all together, over went the fish, to our very great gratification. It was a pleasure to see through a glass how the birds revelled in all manner of creeping things, which their hard won success had exposed to view."

One of the most striking passages in the life of Thomas Edward, the Banff naturalist, tells precisely the same story, how, seeing two of these birds on the beach near Banff, he crept through the "bents," till he got so near as to be able to watch them in their efforts to turn over a big fish which had sunk an inch or two in the sand, how they tunnelled under it and under it, till, at last, it fell over to yield them a rich reward for patient perseverance and hard work.

Wonderful, too, is the adaptation in the eggs of some of these birds. Many of them build what of a nest they have on the almost flat ledges of these lofty rocks—it may be midway between the base and the top—and as they do not have the protection of the soft encircling walls of nest that most other birds' eggs have, the egg is in form large at the one end and small at the other. Some lay only one egg, others more, and in this case, when one or two of them are laid together, they will not have so much the tendency to roll away. If you try the difference between an ordinary egg and something the shape of the egg of the guillemot, you will find how the eggs are in this respect protected. The sea-bird's egg will much more decidedly roll round within a small circle than will the other, and when you set two or three objects of this form together, the small end inside, as the birds lay them, they will hardly roll away from each other, even though touched. When you have put six or seven of them together in this way, they seem veritably to act as wedges to each other.

It is quite a business at some parts to go in search of the sea-birds' eggs or young, and many are the adventures and the perilous positions in which the searchers have found themselves. The plan, in many cases, is to lower the searcher down by ropes and pulleys to the exact ledge or ledges where the nests are, but so determined are the old birds, and such onslaughts have they made sometimes on their assailant, both with beak and wing, that they have compelled him to retreat unsuccessful; and there is even record of their having so driven the man in defending himself against the stroke of their wings, that he has lost his balance, and fallen down, to be picked up maimed and contused on the beach below, or in the sea if the tide were high.

In the winter, when the weather is very severe, flocks of these sea-birds will come up the rivers in search of food. Very beautiful it is to see them poising themselves over the water of the river, and then perhaps descending and diving. The Thames, during the severe weather in January 1893, was invaded by flocks of these birds, which sailed about and showed so many exquisite manœuvres that not a few stood to watch and to admire them. There were, alas! a few, too, who were fain, with the perverted instinct of the sportsman, merely to maim or kill them. A well-known writer on natural history subjects gave an account of his observations in one of the illustrated weeklies. He told how these beautiful birds hung suspended over those who held out food, and descended almost to obtain it from the hand, and then when it was dropped, seized it in mid-air with amazing quickness and precision.

But not only are the sea-birds an element of beauty and attraction about our coasts, they have their uses too. They take their tribute of the sea, but they do their service for man also. They are the great scavengers of the shore, of the pools, bays, and eddies, which but for them would often not be so pleasant. "Any one," says Mr. H. D. Rawnsley in his "Plea for the Birds," "who has watched them at work after the herring boats have come in at Whitby, or at low tide has seen what public service they do by the Bristol quays, will realise that the 'ocean, at her task of pure ablution' round our English shores, has in the sea-gulls [and other sea-birds] a very competent and assiduous band of helpers."

In another way the sea-birds are man's helpers. The fisherman has often to take his cue from them. In 1867, the Tynwald Court of Keys in the Isle of Man passed a bill to prevent the feather hunters from destroying the wild-birds of their coast, and they urged this on the ground, among others, that from good evidence they considered the gulls of great importance to the herring fishers, as indicators of the localities of the "schools" or shoals of fish, and they added that they were "of much use for sanitary purposes, by reason that they remove the offal of fish from the harbours and shores."

The sea-birds have been, and indeed continue to be, favourite subjects with the poets. Their airy, graceful, bold flight and powers of holding themselves suspended, as it were, in the air for so much longer a time than any other bird, unless it may be certain of the eagles, their capability of floating on the waves, and their wonderful powers of diving, have strongly appealed to the tuneful brethren. And no wonder. Here is a verse from one poem, which we much admire for its freedom, swing, and fine sense of the sentiment of the subject :—

> " Birds of the sea, they rejoice in storms ;
> On the top of the wave you may see their forms ;
> They run and dive, and they whirl and fly,
> Where the glittering foam-spray breaks on high :
> And against the face of the strongest gale,
> . Like phantom ships, they soar and sail."

And here is another from a poem almost equally good :—

> " Oh, where doth the sea bird find a home,
> When the loud winds lash the whitened foam,
> And the rage of winter with booming swell
> Is heard like the tones of a demon's yell ?

Is it far in the depths of some inland bower,
Away from the scene's of destruction's power?
Not there is the sea bird's home.

When the fire-winged lightning flashes by,
And the thunder rolls o'er the blackened sky,
When terror sits brooding o'er air and earth,
As if to hail a demon's birth,
Away, away, on the shrieking wind,
Leaving the thoughts of fear behind,
Doth the hardy sea bird roam.

Not on the topmost bough of the tree,
Away from the sound of his native sea,
But like a king on his craggy throne
He seateth him, and there alone
Watching the wrecks of grandeur made,
When the storm-fiend o'er the waters played,
Doth the sea bird find a rest."

Mr. Alexander Maclagan has these two fine stanzas
in his poem, " To a Wounded Sea Bird " :—

" Alas for thee, poor bird ! no more
'Twill be a joy with them to soar
Through sunshine, calm, or storm ;
Nor on the shelly shore to land,
And sit like sunshine on the sand,
Pluming thy beauteous form.

.   .   .   .   .

Cold, nestled on the black sea rock,
I hear thy little feathered flock
In piteous accents mourn
For thee and food ; but all are gone,
And thou art drifting on and on,
And can no more return."

We might almost have included the stately heron
among the sea-birds, for at certain times it will make
its way to the sea-shore, and set itself to work in the

pools and shallows, just as it would in the inland waters. There it may be seen, standing, as it always does stand

HERON.

when fishing, on one leg, the other leg partially drawn up, with its half-foot long lance-like beak, so nicely notched, all ready —a beak which it drives right through its prey with the utmost precision. This prey it tosses up and then seizes in its mouth; but it has happened that when a heron struck an eel and lifted it thus to swallow it, the eel was quicker than it was, threw its tail round the bird's neck, and so held till the heron died from want of breath— the head of the eel having been half gorged, caused it also to die, and both were found locked together. The extensive draining of lands, and the clearing out of marshy fens and commons, has perhaps had a tendency in places not far from the sea-shore to drive the herons there. In such districts they may often be seen proceeding with swift, yet seeming lazy easy flight sea-wards to find tit-bits in favourite feeding grounds.

The heron likes to nest in fir trees, and when he has young ones he has a very busy time of it, and busiest at the time when other birds get rest, for the young herons get hungrier as night comes on; and thus it is that more especially in the spring-time the grey or black and white heron, his white breast most exposed, may be seen like a wisp of foam in the twilight in the sheltered corner of pond or stream. He was once of great account, for it was a lordly sport to hunt the heron with the falcon, as Mary Queen of Scots knew well; and not seldom the hunted was the victor, for the heron, with its instinct, would make a dart at the falcon's eyes and blind it.

Like the crow, in always making at the eyes of an enemy, the heron also resembles the crow in its keen eye for a gun. It knows the difference between a stick or anything else held in the hand and a breechloader. The shine on the barrel from afar is enough, and the heron is off before the sportsman can get aim. The heron has some other claims to notice. He is at once swimmer, wader, and percher. You may see him taking his flight from the lonely pool and making his way on that easy wing of his to the distant fir trees, where, owing to the fine instinct and the great knack he has in choosing his post, he will perch so that, large though he be, you will hardly detect him as he rests quietly after his long and patient labours at pool or stream side.

XVI

ASHESTIEL AND SIR WALTER SCOTT.

> " Great nature mocks us if the heart can take
>   No tribute of high memory to invest
>   Her beauty with the sense of love and good :
>   I think of one who here did offering make
>   Of heart and hope—within whose gentle breast
>   Stirred thoughts for all that moved to higher mood."

THIS is precisely the feeling with which we look at Ashestiel.   It is not by any means the most romantic and beautiful portion of the Tweed.   The heights are here too far removed from the river, and the banks, though well wooded, do not rise to a sufficiently high slope, as they do above Neidpath Castle, for instance, or below Peebles.   But it is full of association and romantic interest, because it was here that Sir Walter Scott for several years found a home, and spent a very active and interesting portion of his life.   The constant journeyings from Lasswade, where he had had a cottage on a picturesque bank of the Esk, to discharge the duties of the Sheriffship of Selkirkshire, ran away with too much of his time, and the good folks of Selkirkshire too, not unnaturally, grudged so much of the " Shirra's " presence to other parts, and so he resolved to find a house within the sphere of his judicial duties.

On the 4th May 1804 we find him writing thus to his friend Ellis :—

" I have been engaged in travelling backwards and

forwards to Selkirkshire upon little pieces of business, just important enough to prevent my doing anything to purpose.   One great matter, however, I have achieved, which is procuring myself a place of residence, which will save me these teasing migrations in future, so that though I part with my sweet little cottage on the banks of the Esk, you will find me this summer in the very centre of the ancient Reged, in a decent farm-house

overhanging the Tweed, and situated in a wild pastoral country."

Could a more desirable residence have been found for the Magician of the North?   Within sound of the romantic Tweed, with its scores of ballads and legends ; with its beautiful and suggestive associations, and its health-giving air.   The house in which Scott lived is approached through an old-fashioned garden, with holly hedges and broad green terraced walks.   Close under the windows, on the one side, is a deep ravine, well wooded, and down this tumbles a little brawling rivulet to join the Tweed. All around are the green hills, silent, reposeful, looking from the level like a billowy sea. The hill heights behind are those that separate the Yarrow from Tweed, the former stream being within an easy ride of Ashestiel—a ride on which some of the finest and most romantic mountain scenery is to be seen.

It was here that Scott wrote " Waverley " and " Marmion ; " here that he corrected the proofs of the " Lay of the Last Minstrel ; " here that " Rokeby " was begun, and " Dryden " and " Swift," in his Edition of the Poets were prepared ; and here too that he fully learned the difference between " long sheep " and " short sheep "—on which distinction a fine joke is founded, for on a native being asked what a " long sheep " must measure in body beyond a " short sheep," was told, " Weel, it's no' that ava', ye ken', it's a' i' the oo'," the contrast really being between the length of the wool in the Cheviot and the native breed.

But Scott's life was never that of the literary recluse, of the absorbed student or antiquary. The claims of human nature were too strong. Lockhart tells us that Camp—his favourite dog then, and the predecessor of the more famous Maida—and the children had free access to his study at all times ; that the " bairns " would often intrude and interrupt him in the midst of a sentence, and demand that he should tell them a story, when he would invariably take them on his knees and comply, always giving them more than they had asked ; and often, too, they would tempt him out to wander with them in the garden or by the stream side, or even further a-field, Camp bounding before or trotting discreetly at their heels.

At first Scott was fain to be his own coachman, and to drive Mrs. Scott about the district; but he was so awkward in this bit of business, we learn, that more than once he put his wife in jeopardy through the threatened overturn of the little phaeton, and a coachman—a relative of Tom Purdie, his trusty servant—was engaged. Often, no doubt, he walked or drove over that bridge we see in the picture that lay, indeed, on the direct way to his house from important points, and delighted in the view from it up the water when the sun shone bright upon it.

Here, James Hogg, rapidly rising into fame, visited the "Shirra," and not a few other men of note.

His lease ran out in 1811, and then he was somewhat uncomfortable; and as he was now in a position to buy a house, we find him writing—

"I now sit a tenant at will, under a heavy rent, and at all the inconvenience of one when in the house of another; I have, therefore, resolved to purchase a piece of ground sufficient for a cottage and a few fields."

After looking at various places, he fixed on a small estate at Abbotsford, where by-and-by the stately mansion arose which is so associated with his name; but it was not so far distant from Ashestiel but that the removal was accompanied with little pictures and associations which must have been dear to the heart of Scott, and often recalled by him and talked of by him and his.

The "flitting" from Ashestiel, we read, "though so full of delight and pride to themselves, was a sad one for the poorer neighbours they left behind them, for they had been the kindest of friends to all whom poverty or sickness reduced to need aid or counsel, Mrs. Scott having even some knowledge of the treatment required for ordinary ailments, so that she had been a Lady Bountiful of the most useful kind ; and the sorrow of the peasantry of the village was universal, though to the younger portion of it, this was relieved by the amusement caused by "the procession of the furniture from the old to the new dwelling. Old swords, bows, targets, and lances, made a very conspicuous show. A family of turkeys was accommodated within the helmet of some *preux* chevalier of ancient Border fame ; and the caravan, attended by a dozen rosy peasant children, carrying fishing-rods and spears, and leading ponies, greyhounds, and spaniels, would, as it crossed the Tweed, have formed no bad subject for the pencil, and really reminded one of the gipsy groups of Callot on their march."

Lockhart says that he retained to the end of his life a certain tenderness of feeling towards Ashestiel, which could not perhaps be better shadowed forth than in Joanna Baillie's similitude : "Yourself and Mrs. Scott and the children will feel sorry at leaving Ashestiel, which will long have a consequence, and be the object of kind feelings with many, from having once been the place of your residence. If I should ever be happy enough to be at Abbotsford, you must take me to see Ashestiel too. I have a kind of tenderness for it, as one has for a man's first wife when you hear that he has married a second."

XVII

IN DURHAM AND NEAR IT.

DURHAM city stands on the line between north and south, and is, as it were, the key and entrance to the debatable land. Even its present-day outward aspect suggests the fact. It is a city of heights and valleys, beautifully relieved by unconscious devices of old-world architecture, in which quaint simplicity and suggestions of refinement are oddly mingled. Its mixture of grey stone houses, with here and there lath and plaster fronts and wooden carvings below; its long closes, and its strange winding vagaries of lanes and streets; its modern shop fronts and ornamented old pillars and balustrades, is quaint and wholly striking to the traveller, either from the south or the north. The beautiful and picturesque river, with its sloping banks rising high just where they should, to set off fully the Cathedral and the Castle with the finest effect, adds exactly the romantic effect that is demanded.

From whatever point you look, you have varied outlines, towers, or turrets rising high, and forming a kind of crown to the whole. No doubt, like all old towns, Durham has its share of dirty corners, but it is ill the part of the stranger to go poking and nosing about for them. We were in this but too like the ill-disposed critic who, seeking for little faults or flaws, is sure to find them, and, having found them, can then see nothing else.   No, we shall not here follow his example, but, in the clear brightness of the spring morning, take our reader by the hand and lead him along for a general view of Durham city.

DURHAM CATHEDRAL.

As we pass from the railway station down by North Road, &c., to the bridge, the city is just awakening. A keen air blows through the winding streets, and a faint morning light catches the highest towers of the Cathedral, and runs a ribbon of white round the grey rugged high lines of the Castle walls and turrets. We pass on and on over the Bridge, and look up the river, to hear it—yes, we can in the comparative silence almost hear it—rushing over yonder weir by the mill, and then come purling onward, as the trees by its borders on the left faintly outline themselves in the water. Up and up we then ascend the climbing street before us, round by the Market Square, with its two quaint statues, and round again we turn and make our way to the Cathedral, and walk about it. None of the good folks in the precincts are yet astir; but a dog has found its way out, and comes and sniffs suspiciously at us strangers, and then goes off, surly and dissatisfied and doubtful, to inform his master of our intrusion, for he scrapes at one of the doors. Even the dogs in Cathedral precincts take on a kind of stiff self-restraint and official wariness. The rooks and jackdaws are busy at their nest-buildings, and caw and chatter in the oddest manner among the trees and shrubs about.

We walk from point to point, gathering quite a new idea of the extent of this reverend old structure, with its great central tower, and its unique twin-pair of towers almost overhanging the river, and its tapering turrets at the other end. We pause and admire their admirable pose, so striking near at hand, so insignificant seen from afar, dwarfed entirely by their greater brethren. Then we go and look, and are lost in admiration of the fine Catherine or wheel-window. The masons are at work at this side of the fabric, for there is weathering in this fine pile, and stones are being cut to replace those that are here hopelessly wasted.

We might tell much of the history of this old

edifice : how Carileph founded it so early as 1093, but did not finish more than one half of it, as we now see it ; how the transepts, the greater part of the nave, the Lady Chapel at the west end, and the Nine Altars at the other, were the work of later days—how Flambard and Pudsey laboured to extend and beautify ; how the choir was vaulted by Prior Hoton (1283), and the aisles by Prior Algar earlier still (1100–37), how the great west doorway, with its medallions and grotesque devices, was gifted by Bishop Rufus, and how the wonderful Catherine window and the famous screen were added. But these things can all be read in the guide-books, especially in the cheap and handy guide-book of Mr. J. H. Veitch in North Road, with full relay of facts such as we need not dwell on, our business being confined, as our space demands it should be, to giving merely general impressions. .

We therefore turn down the South Bailey, with its many quaint but powerful reminders of olden times, and find our way to the river banks. There modern improvement has indeed made a garden. The slopes are umbrageous with trees of many kinds ; the walks, well laid out, are liberally supplied with seats where the wanderer may rest and be thankful, and listen to the birds sending forth as varied and sweet a concert as could be heard in the deepest recesses of many remote woods. The sense of quiet and retirement is such as could not be realised in many cities. As you sit and look up, you cannot but be struck by the great height to which the Cathedral towers rise above the level of the river ; and, as the eye runs along, following the lines of the castle heights, this is still more impressed upon you ; you feel that Durham is in its own way unique. You may visit the University and rejoice in its wealth, the richness of the museum, and the quiet of its halls; you may admire this and that in some of the city churches; you may find much that is quaint in the Grammar School and the Blue Coat School and the Old Exchequer, and much to interest you in the wealth of picture and carving in the Town Hall and the Guild Hall, but your mind will return to the first view you had of the Cathedral and the Castle, and the impression you gathered on your first walk on the leafy terraced slopes of the river banks below them.

One building, for personal reasons more than aught else, particularly attracted our attention. It is the Durham Miners' Hall in North Road—a solid and unpretending building, entered by a wide doorway leading to a broad staircase. In front are impressive white marble statues of two leaders of the Durham miners, that of Alexander MacDonald, M.P., and William Crawford.

On making inquiries, we were told that here and there considerable portions of the old city wall still remain; and we lost no time in making our way to see them. Our engraving gives a very good idea of one of the most important portions which still remain to show the solid masonry by which the city was at one time surrounded.

There are three very delightful walks near Durham, which the visitor on no account should miss. The first is that to Brancepeth Castle, the second to Finchale Priory, and the third to Sunderland Bridge. Of course there are many more, as to Langley Old Hall, Butterby, and Maiden Castle Scar; but the three first named most interested us, as we most enjoyed them. It is not only what is found at the end of the journey, but what the

road itself supplies, that is here enchanting ! The road
to Brancepeth winds in the most delightful way; now
you are almost closed in by woods and gentle heights,
and again you emerge to enjoy the most exquisite
glimpses of distant hills with fringes of wood, and at

length when a view of the castle, which so finely combines the old and the new, bursts full upon you, you
feel that it is a fitting finale to your ramble. Like a
true poem, the last lines crown the whole. It is finely
castellated with six great towers, two of which—those

on the west and south side—are of ancient construc-
tion, the projecting buttresses gradually emerging and
impressing themselves on the eye, and breaking the
lines with fine effect. The restorations, carried out by
Mr. John Patterson of Edinburgh, and finished in 1818,
were in the fullest degree possible in the spirit of the
original portion; and the whole is in the highest degree
imposing. Walls and turrets relieve each other along
each side, and enclose a spacious courtyard, which is
entered at the north-east angle by a Norman gateway
with a portcullis, and flanked by rounded towers. We
can well believe what is said, that it is superior to any
other battlemented edifice in the north of England. The
parts now inhabited lie on the south-west side, and rise
from a high rock. Inside the castle there is much to
interest the visitor, alike in the way of ancient armour
and splendid pictures, besides some fine remains of old
work in groined ceilings, and so forth; and the stately
entrance hall is filled up with massive oaken seats with
strong arms which terminate in boars' heads, delightfully carved. And for the lover of antiquities, there is
much to attract, both within and without the castle, which
is surrounded by a splendid park and gardens, where
days might be spent both profitably and pleasantly.

To reach Finchale Priory, the best way is to go by
foot-road through Frankland and Brasside Moor. The
scenery, if not very romantic or striking, is varied and
interesting; and the more distant views, in many cases,
are fine. It is with a sense of surprise that, after some
windings, a view of the Priory is suddenly gained lying
half-hidden in a lovely dell—the Wear here sweeping
boldly round and forming, as it were, a little peninsula
on which the Priory stands; the high cliffs of Cocken
rising almost opposite, with no little grandeur, and giving

effect and picturesqueness. The ruins are now in many places ivy-grown, but are everywhere touched as with the finger of romance and tradition, interesting, as Mr. W. S. Gibson says, " to the architect no less than to the antiquary, and the more so, because there is not another building of decorated work worthy of note in the county of Durham. Indeed, there are few specimens of it as added to buildings of an earlier period in this part of Old Northumbria, owing perhaps to the incessant wars between England and Scotland, in the age when the decorated style prevailed in this country, and to the active part which the ecclesiastical princes palatine of Durham, and their obedientaries and vassals, monastical as well as lay, were obliged to take in these desolating contests. Unpeopled and desecrated for three centuries, time has spread over the chief portions of these grey walls a mantle of venerable and luxuriant ivy, whose roots entwine about the foundations, and whose branches have penetrated the interstices of the masonry, rearing their perennial foliage where all beside is crumbling to ruin."

Once well clear of the town, the road to Sunderland Bridle is delightful, quietly picturesque, with the sweet relief of strips of wood here and there on the right, running along its borders, with fine specimens of birch and beech and fir interlacing their branches. At the time we last journeyed o'er it (April, 1893), the larks in the fields on the left were rising, circling upwards, making the air vocal with their sweet and unceasing song ; the lapwings circled round, their crests just beginning to be brightened with tufts of deeper colour, and uttering their familiar cry, *pees-weet, pees-weet ;* and blackbirds and thrushes were very busy near to the more wooded and cultured policies that led up to

SUNDERLAND BRIDGE.

the seats of the landed gentry. The hands of men, at all events of all fruit-cultivating men, are against this brotherhood; yet they survive, insist on being his neighbours, and fain would conciliate him by the sweetest of songs at mid-day, and at eventide, after most other day songsters have ceased their song.

Sunderland Bridge is one of those old-fashioned structures, with angular recesses at its sides, V-shaped ; and when anything is going on, parties of anglers starting up the stream for instance, each of these at the sharp point will be found occupied by an interested rural spectator, unwilling that anything should escape him. And often there is a good deal going on here, for it is a very favourite spot for parties of anglers making a start for fishing on the Wear. And no wonder. You have only to pause for a moment, like the rustics, and lean over at the sharp point of one of these angular recesses, and you will get assurance of this. Just below the bridge the water passes foaming over and between the breaks of a high strata of big flat boulders, and then trots smartly down into a fine pool where big fish must sometimes lie. Immediately above the bridge is the spacious railway viaduct, with many spans.

At the furthest end of the bridge on the height is the village of Sunderland Bridge, with its church so nicely and picturesquely set on the hill amid its screen of trees, like a picture. We may note, in passing, that the houses represented in our illustration are not in Sunderland Bridge village at all, but are really in Spitz Hall parish; but that will not probably be of much consequence or interest to the traveller, who will be more concerned to know that Mrs. Mortimer at the Inn, whose signboard you see in the print, can supply really sound refreshments, and is in every way a good and honest hostess.

A little further on is Croxdale, where there is a station on the Darlington and Durham Railway, and by this the pilgrim, should he feel wearied or footsore, can do, as we did, though not weary or footsore, but only pressed for time on that last visit, take the train, and either return to Durham or go to Darlington as he may be inclined.

XVIII.

IN COQUETDALE.

THE Coquet has been so often celebrated alike for its picturesque and varied scenery and its " wale o' trout," that it may seem somewhat late in the day to deal with it as we now propose to do. But, after all, it is not yet so well known to general readers, at all events in the south, as it deserves to be, and the hope of interesting them and sending some of them to see it is our justification. Scenery in which the wild and romantic is at parts mingled with the sweetly sylvan and pastoral may be found in Coquetdale in almost as striking a measure as on some of the favourite streams of Scotland. Many who rush past it, and thus reduce the time they have for enjoyment on the hills in the open air, might pause, and find the Highlands nearer home than in the north and west of Scotland. And this we say though, as the reader knows from what we have already written, we are bound to Scotland by the nearest and dearest ties. But many might comfortably reach the Coquet and enjoy a few days there who would not for the short time they have at their disposal think of going so far afield as Deeside or Inverness or Argyleshire.

Well, then, let us start on our journey. We might spend a good while in tracing the Coquet from its rise in the Cheviot Hills, clearing its way " through moors and mosses many," now spreading out into gentle pools, and again leaping through narrow gorges, and in descanting on the beauties of the many tributaries that come tumbling down the little glens and hillsides and go to swell its current; but beyond Rothbury there is no railway, and the numbers who would adventure far up are limited to the more leisured persons, fond of novelty, and enthusiastic fishermen, and, it may be, an artist or two in search of remote nooks and wild romantic corners that will suggest striking pictures. Rothbury lies on the side of a hill, just where the Coquet makes one of his finest sweeps, and is in its own way unique. It is the capital of Coquet-land, and is indeed like one who lifts up his head proudly and looks pleased over the fair and romantic lands he owns. It is far from being a dull or stupid place. There is a good deal of life in it. I learned that there were several societies, though with regret I heard that a golf club lately formed had not been a great success. The church is a fine structure, and the hotels are good. Personally we found the Queen's Head attractive, and Mr. Lawson an admirable and hearty host. Many delightful drives may be had within an easy distance, the most exquisite of which is perhaps that to Simonside and Great Tosson.

All the country round is rich in springs—some of them chalybeate, some of them sulphur, and others iron. All the country round Rothbury, too, is rich in antiquarian remains—British dwellings, Roman causeways, peel (or pil) towers, ruins of camps and fortresses, telling how the waves of Border invasion swept on and retreated and swept on again. Mr. Dixon quotes a song composed by a Newcastle gentleman well known in Coquetdale, as spirited as it is faithful to fact and the feelings of those into whose mouth it is put :—

"Waes me !—God wot,
But the beggarlie Scot
Through the 'bateable land has prickit his way,
An' ravaged wi' fire
Peel, haudin', an' byre,
Our nowte, sheep, and galloways a' taen awae ;
But by hagbut an' sword, ere he's back owre the Border,
We'll be het on his trod, an' aye set him in order.

Nae bastles or peels
Are safe frae the deils,
Gin the collies be oot or the lairds awae ;
The bit bairnies an' wives
Gang i' dreed o' their lives,
For they scumfish them oot wi' the smoutherin' strae.
Then—spear up the lowe—ca' oor lads thegither,
An' we'll follow them hot trod owre the heather.

Weel graith'd, sair on metal,
Oor harness in fettle,
The reivers we sicht far ayont the wa',
Gin we bring them to bay,
Nae saufey we'll pay.
We'll fangit, syne bang it—we'se see them a' ;
Then on, lads, on—for the trod is hot,
As oot ower the heather we prod the Scot.

We'll harass them sairly,
Nae hoo gie for parley.
Noo the spurs i' the dish for their hungrie wames,
Do your slogans gie mouth,
An' we'll sune lead them south.
Gramerce—gin we cross them, we'll crap their kames
Then—keep the lowe bleezin', lads—ca' to the fray,
Syne we're up wi' the lifters we'll gar them pay.

Fae to fae—steel to steel ;
Noo the donnert loons reel,
An' caitiffs cry ' Hoo !' but it's a' in vain :

> See a clatter o' thwacks
> Fa's on sallets an' jacks.
> Till we've lifted the lifters as weel as oor ain,
> Then wi' fyce to the crupper they'll ride a gaie mile
> To their dance frae the Wuddie at merrie Carlisle."

In the Jacobite risings of 1715 and 1745 Coquetdale had its own part, and the distress and disturbance experienced by the good folks there are commemorated in these lines, often heard by Mr. Dixon on Coquet Water—lines which wonderfully recall one of Mr. Allingham's fine poems, if not indeed, the finest of his shorter poems :—

> " Up the craggy mountain,
>   An' doun the mossy glen,
>   We daurna gan' a-milkin'
>   For Charlie an' his men."

Rothbury contains between 800 and 900 inhabitants, and is mainly limited to three streets—the Front or High Street (the longest), and Bridge Street and Church Street.

We learn from Mr. Tomlinson that the name of Rothbury is supposed by some to be derived from the Celtic word *rhath*, meaning a cleared spot. If any weight is to be laid on the old rhyme which we owe to Mr. D. D. Dixon, it is clear that Rothbury in old times largely put the wild heights about it, unfit for other use, to the rearing of goats, as did many other places in Northumberland :—

> " Rothbury for goats' milk,
>   The Cheviots for mutton ;
>   Cheswick for its cheese and bread,
>   And Tynemouth for a glutton."

But our plan, having seen Rothbury and neighbourhood, was to drive down the thirteen miles to Acklington, there get on the train to Warkworth, and spend a little time at Coquet mouth.

Nothing could be finer than the views that unfolded themselves just as we turned out of Rothbury. Our road lay as if on an upper shelf on a high rocky slope, above us still rough heathery hills, and below the glancing glistening river. Soon the rocks below

THRUM MILL.

seemed to close into a ravine, where the water narrowed and deepened into a kind of gully, and forced its way with foam and noise through barriers of rock. This is what is called the Thrum, and the Thrum Mill is close beside it, one of the most striking bits of scenery on this part. A footpath leads along from Rothbury to the Thrum Mill, a favourite resort of the visitors who in summer come to Rothbury, and here find welcome change. Mr. James Ferguson of Morpeth has given us the following about the Thrum :—

"About a mile below Rothbury, at the Thrum Mill, the river yields a little snatch of bold and romantic scenery. There, in earlier times, the pent-up waters had to force their way through a barrier of sandstone; and the river is at the present time showing how it was done, for at one point the entire body of water forces its way in a serpentine course between rocks so close that a steady brain and sure foot can step across, but not without risk, which should not be lightly taken, for it is evident that, beneath, the rocks must be scooped and grooved out into huge tunnels and dark recesses from which escape would be impossible. Here the southern bank is an almost perpendicular face of rugged rocks, festooned and wreathed with the foliage of nature-planted bushes, and crowned with stately trees."

In one of Wilson's "Tales of the Borders," Willie Faa, the gipsy king, is represented as leaping across the Thrum with the stolen heir of Clennel Castle, and leaving his pursuers behind.

In old days it is said that much poaching was practised here. Mr. D. D. Dixon, whose art it is to combine business with pleasure, and delights to gather up the folklore, old traditions, and local tales as he goes his rounds, never failing to furnish us with new and racy material, has some little records which abundantly prove that the practice has not yet been discontinued. And despite the custom so long carried on, it is apparently profitable enough to entice men to the adventure, even if the Coquet is not so rich in fish as it once was, at all events, according to this report :—

"Talk o' fishin'," said an old Coquet angler, "there's

no sic fishen' in Coquet now as when I was a lad. It was nowte then but to fling in and pull out by tweeses an' threeses if ye had sae mony heuks on, but now a body may keep threshin' at the water a' day atween Hallysteun an' Weldon an' hardly catch three dozen, an' money a time no that. Aboot fifty years syne I mind o' seein' trouts that thick i' the Thrum below Rothbury that if ye had stucken the end o' yor gad into the watter amang them it wud amaist hae studden upreet." *

These halcyon days, if they ever existed, have gone, never to return, but still poaching in Coquetdale is not a lost art. Gangs of men work the torches and the leisters, while those who like to be solitary prefer to work the gaff or the cleek. Mr. Dixon, in his account of salmon poaching, gives this incident :—

"One dark November night about eight o'clock, a few years ago, I was returning home from the country, when, walking along the highway, a few miles from Rothbury, I heard, but could not see, that some one was approaching ; suddenly, with a bang and a rattle, something was thrown into the roadside ditch ; then I saw a form looming through the darkness. According to the fashion of us country folk, I shouted, 'It's a dark night;' immediately the well-known voice of a country-man (who lived close by) replied, 'Oh ! that's ye, Mr. Dixon, aa' thought ye war somebody else: wait a bit, or aa' git thor things oot the dykeside.' Thereupon, after grappling about in the dark, he produced a lantern, a salmon gaff, and a poke : shouldering these implements, we went chatting along the road together until we came to a small burn—a tributary of the Coquet— the spot where my poaching friend was 'gan te try for

* "Rambles in Northumberland," by Stephen Oliver, the younger.

a' fish;' here I left him, as I did not care to be mixed
up in a poaching expedition."

Mr. Dixon also tells that the gangs for leistering
were fond of adopting disguises to aid them against
the water-watchers, and he gives this little bit of character and humour in illustration :—

" Some had their faces blacked and their eyes white,
others these colours reversed, a third, with a yellow
face, had, perhaps, red eyes and a red chin, and so on.
All wore the oldest and the duddiest of clothes they
could procure : their head-dress was often a battered
long hat or a woman's straw-bonnet—the latter was
the favourite head-gear, as the protecting front of the
old-fashioned coal-scuttle bonnet shaded the eyes from
the flare of the tarry-rope lights. An amusing story
is told of an old weaver, who, from all accounts, did
not spend much time in the performance of his daily
toilet. There were going to be some fishers on the
water, and he was to be one of the party, so, on asking
his wife—' Nanny, how shud aa' 'guise meesel the
night ?' she replied, 'Aa'l tell ye what, John, just
wesh yor fyce, an' a'm sure nebody'll ken ye.'"

As we pass on, we look up on the left, and find that
the scene has changed, not that the mountains are less
lofty or less stern in their native character, but that
skill and culture have been applied. We are looking
on the rocks which the wise and liberal expenditure of
Lord Armstrong have converted into hanging gardens,
not perhaps so magnificent as those of ancient Babylon,
but certainly very beautiful and striking. He chose
in this region to fix his abode—has built a splendid
mansion, Cragside he has named it, and made the bare
hills all about it to blossom like the rose. He has
prudently planted only the kind of growths that would

flourish on such ground and in such a situation: firs, pines, rhododendrons, ferns, and so forth, and not only has he his reward, but every passer-by has his share in it. Such a man is a great benefactor, and every visitor to Rothbury is indebted to him.

As we drove along beyond Cragside grounds a strange sight met our eyes. On a field on the side of one of the gentle slopes to our left, lying as it were between two swelling heights, fit probably only for grazing sheep, we saw what seemed to us two figures in women's dress—the one at the plough, the other at the harrow. The horses seemed under complete command, and the work was proceeding apace. In surprise we turned to our intelligent driver, who said, in answer to our queries: "Yes, they are women, and the people round about here regard it only as an ordinary matter to see them out at work. That is Todsted farm; it is held by a man who has four daughters, and up to quite a recent date they themselves did the whole work of the farm, ploughing, harrowing, sowing, reaping, and attending to the stock. The bulk of the farm, which is between 300 and 400 acres, is in sheep runs, but certain things have led the father of late to turn a little more into arable, and he has now got the assistance of a young man, but the daughters still take a turn at every kind of work, and very good hands they are too." It was very odd to have gone to the wild and picturesque neighbourhood of Rothbury to see something in this line so entirely new—to see something more than a practical working out of the old saw which it is so often said has now got antiquated—

> " Man to the mow,
> Wife to the cow,
> Son to the plough,
> Girl to the sow."

We pass by the quaint little village of Pauperhaugh or Pepperhaugh, as it is locally called, with its unique post-office, and see on our right the remains of Brinkburn Ironworks, where many thousand pounds were sunk years ago (for coal and iron are to be found in the valley); but it was a failure, and the works abandoned —another proof that no such enterprise can prosper unconnected with a railway, and this was before the railway was brought so near as it is now-a-days.

As we proceed onward, the valley gradually opens out, throwing its wooded heights further from the stream; the river widens and winds, forming fine sweeps and greeny reaches in the loops it makes. We see, from the depth and colour of the water just after it has passed over brawling shallows and forms pools, that there the fisher will love, in a sweet west wind that gently stirs it, to ply his "triple floating flies," or cast his minnow in the early morning sun, or the mellower afternoon light. So it flows on, murmuring and singing to itself, till we reach the famous Brinkburn, with its Priory set sweetly on one of the greeny loops we have referred to, as though it had been prepared precisely for just such a structure. Very beautiful is the whole picture here presented—the Priory, with its gardens and woods gathered round it, as though nestling there; and looking on the water where its outlines are faintly reflected in the stream that here flows calm and clear. Those who wish to know all the details about this historical priory must go to the guide-books—to Mr. W. W. Tomlinson's very admirable "Comprehensive Guide to Northumberland," published by Mr. Walter Scott, or to the everyway excellent little guides by Mr. D. D. Dixon and Mr. James Ferguson of Morpeth.

Another very famous point on the river is Weldon Bridge, where there is a quiet and homely inn much

patronised by fishermen in the season, and by bicyclists
and parties of men on walking tours.   We have good
reason to speak of the cleanliness and order of this
inn, for we rested there and found ourselves in good

BRINKBURN.

company, from which we did not seek to stand aloof.
True, indeed, is the old rhyme still :—

> "At Weldon Bridge there's wale o' wine,
>   If ye hae coin in pocket ;
> If ye can throw a heckle fine,
>   There's wale o' trout in Coquet."

Here the river widens out, the banks becoming
flatter, and so continue for some distance with little
variation, till we approach the very beautiful village of
Felton, where again the banks rise, the river in some
degree narrows, and you have one of the finest effects
imaginable. Felton lies as if in a half cup-like hollow
on the left side in a series of irregular terraces, some

WELDON BRIDGE.

of the houses appearing almost to be hung nest-like
on the slope amid trees and delicious greenery, while
the main road, now high on the right bank of the river,
runs through another village higher up, and looking, as
it were, lovingly down across upon Felton. The scene
is indeed delicious. From the blue and red roofs, the
smoke, as we looked, rose straight into the blue, for
not much wind was then stirring. Had we the power

of choosing the spot where we should spend the two most charming months of the year, we are not sure but we should say Felton, and would give it a fair trial, sincerely hoping that it would not verify the truth of the line, that " distance lends enchantment to the view."

There is not much more to make note of till we reach Acklington, which is rather a cold-looking little village, and here we leave the river to return to it when we reach Warkworth. This is one of the quaintest of old towns. Driven from the station, we find the road goes right round the greater half of the town, and you enter it by the further side, crossing the river, which almost winds round the little town, by an old two-arched bridge with many angles, and passing under an old and picturesque gateway that directly recalls mediæval times. Going forward, you come to the main street, and the Castle lies on the height right in front of you on a flat greeny knoll. It is much more of a ruin than might be fancied from the picture. The keep, built on an artificial mound and thus overtopping the rest, is the portion in best preservation, if we except the great gateway on the opposite side from the town, which is one of the oldest parts, if not the very oldest ; and by its powerful build and fine machicolation tells how in these days use and ornament went hand in hand. The keep was built on the site of an earlier one by the son of that Hotspur celebrated by Shakespeare in " Henry IV.," between the years 1415 and 1454. Mr. Freeman says " it is a good study of the process by which the purely military castle gradually passed into the house fortified for any occasional emergency." All round the Castle, in the olden days, there ran a wall ramparted and with round towers at certain points, but this wall has been in parts destroyed,

or has mouldered away, so that the two parts of the
Castle, as seen in our illustration, seem to be almost
disconnected. The arms of the Percys, and many
other devices, are engraven on the walls here and there,
and we see many traces of draw-wells and dungeons,
deep pits and descents, in some of which, no doubt,
men were imprisoned, or it may be, shut from the light
of day and tortured.

WARKWORTH CASTLE.

All round about Warkworth are the most delightful
walks, and bits on the river are simply charming. The
steep banks on the side opposite the church are laid
out in the most attractive pathways; and, as we stood
there in the sunset admiring the effect, we heard the
big fish leap in the still pools with the big bouldery
margins beyond and nearer to us. Nor should the

parish church, dedicated to St. Lawrence, be left without some examination. It is a fine structure and well worth attention, as specimens of all the various styles of English architecture are to be seen in it. Mr. Tomlinson (p. 408) gives these excellent hints regarding the most interesting points in connection with it :—

"The features most worthy of special notice are, the Norman windows of the nave, the original groining of the chancel, and the Norman triplet filled with modern stained glass at the east end, and the chancel arch with its singular and perhaps unique fan ornamentation ; the old staircase for the ringer of the sanctus bell at the north-east angle of the nave ; the cross-legged effigy of a knight in the south aisle ; and a curious window in the vestry composed of three narrow slits, through which it is believed an anchorite inhabiting this chamber communicated with persons outside. The porch on the outside is well peppered with bullet marks. Within it is laid the opening scene of Mr. Walter Besant's story, 'Let nothing you dismay;' the hero of the narrative having to do penance in a white sheet before the congregation entering the church."

In speaking to some of the more intelligent inhabitants I met of the facility with which the castle might be restored, after the manner in which the Earl of Moray restored Doune Castle, I was somewhat surprised to find that the suggestion met with no encouragement from them.. They shrugged their shoulders ; and said that it was better as it was. The Duke of Northumberland had a splendid seat not very far off —Alnwick Castle, namely—and they knew that were Warkworth Castle restored, and the ducal family settled even for a part of the year there, it would soon come to be a heavy tax on the good folks of Warkworth, by a curtailment of their freedom in many ways—no doubt a very sensible view to take, but certainly not savouring much of feudal devotion, which just shows how far and how fast we are now travelling from the romance and sentiment of the feudal times.

Looking out from the ramparts of the castle seaward, we could behold Coquet Island lying perhaps a mile out, like a vast black-backed fish basking in the sun, with the lighthouse, dwindled to a small point, like a high whitish fin just behind the head. We made inquiries about the best means of getting out to it, but were told that unless when the boat goes out with supplies for the lighthouse men there is no course but specially to employ a fisherman or boatman to row one out. But on asking whether Coquet Island Cell was worth the journey, all to whom we spoke answered decidedly no, that Coquet Island was, in their idea, best looked at from a distance, that the only portion of the famous cell that. remained was now a part of the foundation of the lighthouse or keeper's house, and that if it could be seen at all it was with difficulty, and they dissuaded us from the enterprise. Wrecks, in old days, were all too frequent on Coquet Island, so that it was a cause of great rejoicing when on 1st October 1841 the first light was exhibited from the lighthouse. In 1643, during the Civil Wars, the place was taken, with all its garrison, by the Scots, and thus attained for the time some importance.

Instead of rowing to Coquet Island, therefore, we acted on the suggestion received and visited the Hermitage, which lies about a quarter of a mile up the river from the castle in the centre of a wood, one of the most remarkable places we have ever visited. As we approached, and came within view of this interesting structure, I could not help thinking of Coleridge's lines in " The Ancient Mariner " :—

> " The hermit good lives in the wood . . .
>   He kneels at morn, and noon, and eve—
>   He hath a cushion plump :
>   It is the moss that wholly hides
>   The rotten, old oak stump."

The hermitage itself is cut out of the solid freestone rock some twenty feet in height, and is approached by a flight of some seventeen steps also cut in the rock. It contains three apartments, the cell, the chapel, and the dormitory. The first is about twenty feet in length, and about seven and a half feet in height, and it is certainly not to be matched elsewhere in our country.

Here and there are relics of sculptured effigies of angels and cherubs, and crosses and other emblems. The ceilings are beautifully groined, the arches springing from highly wrought pilasters. On an altar tomb, to the right of the altar, just before a two-light window, is the recumbent figure of a lady, her hands upraised. On the inner wall over the entrance is inscribed, in old English characters, the Latin, *Fuerunt mihi lacrymæ meæ panes die ac nocte,* " my tears have been my meat day and night." Built up against the side of the rock is a little chamber about eighteen feet square, and in it is a wide fireplace. It is supposed that this was the residence of a chantry-priest, who lived here at a period subsequent to the original date of the hermitage.

The solitude of the place, the sense of sanctity, reinforced by the wealth of foliage, the shrubs, mosses, and ferns surrounding it, combine to awaken feelings new and unique ; the mind is filled with emotions kindred to those which animated the men who sought such a retreat in days long gone by, and desired to make it mirror as far as might be the feelings of reverence and worship that dwelt in them. Antiquarians give the date of the structure as the middle of the fourteenth century.

XIX

ABOUT WOOLER.

WOOLER is the centre of a world of its own. It is, as it were, the queen of its four streams which, so to speak, knit themselves about it, and look on it from near and far as their presiding and tutelary patron. At its feet the Wooler Water, flowing gracefully on; further off, the Beaumont and the College streams that wind down to meet and form The Glen, one of the most delightfully wooded and most picturesque of Northumbrian streams. I had come to Wooler from Warkworth, and reached it rather late in the evening, for some of the trains on that line are not only slow, but apt to be rather behind time, and it was too dark to see much that night. But as I took a turn, and picked my way along at the risk of a fall, I could see that the place was pretty, and had a character of its own. But more than this was not possible then. I put up at the delightful Tankerville Arms (locally called " The Cottage Hotel "), which combines in very truth the character of a cottage with that of a town hotel. You are served in a hearty and homely way, for Mr. and Mrs. Aitchison are the true old-fashioned host and hostess; and you soon find that the inn has many memorials of famous fishermen who have made head-quarters there, returning to it again and again, as though it were to them a kind of second home. It is not much to look at—two long rows of building meeting at right angles, and really forming half of a square, with pretty bits of garden seen from some of the windows. Our little cut gives a very fair idea of it; but the interior is much finer, and is full of character in many respects.

I found in the list of visitors and in other records in the public rooms much to interest and amuse me, and

THE COTTAGE HOTEL, WOOLER.

retired to rest early, that I might be up in the morning fresh and able to make the most of my time.

In the morning I strolled round the little town, admiring what nature had done for it, and what unconscious art had done also—so settling some houses here and there in nooks and corners that no view of Wooler can be got that will give more than a fragment of it. It is hung on the slope of a gentle hill, its main street along a kind of ridge, and the back gardens on the one side deliciously sloping down towards the Wooler Water, which flows at its feet. This street is the only long and straight thoroughfare in it, and at the upper end it opens out into a kind of triangle, in the centre of which stands the picturesque and beautifully ornamented fountain erected by public subscription to the memory of William Wightman, Esq., who was a banker in the town, and much loved and respected. Just round from the corner of this triangle stands the parish church —a slightly irregular and not very imposing structure. Towards the other end is the handsome Roman Catholic Church erected in 1855.

I was a little surprised at the presence of so many churches and chapels in so small a town, which led me to remark to a residenter, with whom I talked, that the good folks of Wooler must either be very good or very bad people, which caused him to put on a questioning look. By way of reply, I quoted, in a laughing way, the lines of Defoe—

> " Wherever God erects a house of prayer
> The devil is sure to build a chapel there,"

and added, " the nearer the church the further from grace."

" Well, yes," he said, " we have enow o' them ; and, as you say, we should be good people if stone and lime and the preachin' of the word could do it."

" Why," I said, " you must have a church or chapel for every score of people in the place. How many churches and chapels are there in this small town ? "

" Well," he said, " let one see : there mun be six at least. There's the Parish Church *there* and the Roman Catholic Church *here*. *There's* a Presbyterian (pointing with his finger), and down that entry is inother

Presbyterian, and there's a third Presbyterian at the other end of the town. And we have a Primitive Methodist Chapel, and a hall where the Plymouth Brethren meet. Yes, we *should* be 'good people,' if stone and lime and preachin' the word could do it; but I'm afraid there's a good bit of the old Adam left still hereabout in spite of all that."

And then he proceeded to tell me how it came about that the keen Presbyterian spirit could not be content with fewer than three churches—one had originally belonged to the Established Church of Scotland, and one had been a Burgher meeting-house, but both were now connected with the Presbyterian Church of England. The independence of the Border spirit thus comes out very illustrative in the field of religion; the people are, or have been, keenly influenced by the religious and theological differences that prevail in both countries. The Roman Catholic church, he told me, was built at a time when not a few of the landed gentry in the region leaned that way; but now many of them had died out, and the numbers attending this spacious church were so few, that when a much esteemed priest died some years ago no new priest was settled in Wooler, and they "begged or borrowed" a priest, as he said, now and then from neighbouring churches.

As we talked, the beauty of the morning was, as it were, blighted by two or three ragged, wretched-looking, filthy creatures creeping along with that peculiar huddling together of the figure that tells of too scanty clothing for the keen morning air. Hands in pockets, and nondescript caps drawn as far as might be over their eyes, they crept on, ill-shod, as though the sunlight were a burden; and they were followed by another couple with better bearing, much more independent air, and cleanlier look—they had little bundles in their hands. My eyes turned from them to him with inquiry.

"Oh!" he said, "these in front are tramps just come from our workhouse over there behind the church, and they are just on their way to the next one. They go a regular round, and that makes up their lives, poor devils—'tis little better than a treadwheel, yet they don't commit suicide. The two behind, if I judge right, are not tramps, but respectable working men out of a job moving on to try and find one. They look very different from the others, and may work into better luck yet."

I looked again as those in front turned a corner, and saw the last of them—one was just borrowing a rag from another, probably all they had for a handkerchief among the lot. In these days of accumulation and care for the things of to-morrow, these men, at all events, illustrate complete dependence on Providence, laying up no treasure for themselves here below, nor carrying scrip nor cloak—the saddest spectacle almost to be seen in our Christian country, and strongly emphasised here by the freshness, greenness, and sparkle of nature all around.

Before I parted from my good informant, a gentleman with an air of business came along, whom I was informed was Mr. Brand of the "Atlas" Printing Works, who could supply me with the "guide" I wanted. I went with him to his place to get Mr. Hall's very excellent "Guide to Glendale," which I found most interesting and useful, simple, clear, and nicely illustrated.

This enabled me to choose my walks whilst at Wooler; and of two of them I must make special mention. The first was to Haughhead, by a delightful road. You turn round the upper side of the town down a delicious descent to Wooler Bridge—another with many angles—and then crossing it, enter a wide plain with a steepish hill on one side near Wooler laid out in pretty walks, and then you pass on to a region of gentle swelling hills. The road winds, and the Wooler Water spreads here and there over gravelly reaches, and chatters and sings to itself, and then passes into deeper pools, and, like deep things, is then silent. Haughhead is a good place for picnic parties to go to if they wish quiet, and they had need to *picnic*, for the inn there is not now what it was in the olden coaching days. But what gives its main interest to the place is the fact that here the English army lay encamped for two days just before Flodden. It was from this place that the Earl of Surrey sent that letter of 7th September, upbraiding the Scottish king for breaking his promise to meet the English forces, and offering to give him battle next day on Milfield Plain.

The second was to Humbleton, to see what is called " The Cup and Saucer Camp." It is an intrenchment which is said to have been one of the strongholds of the ancient Britons. Mr. Hall gives a very full description of it: " It is 180 yards in circumference, having a hollow in the centre of the area, and is surrounded by a rampier of stone and earth, which is yet in some parts three feet high." There is not a little here to interest the lover of nature as well as the antiquarian, for some of the views from this point are fine, and the fact that numerous skeletons have been dug up here exceedingly well preserved gives it a kind of claim upon the regard of ethnologists.

A letter from Sir Walter Scott to his friend Clark,

in 1791, when he paid a visit to Wooler and its neighbourhood, is of value, were it for nothing else but
showing that in these days here, as in Coquetdale,
the keeping of goats for the sake of the milk, &c.,
was common, though now the hill farmer has turned
his attention to the more profitable occupation of sheep-
rearing, and the lowland farmer to the more scientific
cultivation of the soil, which has led to a great change
in the landscape in many ways. But we must give
ourselves the pleasure of quoting a part of Sir Walter's
most characteristic letter :—

"I am very snugly settled here in a farmer's house
about six miles from Wooler, in the very centre of the
Cheviot Hills, in one of the wildest and most romantic
situations which your imagination ever suggested. And
what the deuce are you doing there? methinks I hear
you say. Why, sir, of all things in the world, drinking
goats' whey: not that I stand in the least need of it,
but my uncle having a slight cold, and being a little
tired of home, asked me last Sunday evening if I
would like to go with him to Wooler, and I, answering
in the affirmative, next morning's sun beheld us on
our journey through a pass in the Cheviots, upon the
backs of two special nags, and man Thomas behind
with a portmanteau and two fishing-rods fastened
across his back, much in the style of St. Andrew's
cross. Upon reaching Wooler we found the accom-
modation so bad that we were forced to use some
interest to get lodgings here, where we are most
delightfully appointed indeed. To add to my satisfaction, we are among places renowned by the feats
of former days : each hill is crowned with a tower, or
camp, or cairn, and in no situation can you be nearer
more fields of battle—Flodden and Chevy Chase, Ford

Castle, Chillingham Castle, Coupland Castle, and many another scene of blood are within the compass of a forenoon's ride. . . . All day we shoot, fish, walk, and ride, dine and sup on fish straight from the stream, and the most delicious heath-fed mutton, barn-door fowls, poys (pies), milk-cheese, &c., all in perfection."

To those who are interested in cattle a visit to Chillingham to see the wild cattle there will be most enjoyable. It is an easy matter from Wooler, being only six and a half miles off. The poet has thus enforced the attractions of such a visit in May :—

> " The wild bull his covert in Chillingham wood
> 　Has left, and now browses the daisy-strewed plain ;
> The mayfly and swallow are skimming the flood,
> 　And sweet in the hedge blooms the hawthorn again."

I left Wooler to proceed up the glen, beloved of fishermen. It becomes more and more picturesque and nicely wooded as you advance into it, the views being here and there very varied and extensive. At one point you look over ranges and ranges of hills rising in wave-like forms, till you catch the high flat head of Cheviot himself overlooking all, and, unless in the heat of summer, you will see the streaks of snow still lingering on his higher ridges. Very faithful and very beautiful is the picture which Story, the shepherd-poet of Lanton, has sketched of the hills as seen from his abode on Lanton Hill :—

> " ' These mountains wild,' began the maiden, ' claim
> 　Each for itself a separate local name.
> 　We stand on *Lanton Hill.* Not far behind,
> 　The verdant *Howsden* woos the summer wind ;
> 　That mountain with its three wild peaks before
> 　Is styled by dwellers near it *Newton Torr ;*

The oak-clad ridges there of *Akeld* swell,
And here the bolder slopes of *Yeavering Bell*,
While towering yonder, with his patch of snow,
And proudly overlooking all below,
Is CHEVIOT'S mighty self, his throne who fills,
The admitted monarch of Northumbrian hills.'"

Yeavering Bell can be seen very distinctly from the
railway, its upper part like a cone, with two wide-

COUPLAND CASTLE.

spreading shoulders, shining green and purple in the
sun.

Further on the valley widens, the river gliding under
gentle wooded slopes on the northern side, and, amid
the most exquisite of these woods, rises the beautiful
Coupland Castle, with its square towers and angles, fitly
placed if ever castle were. There is a dreamy grace

about it, so different from many of the Northumbrian Border castles, as though it should have been at all times the refuge of refinement and peace. Mr. Tomlinson tells us that "when the survey of Border towns and castles was made in 1552, there was no fortress or barmekyn at Coupland;" and yet he goes on to add: "The fact of such a stonghold being raised sixteen years after the union of the two kingdoms is a remarkable proof of the unsafe and unsettled state of the Borderland at that time. The oldest portion of the existing castle consists of two strong towers, containing eleven rooms and a remarkable stone corkscrew staircase. The walls are in some places six and seven feet thick. At the corners of the castle are 'pepperpot' turrets, the only other examples south of the Tweed being at Dilston and Duddo."

But our time in the glen is exhausted, though we are loth to leave it, with its soft pencilled beauty here and there, and its wilder breaks and ravines and distant romantic glimpses. We must make for Kirknewton, there to get the train to take us south again, for we are already almost due in London town.

APPENDIX.

APPENDIX.

I.

IMITATIVE BIRDS AND THE NIGHTINGALE'S SONG.

IT is well known that there are whole classes of birds which, instead of keeping to a definite song of their own, are apt to imitate the songs of other birds, and bring it in into their own in the most arbitrary way. The mocking-bird is the typical bird of this class. But some of our common birds, such as the starling and blackbird and thrush on the one hand, and the little wren and the bullfinch on the other, are apt to surprise those who closely watch them by occasional departure from the ordinary notes and the introduction of something quite fresh. This was brought before my mind in the oddest way. As told in chapter vi., I had gone one summer evening, about ten o'clock, to the vicarage park, about a mile from the little house where I live in the country, to hear a concert of nightingales, a concert which was indeed richly enjoyable, the birds coming out in the fullest songs with their trills, warbles, gurgles, *jug-jug-jugs* as though in honour of our presence. When we left to return home, it was near midnight ; and, strange to our ears, as we trudged along in the moonlight, it seemed as though from many distinct points the faint echo of nightingales' songs came on the low wind. We could not have believed that there were so many nightingales about in that district. We published an account (abridged, compared with what it is in this book) of our visit to the nightingales at the vicarage, in the *Argosy;* and that article brought us some correspondence, a portion of which, as it certainly embodied original observation, and was suggestive of new explanations of certain facts, may be welcomed—the more that it may lead to further and fuller observation, comparison of experiences, and definite results in what are at present doubtful questions. At all events, some very interesting questions will be raised about the nightingale's song and its effect upon other birds. Some of the observations of my correspondent may do something to explain the very conflicting evidence we get about the earliest or the latest dates at which nightingales have been heard in a definite vicinity; for, if other birds can, by continuous effort, come to imitate the nightingale, perfecting their imitation even after the nightingale has ceased, these songs might well be mistaken in many cases for the song of the nightingale itself. My correspondent not only speaks for himself, but for others; and it would be very valuable, and help towards a settlement of the questions, if others would give the result of their observations.

I.

"NORTHAM, DEVON, *December* 8, 1890.

" DEAR SIR,—In your article on nightingales in September *Argosy*, which has just come under my notice, you say, ' How the other birds can sleep soundly in their beds is indeed a wonder.'

" The following facts may raise a doubt *whether they do.* I have never seen observations of the kind in any Natural History work, and therefore *they may have an interest for you* and Mr. C. Wood, as naturalists.

" In '72, I went to live on Shooters Hill, Kent. The nightingales were very numerous, and as many of them were in the garden, and when singing were often on trees within a few feet of my bedroom window, and as my duties also kept me from retiring till late, I had good opportunities for observing.

"I found frequently that when the song was long continued, and the nightingales numerous, other birds gave evidence of unrest; but, on many occasions, when the nightingales' tones were prolonged till twelve or one o'clock, especially on nights of great brilliancy, the moon being near the full, all the songsters joined in, and a concert of great power took place for about twenty minutes. In some cases there must have been hundreds of birds over scores of acres singing at the same time.

"About '83 I heard a similar night concert at Lee Woods, opposite Clifton Downs. Contrary to usual idea, nightingales are not rare in some parts of Devon, and within the last two years I have repeatedly heard their songs. I could distinguish the singing of from five or seven to eight birds end in one of these general night-concerts of various singing-birds. One of these took place in '89; it began at 11.10, and lasted, with some intervals, three-quarters of an hour. This is the earliest I have heard. The latest was about four in the morning. I have never heard the singing-birds give such concerted masses of sound by day.—Yours truly,

"T. MANN JONES, F.G.S."

In replying to this letter, I mentioned that the sentence which Mr. Mann Jones has quoted was meant to lead up to a reference to that legend of Sultan Solyman the Magnificent (supplied in the foregoing chapter), which represents the birds as coming to him and claiming his aid on their behalf against the nightingale for disturbing their slumbers by his notes during night, so that they could not from weariness sing so sweetly through the day as otherwise they would do. Of course the Sultan's decision was that he could not silence the nightingale to procure unbroken sleep for the birds.

X

II.

"Northam, Devon, 17th January 1891.

"Dear Sir,—In reply to yours just received, you are heartily welcome to use my letter of the 8th December in the way you propose, and I shall have great pleasure in receiving a copy of your intended paper.

"Your letter recalled the fact that the observations were wider than I stated in my letter. I first noticed these concerts in Sussex, and, mentioning the fact to my mother, I found that she had observed the circumstance many times, and for some years. The only other person I have ever known who had observed them was a totally illiterate but remarkably intelligent woman of great age, who had never been out of Sussex. I have searched "nightingale literature" in vain for any allusion to these night concerts.

"It is my conviction that the nightingale produces an impression on the birds somewhat analogous to that produced on the mind of man rather than that referred to in the legend you mention. As you are doubtless aware, individuals among many of the songsters learn the songs of other birds. So far as my observation goes, the nightingale's song is the most frequently imitated.

"A blackbird sang outside my bedroom window last summer, beginning about two hours after the nightingale ceased. He made many attempts to imitate the nightingale's song, but for some time the success was very small, though finally it was difficult to distinguish the imitation from the original. His observation must have been very close, as he only perfected the imitation some six weeks to two months after the nightingales had left the neighbourhood. For a considerable time after he continued to sing, interrupting his own song at intervals to take up the nightingale's.—I am, dear sir, yours very sincerely,

"T. Mann Jones."

In one of a series of letters which appeared in the *Standard* some time since on the question whether the nightingale is heard in Devonshire, " H. B. F. " said—

" I have known Devonshire intimately for forty-two years, during ten of which my people lived in the outskirts of Exeter, but none of us were ever lucky enough to hear a nightingale ; in fact, the nearest point to Devonshire in which I have heard it is the Somerset side of Exmoor, near Minehead. In saying this I by no means intend to imply the shadow of a doubt on what " R. C. " says, but I welcome his fact as proving my own idea, which always has been that the nightingale is to be heard in Devonshire. It would be very interesting if observers are found who have heard it in other parts of the country where it has been considered unknown."

Mr. Mann Jones's evidence is precisely of the kind that H. B. F. desiderates, and may be of some value—more especially in leading others to observe and to tell the results of their observations. But it is evident that the greatest care is necessary in the start to distinguish between the genuine and the imitated song, for, if other birds can recall and reproduce the nightingale's song months after he has ceased, then no end of mistakes are possible on mere first impressions. And this may affect reports of other birds' songs than that of the nightingale. The starling often imitates the notes of the oyster-catcher and curlew with the greatest accuracy, that of the sandpiper too ; and will often so reproduce the cry of the corncrake or landrail as to deceive even careful observers. And not only so, but he will do this in advance of the arrival of some of these birds, so that the clever rascal must, just for the fun of the thing, have been reproducing a note learned during the previous year. So that, in all such matters as these, it is very needful to be wary and make sure of your bird, just as in the case of disguises assumed, the detective needs to make very sure of his man.

The Rev. A. Rawson, who has paid close attention to the nightingale and the nightingale's song, is inclined to limit very specifically the portion of Devon in which the bird is found. He says—

" Its partial distribution over England is exceedingly curious and unaccountable. In the South, the western limit of its migration would appear to be the valley of the Exe, and even in this part of Devon it is extremely rare, though of all counties this seems exceptionally suited to its requirements. It is found in Glamorgan, is plentiful in the valley of the Wye, but is unknown in the Channel Islands and Ireland. Apparently its migration is due north and south within defined limits, and outside these limits a few stragglers only are found. Its habits are well known in localities where it breeds, and the regularity of its return to old haunts is remarkable. In my own garden in Kent, where I spent forty years of my life, in a parish notorious for the abundance as well as the quality of its nightingales, the arrival of this bird was regularly recorded under most favourable circumstances, and I find by my note-book that ten days mark the extremes. It built always in my garden, and the nest was usually in low underwood, near or on the ground, but I found that a good mass of old peasticks was also a favourite situation. The song lasts till the young are hatched, but I noticed that when the nest had been taken and a second brood hatched, the song was not nearly so continuous ; it is at its best about the second week of May. . . .

" The nightingale is becoming much scarcer in England and in Europe generally, owing to the bird-catchers. In this country it is now protected by the Wild Birds' Preservation Acts, which were passed not a moment too soon. It is a well-known fact that one year, between April 13th and May 2nd, no fewer than 225 nightingales, all cocks except six, were sent to a dealer by three bird-catchers. The ease with which it is caught on its first arrival is remarkable, for it cannot resist a meal-worm, but this is compensated in some measure by the equal difficulty with which it is caught a second time should it once escape. The knowledge of this has led, in some localities, to a practice called 'sparking,' *i.e.*, capturing the birds and then releasing them. As much as £5 has been paid by the residents in Epping Forest in spring to a professional bird-catcher to 'spark' all he could. They must have been plentiful enough in days long past, as we read of a Roman emperor regaling himself on a dish of nightingales' tongues! Attempts have been frequently but unsuccessfully made to introduce the bird to localities where it is not found. Evidently some 'environment' is wanting to induce it to take up its abode in any place in which food, climate, and surroundings are not suitable."

"An East Kent vicar," writing to the *Standard* on April 3, 1893, respecting "Early Flowers," adds: "Is it quite certain that the nightingale has been heard at Torquay? It used to be an article of ornithological faith that that sweetest of songsters never visited the counties of Devon and Cornwall." But from the facts we have here presented, it is almost certain either that stray nightingales do now visit certain parts of Devon, or else that natural history observation in these regions is more thorough and exact than it used to be.

One of the most interesting and amusing natural history sketches produced is that of Mr. John Burroughs, titled, "A Hunt for the Nightingale," republished from the *Century*, in the volume "Fresh Fields" (David Douglas). Though Mr. Burroughs reached England in the middle of May, it did not strike him to go in search of this minstrel till the 17th of June, by which time the full song is over. If it is ever heard after that, it is in the case of a second nesting and brooding, and the song in this case is invariably weaker, more broken, and disconnected than the earlier song. It is even very doubtful if that five minutes' song which Mr

Burroughs did hear was, after all, the song of the nightingale, seeing that the song by that time has so many imitators ; and it does not appear that Mr. Burroughs saw the bird which gave the short shower of notes he set down as those of the nightingale. "Its start," he says, "is a vivid flash of sound. On the whole a highbred, courtly, chivalrous song : a song for ladies to hear leaning from embowered windows on moonlight nights ; a song for royal parks and groves, and easeful but impassioned life. We [Americans] have no bird-voice so piercing and loud, with such flexibility and compass, such full-throated harmony and long-drawn cadences, though we have songs of more melody, tenderness, and plaintiveness. None but the nightingale could have inspired Keats's ode—that longing for self-forgetfulness after the oblivion of the world, to escape the fret and fever of life—

'And with thee fade into the forest dim.' "

One very common error about the nightingale, as observed in the text, is that it sings only at night. But it is to be heard through the day also—only, the chorus of other birds' songs then make it less emphatic and noticeable. Another error is that it is only to be heard in remote places, and in the depth of woods and great gardens. Nothing could be farther from the fact. The nightingale is often to be heard by day singing in the most exposed places ; often by hedgerows, the edges of plantations and underwoods, by the very sides of much frequented roads and pathways.

A writer in the *Spectator* of May 13, 1893, has thus described the nest and eggs of the nightingale, though he fails to note some of the places in which Mr. Rawson and others have found the nest :—

"The eggs and nest of the nightingale are both so beautiful and so unlike those of any other English bird, that it is impossible to mistake them when once seen. The site is nearly always chosen among the brown and dead oak or Spanish chestnut leaves which lie on the ground among the bramble or wild rose roots, or have drifted into some hollow of a bank. Sometimes, though rarely, the position is open to every passer-by, with nothing to conceal it but the resemblance of the nest and sitting bird, with her russet back to the surrounding colour. The outer circle of the nest is built of dead oak leaves, so arranged that the rim of the cup is broken by their projections, a mode of concealment practised, so far as the writer knows, by the nightingale alone of English birds, though a common device in the nests of tropical species. The lining is made with the skeleton leaves that have fallen in the previous winter, and completed with a few strands of horse-hair, on which the shining olive-brown eggs are laid. There are few prettier sights than that of a nightingale on her nest. The elegance of the bird, the exquisite shades of the russet and grey of its plumage, set in the circle of oak leaves among the briars, suggest a natural harmony and refinement in keeping with the beauty of its unrivalled song."

II.

THE VOLES.

THERE are three varieties of British voles, to each of which we have incidentally referred in the body of the book—the water-vole (p. 52), the field-vole (p. 104), and the bank-vole (p. 61).

They are all partially dormant in the winter, laying up in their holes tiny stores of food against a temporary awakening. They are all very shy and retiring, and till a comparatively late period, were little known, and were vulgarly confused with rats and mice. They belong to a wholly different class, and as we have said, are really more miniature beavers than rats or mice. They are all great tunnellers, and drive their little runs with the utmost precision to the exact point they desire. The two first are strictly vegetable feeders, but some say that the third has learned to try an insect diet.

1. The water-vole (*Arvicola amphibius*) is the largest of the three. He usually has his abode on the borders of a pond or stream, and delights to browse on the herbage on the banks. He is known widely as the "water-rat," and often bears the blame of actions done by the brown rat, which is a good swimmer, but cannot emulate the soft noiseless motion of the vole. The vole's head is broader than the head of the rat, and his tail is shorter.

2. The field-vole (*Arvicola agrestis*) is also abundant; he likes to burrow in the banks of mossy meadows, and is often found in orchards and gardens, as well as in cornfields. He is light-brown in colour, and the under parts are pale greyish. The fecundity of this species is astonishing, and

if they once get a footing it is difficult to clear them out. In a wood they gnaw the tender shoots as soon as they appear, and even eat off parts of the bark of grown trees, and clear off any tree roots that may lie in the line of their tunnels. When food is scarce they run up trees squirrel-like to nibble at the tenderer bark above. The field vole's winter stock is often partially composed of cherry stones, which it gathers at the points where it finds out that thrushes and blackbirds are apt to drop them, having eaten the fruit they have carried.

3. The bank vole, or red bank-vole (*Arvicola glareolus*) is not so common as either of the above species. It is redder in the colouring than the water vole or the field vole, and it is longer tailed. It affects old hedge bottoms with tangled undergrowth. It is said to be a slug, worm, and moth eater, though its main staple is admitted to be vege-tables; and it is generally held to be more carnivorous than either of its relations. It has delicately formed legs and feet, with peculiarly bright eyes. It is not so fertile as the field mole, producing only four or five young ones. But on the point of its food we should not forget the opinion of Mr. Rope, cited at p. 61 (note), that he, having kept this species for long periods in confinement, found they too were vegetable feeders.

III

THE WOODPECKER'S TONGUE, &c.

THE green woodpecker has a tongue perhaps more remarkable than that of any other bird. "The tongue bones are so much prolonged that they pass right over the back of the head, and are inserted in the skull just above the right nostril; these tongue bones, uniting in the lower jaw, become consolidated into a round mass about the thickness of a small straw; this pierces the true tongue substance, and ends in a horny tip, which is barbed on both sides." By means of his powerful bill the woodpecker hammers into the bark of the tree, and then by very rapid and extensive protusions of the tongue, seizes the fugitive insects. To render this horny tongue slimy, and to keep the tip of it constantly moist, two large glands are placed at the angles of the lower jaw, and these, through a special duct, pour out a viscid and glutinous secretion. "This remarkable structure," says the writer above quoted, "is one that is easily displayed by a very simple dissection with a penknife; and the beautiful fittings and marvellous elasticity of the parts can so well be seen in a fresh subject that no one who sees can help admiring."

Another writer says—

"Nature has appointed the woodpeckers conservators of the wood of old trees, furnished them admirably for their office, and so formed their habits that an old tree is an Eden to them, fraught with safety, and redolent of plenty and fatness. So exquisitely are they fitted for their office that the several woodpeckers vary in tint with the general colours of the trees which they select. If it is an alternation of green moss, yellow lichen, and ruby-tinted cups, with here and there a spot of black, then the green woodpecker comes in charge ; but if it is the black and white lichens of the alpine forest, then we may look for the spotted race upon the bark."

The glutinous secretion which we find in practical service in so many birds deserves attention. The swallow uses it in nest-building, the nightjar uses it to assist it to keep in its mouth the moths or beetles it has caught in flight till with them it can feed its young ; the woodpecker uses it for the purpose we have just seen, and the nuthatch with it gums the clay with which it reduces to true proportions the entrance to its nest. The edible nests of China, which are an article of commerce, are chiefly composed of this glutinous secretion which the birds use to supply the lack of other materials for their nests ; and evidently the king-fisher uses something of the same kind to unite together, however flimsily, the fish bones of which he forms his nest. And is it not likely that the chaffinch uses something of this in supplement to the spiders' webs, in so neatly cementing the "lichen" over the outside of its nest? Is it not possible that before differentiation this was even a more important element than it is now ?

IV.

THE ROOKS.

The crusade against the poor rooks is carried on so systematically, the farmers being apt to forget, during the few weeks in spring after corn has been sown, the great services these sable insect-foes render during the other eleven months of the year, that we reproduce here from the *Zoologist* a simple, practical, and inexpensive means of protecting the newly sown seed, without destroying the birds, from the pen of Mr. Henry Reeks, F.Z.S. :—

"In all light soils, where wire-worms (larvae of the genus Elater) abound, also those of the Tipulae and Noctuae, it would be almost impossible to grow crops of corn or roots without the friendly assistance of the rook. In this immediate neighbourhood, where the soil is cold, strong, and heavy, and consequently very free from wire-worms, rooks and rookeries are comparatively scarce; but from my farm at Thruxton, where the soil is light and chalky, I can stand and see seven large rookeries within a radius of three miles. Now, for at least nine months in the year, these hosts of rooks are purely insectivorous, and they may be easily compelled to be so for the remaining three months. When the autumn and spring corn is being sowed, and until after the spire or blade is well out of ground, it is absolutely necessary in large fields to employ a man with a gun, and also when the corn is in the sheaf, but not so when it is ripening; then a very simple device will keep them off much more effectually than any gun, unless always present. I buy a pound of good strong crochet-cotton, which costs, I think,

332

about four shillings ; this is wound off into balls rather larger than a cricket-ball. I cut then a number of sticks about half-an-inch in diameter and two feet long ; these are stuck in the ground by the side of the corn, and about fifteen yards apart. I then run down by this row of sticks, paying the cotton out as I go, and tying it with a double knot at each stick, and about a foot from the ground. No rooks will ever pull ears of corn over or under this barrier. To string a hundred and fifty acres of corn round in this manner is only a summer's evening amusement for two persons—one to carry and stick in the sticks, and the other to follow and fasten on the cotton. Where this, or the gun, has been neglected, I have known a large flock of rooks to carry away and spoil five pounds' worth of corn in a single day! By adopting the simple means I advise, rooks are driven to search behind the ploughs and in pastures for their favourite and legitimate food. Although perhaps the most useful of British birds, it was quite right not to include it in the schedule of "wild birds" for protection ; we could scarcely have done away with our social meeting once a year for rook-shooting, or the cold rook-pie as an after-luxury. I have never known a rookery decrease where the young rooks have been annually shot at, provided the birds are not persecuted more than *one* evening."

A good authority says : " Rooks intermarry every year, chiefly amongst the occupants of adjacent rookeries. If a male should be so bold as to bring home to his rookery a bride from a distance, the other rooks would not receive her, and would force the pair to build some way off. In the neighburhood of the big rookeries outlying nests of this kind can always be found."

V.

FEET OF THE DIPPER AND COOT.

THE fact that the feet of the dipper are still like the feet of
the thrush, and that the feet of the coot have only web-like
expansions, as we have said, on the sides of the toes, gives
Mr. Lydekker ("Phases of Animal Life") the suggestion
that the aquatic habits of these birds are of comparatively
recent acquisition, and have not yet induced any strongly
marked structural peculiarity.

INDEX.

PRINTED BY BALLANTYNE, HANSON AND CO.
EDINBURGH AND LONDON.

www.ingramcontent.com/pod-product-compliance
Lightning Source LLC
Chambersburg PA
CBHW031139120726

47905CB00006B/1750